Grave Concerns

HELL RAISING AND OTHER PASTIMES

JAYCE CARTER

Hell Raising and Other Pastimes
ISBN # 978-1-83943-990-2
©Copyright Jayce Carter 2021
Cover Art by Louisa Maggio ©Copyright June 2021
Interior text design by Claire Siemaszkiewicz
Totally Bound Publishing

HELL RAISING AND OTHER PASTIMES

Dedication

To all my fellow ADHDers:
Move that load of laundry to the dryer!

Chapter One

So, hell was pretty much what I'd expected.

Troy sat across from me in a small cave we'd taken shelter in, still avoiding looking at me, turning the spit with something cooking on it over the fire.

I had decided against asking what it was they were roasting, because I doubted any answer to that would make me happy.

If it were some strange hellbeast, I'd be grossed out, and if it were a cute, fluffy critter, I'd be sad.

Some questions were better left unasked, such as "Do I look fat in these?" or "Do you think my sister is hot?" and "What animal did this come from?"

Hunter came into the cave looking far too happy, as though he'd been waiting anxiously for just this moment. Hell, he was almost *skipping*.

Kase, on his heels, appeared significantly less pleased with the turn of events.

"I love the smell of brimstone in the morning." Hunter set down an oddly shaped cup in front of me.

I took a closer look at the dish, the white of it standing out against the dimness of the everything else. "Where'd you get this?"

"Don't worry about it. Drink. You mortals get parched fast out here."

His answer didn't ease me at all, so I lifted the cup closer to the fire. The white took a moment to place, and once I did, I couldn't unsee it. "Is this bone?"

Hunter groaned and sat cross-legged on the other side of the fire. "I *told* you not to worry about it."

"You can't seriously expect me to drink out of a bone cup."

"I have skulls, if they're more your style."

I was ready to yell at him for the stupid joke until I realized he probably wasn't kidding. Somehow, the idea that Hunter had a collection of fine china made from bones in hell seemed right on par for him.

Especially the way he had no shame over it.

"Drink," Kase said, nodding toward it. "I doubt you want to die of dehydration while in hell."

"At least it'd be a short trip if I did," I muttered before closing my eyes—it'd be easier if I didn't have to actually see the cup—and drank the water in big gulps. I figured if I finished it off quickly, I'd have to touch the thing for less time overall.

Which was a stupid reaction since I'd touched dead bodies plenty of times.

But I'd never use them as flatware. There were some lines a person didn't cross.

The water was warm, stale and tinged with an odd taste that made me want to gag a bit as I downed it.

Still, once I finished it, I handed back the empty cup. "Why would Lucifer drop us *here*? I thought he wanted to see me?"

Hunter shrugged. "He might figure a good test would be worth it. Anyone who can't survive a few days journey in hell isn't someone important enough for him to meet in person. Or maybe he intended for us to get dropped in his Court, but something went wrong. Magic doesn't work quite right on you."

"Things aren't supposed to just go wrong for Lucifer."

"Then you don't know Lucifer. Remember the whole fall from heaven thing? He's had things going wrong right from the start."

And, again, that made me feel no better. I liked the idea that at least Lucifer had his business figured out. The thought that he was as powerless and fumbling as the rest of us gave me a moment of thinking, *If he can't get shit right, what chance do I have?*

I sighed and crossed my legs, leaning forward. *Great.* We were stuck in hell, had no idea why I was where I there and now even the guy who ran it all didn't seem to have a good grip on specifics.

The only person happy about our circumstances was Hunter, who grinned as though he couldn't have planned things any better.

Then again, it was his home.

Grant was still outside, setting wards so we could get a good night's sleep, or at least the best one could expect in a cave in hell.

Not that there seemed to be any *night.* It reminded me of the pocket realm I'd met the fae in, except it didn't get lighter or darker. It remained a constant depressing level of dim, which ranked around the super overcast and rainy level.

When Troy finished cooking the food, he tore free a piece and held it out for me. Instead of thinking too much about it—I was really hungry—I popped it into my mouth, surprised to find it rather good.

As long as I don't consider what it might have been before being spit roasted or how many legs it might have had.

"Do you think he'll try to kill me?" I asked.

"I doubt it," Hunter said. "If he wanted to kill you, he could have done it without this much work. Lucifer doesn't do anything without a reason. He calls it efficient—I call it lazy."

"Maybe he just wants to be able to watch me die in person," I muttered around another bite of food.

"We won't let him hurt you," Kase said.

I gave him a withering glare in return. I didn't get over betrayal so easily. We might have been in an entirely different realm, but I wasn't ready to forgive him for lying to me, for hiring Grant to figure out what I was, for manipulating me. Maybe his words would have reassured me if I didn't already doubt his loyalty so much.

He looked as though he wanted to discuss the matter, but a glance around the cave reminded him we had an audience. Kase's ego would never want to air dirty laundry with others in earshot.

The perfect Kase didn't want to not look so perfect.

"You know, you all don't have to be here." I forced the words out even though I really didn't want to say them. Still, it was only fair to give them an out.

"What?" Grant asked as he came into the cave.

"Well, you can make portals to and from hell, right? You might have gotten sucked in here on accident, but you don't *have* to stay."

"Actually, we do," he said.

"Don't give me that. There's no reason for you all to risk your lives just because I evidently have an appointment with the devil."

Hunter shook his head, a smirk across his lips. "No, shadow-girl, what he means is that when Lucifer yanked us here, it placed a tracer on us. *All* of us. None of us can portal back until Lucifer removes it. The magic just won't work for a portal. I could cross the boundary, but I couldn't take anyone with me."

I blew out a breath, ashamed to admit just how relieved I was by that. Sure, I had to give them an out, but the thought of them leaving, of trying to make my way across hell by myself hadn't been one I relished. They were stuck with me for now, and it was far more reassuring than I wanted to admit.

"How long until we reach Lucifer's Court?" I asked, trying to change topics.

Hunter plucked a piece of meat from the creature and ate it with noisy bites. "Three days? Maybe five if we need a lot of stops. We ended up right at the boundary line, so it's a long walk. If it were just me, I'd make it in a day, but you all couldn't keep up."

Troy snorted. "Maybe not them, but I'm quicker than you think."

Hunter offered Troy a wide grin. "Yeah, but you'd keep up — *maybe* — if you were in your wolf form. Sadly, you've got some performance issues about that one, and on two legs you're as slow as the mortal."

Troy narrowed his eyes but didn't respond.

Fine by me. Honestly, I'd love for them all to shut up.

It was bad enough they bothered me at my house, when they stopped by constantly and threw my life into chaos, but out here, I didn't even have the privacy of a bathroom or the occasional moments of peace.

It was twenty-four-seven testosterone zone.

So I ate another piece of food before a yawn told me I needed rest.

The cave floor was hard and there wasn't anything to use as a pillow around. I groaned and twisted, my shoulder sore from where it dug into the ground.

Troy had taken a spot far away, as though he wanted to avoid me as best he could—just like he'd done since I'd saved him.

The ungrateful bastard. Next time maybe I'd let that freaky shadow take him over.

After checking the wards, Grant had leaned himself against the doorway of the cave, his legs stretched out and his eyes closed. He'd picked there, at the threshold, like a guardian.

Funny, since Grant, with his twenty-year-old appearance, massive number of tattoos and rebel hair style, appeared the least dangerous.

Hunter had chosen to rest outside, like some dog in the yard. He'd taken a large hunk of the meat and claimed to like sleeping under the stars.

Not that there were any stars…

"Come here." Kase's voice was soft in the darkness, and close enough I jumped.

How he could move so quickly, I didn't understand. He'd managed to shift around so he crouched just above where I lay.

I pressed my palm against the cave floor and pushed myself up. With the fire gone, I struggled to see Kase, so I glared in his direction best I could. "Sorry, but that doesn't work."

"What doesn't work? You need sleep, and you won't get any tossing and turning like that."

"You think this is my first time dealing with men? Let me guess, I'll sleep *so* much better all curled up beside you. And I'll sleep better without any pants. In fact, a few orgasms will put me right out." I made sure my voice sounded as insulting as I meant it to be.

Which was stupid, because no matter how much I disliked him at the moment, a few orgasms *would* help me sleep.

Just not from him. Not that he'd proven himself capable of delivering them anyway. His only attempt had been pathetic.

He sighed before sitting on the ground, his back to the wall. He removed his jacket and balled it up in his lap. "I'm not offering orgasms, Ava, and since my body doesn't run warm, there isn't a reason to curl up beside me, naked or not. However, I am, at the very least, useful as furniture."

I wanted to argue that I was sleeping just fine, but the ache in my shoulder called me a liar. Still, the thought of touching him made me wonder how stupid one person could be.

His entire reaction to me was bad enough—I wasn't sure I'd ever live down him spitting out my blood as if it were tainted—but the idea that he'd been lying to me was what really stuck.

He'd hired Grant to spy on me, to go behind my back and figure out what I was. He'd even said the entire thing had been for the coven, not him. How on earth could I just forget that?

Still, his lap was as good as anyone else's, and I *was* tired. I slid up, wincing when it aggravated my shoulder.

He set a strong hand on my back, helping me to adjust, until I was on my side, my head pillowed on his lap, his jacket creating more cushion and a useful barrier between me and any erecting that might happen.

Not that that seemed a problem with him.

When he ran his fingers through my hair, I swatted him away. "Knock that off."

He let out a soft sound, all annoyance. "I'm trying to help."

"I didn't *ask* for help, did I?"

"You haven't ever asked, and yet here I've been, doing it anyway. I am in hell, literally, for you."

I sighed, having nothing to say back to that. When I closed my eyes, he dragged his fingers through my hair again, and this time I let him. Just because I was mad at him didn't mean I had to forgo the nice sensation, did it?

It wasn't like he was getting anything out of it. Might as well enjoy it while it lasted. I doubted many nice things happened in hell.

"I didn't mean to hurt you," he said, voice low as if we could have a private conversation in such a small space, surrounded by others. "I hired Grant before I knew much about you."

"But even after you got to know me, you didn't feel the need to mention it? To call him off?"

"I knew you wouldn't be happy about me invading your privacy like that, and as I spent more time with you, I found out you hold grudges. It seemed a pointless argument to risk, since if you never found out, you would have never been angry."

I shifted and *accidently* elbowed him in the crotch.

He let out a rush of air—it seemed not everywhere on a vampire was impervious to harm—before groaning. "I have learned my lesson, Ava. I do not intend to lie to you again."

"And so I'm supposed to be okay with it? What was this all? What was it when you tried to feed from me? Just more research for the coven? At least that explains why you couldn't keep it up."

"No. It wasn't ever for the coven."

"That was what you told Grant."

"Because I prefer not to expose potential weaknesses."

"So I'm a weakness now?" I went to rise, because his lap was *not* worth me getting any more hurt than I already was.

He set a hand on my shoulder and pressed me back down, reminding me just how strong he was. "Stop it, Ava. Stop fighting with me long enough to listen. I have thought about you since I first saw you in that shop, and that obsession hasn't ended. When I asked around and found out what little I could, it still wasn't enough. So, yes, when given the chance, I hired Grant to discover more about you — not for the coven and not for Colter, but for myself. You can be angry with me for as long as you'd like for that invasion of privacy, for the lies, but do not mistake it for something it wasn't. I hired you for the job with Olin because you could do it, I wanted to feed from you because I couldn't stop thinking about it. I *want* you because I have since I first saw you. Besides, you shouldn't be so angry with me when Grant found nothing useful out."

"Maybe that's why he got kicked out of the guild, because he's a terrible mage."

A snort from the doorway said Grant was listening, but I pretended it was a random sound so I didn't have to think about our audience.

Kase went back to the gentle stroking of his fingers through my hair, and, despite my better judgment, it relaxed me. His voice, smooth and unfailingly calm, was even worse. "He ran every test he could, did everything he knew and he could not identify what you were. No matter how much I researched, who I threatened, I discovered nothing. You are an enigma, Ava."

"And that's why you're still around? Because I'm a very interesting puzzle, and you're old and bored? Or because I could be potentially useful to you?"

"No. I don't think I care what you are anymore. Originally, it was a mystery, but I've discovered you are trouble no matter what you might be."

"That doesn't explain why you're here *now*."

"You're smart enough to figure that one out. I'm not sure there are many reasons a man goes to hell for a woman."

I opened my mouth, but nothing came out. Kase and I, we never talked. We didn't admit anything. Where Troy liked to come out and say what he felt, and Hunter didn't feel deeply enough for the need to have a conversation, Kase and I liked to exchange things in non-speak.

He didn't say he cared, and I didn't say I liked that he was there.

Even still...I couldn't quite accept his words. I recalled Colter, remembered the coven house, and knew I had no idea where his loyalties really lay.

He might be a great piece of furniture, but that didn't mean he wouldn't kill me if he needed to…

* * * *

I wiped my mouth after coughing and gagging some more.

As it turned out, werewolf and vampire physiology weren't as affected by the smoke and ash as mine. Kase and Troy had no problem trekking along, mile after mile, while breathing in that junk.

Hunter lived here, so it didn't bother him.

Grant coughed on occasion, but his immortality made him sturdier, which left me as the one who kept throwing up because the ash coated my esophagus and made me gag.

I wiped sweat from my forehead, already sick of hell.

Hunter passed a waterskin to me, the outside made of a leathery material that looked suspiciously like scales. I'd opened my mouth to ask Hunter what it was made of the first time he'd had it, but he'd told me it was better I didn't know.

That seemed the general theme of hell. What was moving in the distance? What were those things flying above us? What was the shrieking?

Better not to know.

I took the water from Hunter and drank in large gulps, ignoring how warm it was.

Everything was warm. The breeze, the water, even in the shade, the rocks were hot to the touch.

Still, it was better than nothing, and the constant ash meant even warm water was helpful in clearing it away. Plus, he hadn't tried to give me anything made of bone to drink from again, so I'd take the weird scale bag as a win.

"How can you figure out where you're going here?" I handed back the waterskin.

Troy was far to the front, and Grant and Kase had taken up the rear. Hunter moved between the group, as if herding us all in the direction he wanted us to go.

"I feel it." He pointed behind us. "That's the way to the barrier, to the points between this world and the living world, and in the other direction, at the center, is Lucifer's Court."

"I thought you weren't controlled by him."

"I'm not. It isn't his power that draws me, but the fact that it's the center of hell, the draw point of the power in this place. It's where hell connects to the other realms of the afterworld. Lucifer built his palace there *because* it was the center. It isn't the center because he's there, no matter what he'd like to think."

A screaming echoed in the distance, died off to a whimper, then to nothing. I twisted to peer in that direction, even though I knew I wouldn't be able to see it, and I probably didn't want to.

Spindly trees rose around us in each direction, looking like dead things in the middle of winter, but they grew so densely they still obstructed the view.

"Relax," Hunter said.

"How am I supposed to relax when things sound like they're being eaten?"

"Well, they probably are being eaten." He grinned when I offered him a shocked look. "However, the point is that they're getting eaten because I'm not there to protect them. This is my *home*, Ava, and believe it or not, there isn't much here I'm worried about. At least, not anything outside of the Court."

"Forgive me, but you don't look nearly as imposing as those things I've seen before, as whatever is *eating* that poor creature. You're just a man and some smoke. I mean, a good-looking one, but I don't think monsters are going to be like 'he is sure handsome. Guess we won't kill them.'"

"I still look like this because you won't like me as much in my other form. Plus, no usable penis like that, and I'd really love to use mine on you, so I choose to keep looking like this."

The casual way he said such things silenced me and made me think about how much I agreed.

Not about not liking him in another form, but about how I wouldn't mind a repeat of our time together in the tent.

Or in my bed.

Really, so long as we were both naked, I wasn't picky about the locale.

Another howl came through and woke me up.

We were in hell. That was *not* the best time for quickies.

He lifted his head and inhaled, slowly, tension filling him.

When Hunter looked nervous was about the time to panic…

I inched closer to him, unable to help it. I would much prefer to be nearer to him for reasons that had nothing to do with orgasms right then.

Well, other than I'd like to live long enough to have more of them.

"Fuck," he muttered softly.

"What?"

Something in the distance came into view, but just barely. It wasn't a shadow, not like the thing that plagued me, that we chased, but more like mist. It reminded me of my dreams, of the things I saw in them.

It sped over the landscape as if it weren't fully there, the hazy appearance of a spirit.

Hunter pressed closer to me, though he didn't wrap an arm around me, as though he wanted both hands free to face whatever approached us.

The thing slowed when it neared us, and this time I could make out a shape. It was a dark figure, though not wholly corporeal or solid, covered in dark, floating cloth, including a hood that obscured its face. It had sleeves so long, hands couldn't be seen. Nothing but the mist-like robes were visible, floating despite there being no breeze.

It paused before us, and I could *feel* it looking at me. The sensation crawled over me like ice, something frozen and sinister.

A growl left Hunter, but the thing took no notice of him. It came closer, shifted as if to see me better. After another moment, it rushed away with the same speed it had arrived with, and Hunter let out a heavy breath.

Kase came over, Grant behind him. "Please tell me that wasn't what I think it was."

"Wish I could."

"They never show up," Grant said. "What the hell is going on?"

I elbowed between them men. "For those of us who don't have a field guide to hell on hand, what was that?"

Hunter pushed his hair from his face. "A reaper."

"The thing that severs the connection between body and soul?"

Hunter nodded. "Yep. Reapers are one of the few things that *nobody* fucks with. Even Lucifer leaves them alone. Because they aren't alive or dead, they don't belong to the living or the dead realm. They don't *belong* to anyone."

"They're from purgatory." I might not have seen one before, but I did understand what they were. They were, in a way, cousins of mine, something connected to the thing that seemed to make me different.

Kase was the one to answer, nodding. "Reapers don't take notice of the living or the dead. They're more like scavengers than anything else, beings that do their job and ignore everything else."

"It was looking at me."

"I mean, it stopped, but—" Hunter started to say.

"No. I felt it staring at me."

Grant cursed under his breath. "You do not want a reaper taking an interest in you. They're essentially invincible because they aren't alive—never were—and they don't have actual bodies to harm. If they want to snatch a soul from a body, they can do so with a touch and no one can do a thing about it."

I thought about the way it had seemed to look past my skin, into my spirit, into the part of my that wasn't corporeal, and I shuddered. Just when I thought there wasn't anything worse, that we had reached the end of bad shit that could ruin my day, it seemed like the universe wanted to throw another one into the mix.

Sure, soul-snatching mist creatures from purgatory.

What the hell was next?

Chapter Two

I shoved Troy, and the jerk didn't even have the decency to look as if he felt it. He hunched his shoulders forward and wouldn't turn around.

We'd been walking across this depressing wasteland for hours, ever since waking, and he *refused* to acknowledge me. No matter what happened, even when I tried to draw his attention — *nothing*.

As it turned out, I didn't care for being ignored, which was funny given how little notice people normally took of me. Maybe that was why it bothered me so much. I'd spent my life being ignored, so how dare Troy — who I couldn't get to leave me alone before — pretend as if I suddenly didn't exist.

Especially all because of his own insecurity-driven hissy fit.

I leaned down and picked up a small rock from the path, then chucked it at the large target that was his back. I rather enjoyed the deep thud when it made contact.

He stilled and rolled his shoulders, as if centering himself. "Do you really think provoking a werewolf is a good idea?"

"You don't scare me, and neither does your furry little friend."

He turned slowly, and his eyes had that brightness to them that said he struggled with his control. It seemed that after his little run in with that shadow, he hadn't fully recovered. Still, he didn't meet my gaze directly. "You *saw* what I really am."

"And?"

"And I hurt you. I could have killed you. That should explain to even you why this was a horrible idea from the start."

"Even me?"

He huffed softly. "You don't make great choices when it comes to your well-being. You have to realize how dangerous I am now. It's better for everyone if you keep your distance." He turned to walk off, as if our conversation had ended.

It *hadn't.*

I grabbed his arm and yanked, but when I couldn't turn him, I got in his path instead. "What if I don't *want* to keep my distance?"

"Too bad. I have enough control for us both."

I crossed my arms, standing toe to toe with him. If he thought I was afraid, he clearly didn't know me at all. "That wasn't *you.* It was that shadow."

"Maybe the shadow made me act that way, but if you hadn't done whatever you did, *I* would have killed you."

"But you didn't."

"I've already lost one mate!" The words came out on a roar, one that shook the trees around us. Even if the others weren't right next to us, no doubt they'd heard.

Anger didn't make up all that bluster, though. I'd learned that anger was nothing more than fear dressed up all fancy.

He lowered his voice, sounding more defeated that he ever had. I'd annoyed him countless times as his neighbor, but he'd never looked lost before. "I lost one mate because I wasn't strong enough, Ava. I lost her because I couldn't protect her, and it nearly destroyed me. I can't do that again, can't lose another, especially not you."

I cupped his cheeks, the stubble on them unusual for him. Then again, it wasn't as if there'd been time or chance to shave in hell. I lifted his face until I could see his eyes, but he still didn't look at me. "I'm not afraid of you."

"You should be."

I shook my head. "Whatever it is we're chasing, *that* tried to kill me, not you. It wasn't something you did — it was something done to you."

"How can you even stand to touch me after you saw what I really am?"

"I don't know — I kind of like your wolf. I always wanted a pet."

Ah, that disapproving look he gave me was everything. It took me back to before things had become so complicated, back when I was his annoying neighbor, and he was the sexy silver fox next door.

Funny how quickly we'd moved past that, that we'd become closer and yet far more confusing. Then again, the more important something was, the more difficult it was to hold on to.

"I don't like what *I* am," he admitted softly. "For a little while there, I thought I could control it, that maybe I could be whatever you needed, that something between could work. I'm older than I was with my last mate, so I'd thought..." He let out a long-drawn-out sigh before shaking his head. "That isn't how life works, though. I don't just become something because I want to be that. I have to be realistic and what happened was the wakeup call I needed. I could have killed you, Ava."

"But you didn't."

"Because of whatever you did, not because of me at all. I bet you don't know exactly what you did, do you?"

"I saved your ass—that's what I did." Sure, the words came out sullen and annoyed, but that was only because we both knew he was right. I had *no* idea what exactly I'd done, and if I needed to do it again, I'd be hard pressed.

When Troy had been taken over by that shadow, when he'd lost his damned mind, when I'd realized it would destroy everything I had—no matter how little that might be—I'd reached into him and wrapped my fingers around that shadow. I'd *felt* the difference between the other presence and Troy, been able to run along the lines of his spirit and that shadow. It shouldn't have been possible, and yet I'd used some instinct I'd never known about, something deep inside of me to do it.

He finally looked at me, and *damn* that hurt. There was so much pain inside those silver eyes, so much fear. I'd never have looked at Troy and thought fear, yet there it was. He was terrified. Of himself, most likely, of his nature, of parts of him he couldn't control.

I got that more than I ever wanted to admit. I understood that sort of feeling, where I had powers I didn't know how to control, where I wasn't easily definable.

It was a scary place.

"I don't care what you say," I told him. "I'm not afraid of you. I know who you are, and that wasn't you."

He pressed his lips together, a sure sign he didn't believe me one bit.

Then again, people tended to hold onto the negative, to their own hang ups, no matter how much others fought against it. Strange how easy it was to believe the worst in ourselves and how hard to really hear the best.

"I—" he said, and I could already hear his excuses, his nonsense.

I silenced him with a kiss. It was soft, sweet, just an attempt to say what he refused to hear.

For just a moment I thought it had worked. His lips softened, gave, as if instinct alone made him react to my touch.

Maybe there is something to this mate thing.

As soon as it happened, however, it stopped. He pulled backward and shook his head. "I can't," he whispered, as if his actions hadn't said it well enough.

I was left staring at Troy's back as he turned away and shoved his hands into his pockets.

Maybe it would just take time.

Or maybe I'd been right, and I'd never had a shot.

* * * *

Tiny rocks dug into my fingers like slivers of glass. I'd never thought of sand as particularly sharp, yet the knicks and cuts on my hands told a different story.

"You hanging in there?" Grant knelt above me, then stuck his hand out to help me up and over an especially large boulder as we made our way up a steep hill covered in rocks.

"I thought this was going to be a 'stroll down a path' sort of thing," I panted out, breathless.

"I feel like there's a joke here about the road to hell."

"If there is, I ask you keep it to yourself. People should be sent to hell for making puns, but free from them once we get here."

After he helped me up, I rolled to the side and sat on the oversized rock. Whenever I needed to stop—and it had been far more often than any of the others needed—they all slowed. Funny how we could be traveling together and yet somehow be so entirely separate.

The men kept to the peripheral, drifting in and out of my line of sight, each taking up a different point as we went.

Occasionally they'd venture off farther and every once in a while come back more disheveled.

It seemed they'd rather take out dangers before they got anywhere near me.

Then again, I was the only mortal in the group.

Grant handed me water, and I gulped it down. It felt like mud coated my esophagus, like the ash had mixed with just enough water that it only thickened. I had no idea where they were getting water from, but I'd guess it wasn't easy. When Hunter returned with a new supply in hand, he always had a fresh wound. For that reason alone, I didn't complain about the quality.

"Could you just get it over with?" Grant blurted out.

"Get what over with? *Oh*," I said as though I'd just remembered. "You mean the conversation about how you lied to me, betrayed me and stole my blood to run tests on it? *That?*"

He huffed. "Yes, *that*. You yelled at Kase already, but you haven't said anything to me."

"So? If you just want someone to yell at you, I bet you could find something like that here in hell. Seems like a kink you could pay someone for."

He sat beside me, right up against my side. "Silence is far worse than yelling. People don't yell unless they give a damn. Silence comes after that, when they don't give a fuck anymore."

"Speaking from personal experience?"

"More than I'd like to admit." The way he said it told me the conversation was over, and yet there was *far* more to it then he'd let on.

Which again reminded me how little I knew about him. He was a mystery. Funny, charming, but with a darkness inside him that ran deep.

"I don't know what you want me to say. You had every chance to tell me the truth, but you didn't. I know you'd prefer not saying anything that might get you into trouble, but there are limits. It makes me wonder just what else you'd do if the paycheck was right." I frowned for a moment. "Is that sort of behavior what got you kicked out of the guild?"

He snorted. "No, trust me, morals in the guild are a joke. They don't kick people out because of a lack of ethics."

"So what was it? You want me to forgive you? To move past this? You've got to give me something, show you want to change things. Tell me what exactly you did that got you kicked out."

He tipped the waterskin back and gulped like it was a bottle of liquor and he needed to wash away the taste of the unpleasant question. Finally, he dropped it in his lap. "I killed someone. No, that's not right. I killed quite a few someones. The entire council and the Magistrate. It seems that while there aren't a lot of lines that can be crossed with the guild, that's one they don't take lightly to."

"All they did was kick you out? Seems like a pretty light sentence."

"They didn't even kick me out," he said. "*I* left. I walked away, but you know me. I don't like to cross any bridges unless I burn that bitch to the ground."

"How many did you kill?" A sickness in the pit of my stomach made me swallow hard.

"Fifteen, not including the Magistrate." He said it like he was counting fence posts, as if they weren't people he was admitting to killing.

Yes, I knew the four men I'd ended up spending time with had killed people. I chose to ignore it most of the time, but I wasn't stupid. It wasn't that he'd killed, it was how little he seemed to care, as if those people's lives meant nothing.

How can someone be so callous?

"And you don't care at all?" The whole forgiving-him thing had gone out of the window. I had no intention of forgiving him, let along ever trusting him again. "None of them bothered you?"

"One," he admitted, voice soft. "It shouldn't have, but I guess even I'm not quite as heartless as I like to pretend. The Magistrate was harder to accept. Not that hard to kill, not for me, but there? At the end?" He let out a soft sigh. "Yeah, I hesitated."

"What was so special about him?"

Grant rose from the boulder, hopping to his feet and brushing his hands off on his jeans. I didn't think he'd answer at first, as he readied himself to get back to the trek, but then he turned toward me, an expression on his face so unlike any I'd seen on him before. *Regret?* As close to it as I could guess.

"The Magistrate was my father," he said, then handed me the water. "Drink up. We've got a long day ahead of us still.

His answer didn't make me feel any better about him…

* * * *

Something moved just outside the edge of the campfire light, where everything went from an orange glow to the dimness of the realm.

Whatever it was shifted around like a creature stalking prey.

How did no one else notice it? How did they not see it? I didn't have the same predator senses as they did yet I sure as fuck saw it.

Hunter wasn't at the campfire, but the other three were pressed in tight, as though we were on some wonderful camping trip—one big, happy, dysfunctional family.

I opened my mouth to mention what I kept seeing, the rustling of twigs and leaves that was barely audible above the crackle of the fire.

Kase cut me a sharp look with an almost imperceivable shake of his head.

So maybe I wasn't the only one to notice.

Ignoring it seemed stupid, especially from men who were more than capable of doing *something* about whatever it was, but what did I know?

I could play their little game, too, and somehow act as if I didn't notice the massive thing shifting around, readying to strike, to devour one of us.

Probably me, with my luck.

The thing was big, whatever it was. It crept along the darkness, a smoothness to its movements that screamed danger.

"You should eat," Grant said, though an odd tone in his voice said he paid little attention to me despite speaking to me. "You don't want to lose your strength. There's still a long walk ahead of us."

"I think I've had all the hell critters I can stomach."

I expected a snarl before the thing in the dark attacked. That was how it always happened in the documentaries.

However, as was often the case, reality was a lot different than the shows. Something dark and shadowy came barreling at me without the decency of a warning.

Before it struck me, however, Grant lifted his hands, those strange words falling from his lips. The creature stopped mid-air, but it wasn't the shadow I'd dealt with, the one that plagued my every step.

Instead, this thing was better formed, like a creature combined with smoke rather than made of smoke. It wasn't a dog, and light hit the edges of the creature and reflected like...scales?

Kase grabbed my arm and yanked me backward, tucking me behind him with a hold that couldn't be broken.

Not that I was planning on breaking it. Troy could say all he wanted about my lack of self-preservation, but I also knew when I was outmatched. I wasn't about to try and face off against some sort of...smoke creature.

Whatever it was wouldn't be held by Grant's spell, though. It twisted, horrible sounds coming from its writhing body.

It broke free, but before it could strike me — and why I was its target, I had no idea — another flash of black and red struck it. The two figures tumbled to the side, the smoke combining so it was impossible to tell where one creature ended and the other began.

Well, other than the snapping fangs.

As the smoke creatures moved, striking trees and rocks, I managed a better look.

Dragon was the best I could come up with to explain them. Black smoke covered their bodies, and sharp white fangs lined their long muzzles. Huge hands tipped with gleaming claws slashed, and red flames danced in their eyes and along their spines.

One pinned the other, but I couldn't tell which had won.

Did it really matter? I didn't feel much like trusting *either* of them.

The one trapped beneath spoke in a gravelly voice that could have come from no human. "I yield. You were always quicker than me, Hunter."

Hunter?

They broke apart, the shaking of the ground beneath their massive weight making me cling tighter to Kase. Once they'd separated, the one who had triumphed shimmered, the smoke twisting until a human form swallowed up the massive body of the dragon.

Standing there was no monster—at least not the kind that could be seen—but Hunter.

I'd recognize that ass anywhere…

His words came back to me, when he'd said his true body resembled a dragon—I just hadn't believed him.

The other creature rolled and rose to its feet, standing far taller than Hunter.

"What are you doing here, Jerrod?" Hunter asked.

The creature stretched, then shook its head like a dog. "I was tracking *that*." It gestured at me. "What have you brought here, brother?"

"I didn't bring anything. Lucifer summoned her here." Hunter turned to peer at me, then back. "And she isn't used to hell or our other form, so why don't you change?"

Jerrod—or at least I assumed that was his name, given the conversation—made an unhappy sound before doing as Hunter asked. When done, he stood around six feet, covered in thick muscle much like Hunter, and with the same tattoos wrapped around him. However, his hair was shaved off, and he had an unhealthy, pale glow to his skin. He had eyes that were almost yellow, close enough to amber that a person wouldn't immediately assume they were fake but far enough that anyone would take notice.

He was naked and had the same 'I don't give a shit' attitude as Hunter.

It seemed modesty wasn't an issue for hellhounds.

"Why do you like to look like this so much?" Jerrod asked, his lip curled up as if it was all together unacceptable. "It's small and weak and *soft*."

"It has its advantages," Hunter said, and I could hear his smirk even without him turning toward me. No doubt he was talking about *advantages* that I didn't care to discuss with company around. He moved on before I could scold him. "Besides, it isn't like our other form can go inside."

"Who wants to go inside? Give me the open air anytime." Jerrod leaned to peer past Hunter, and the moment those freaky yellow eyes landed on me, I pressed closer to Kase. "Lucifer wants her? What for?"

"I don't ask things like that," Hunter said. "But more importantly, she's under my protection."

Jerrod snorted, as if that meant nothing. "Keeping a mortal alive here is a losing feat, even for you."

"Maybe, but I have a feeling that anyone who fucks with Lucifer's guest will have problems even bigger than me. He wouldn't call a mortal down here unless he wanted something from her pretty badly."

Jerrod huffed and crossed his arms. "Lucifer is fickle. He may want her now, but give him a few days and he'll have moved onto something else. You're away too much, brother. Lucifer is *always* bored now."

"Maybe, but you remember the time he had that pretty girl here? The one with the white hair?"

Despite the fair complexion, Jerrod paled as he gulped. "The girl caught a portal topside."

"The idiot who let that happen didn't get off too easily, did he?"

I didn't *need* to hear exactly what Lucifer had done to the poor person. Even without all the knowledge, I could venture a guess based on the fear in Jerrod's eyes.

Which made me wonder, yet again, just what the fuck I was doing in *hell* headed toward the very person who had put that fear into a *hellhound's* eyes.

Some rules people had to be taught, but some should have been basic knowledge.

One of those *had* to be that if a hellhound was afraid of something, maybe don't go looking for it.

Of course, that implied I had a choice in the matter, and I wasn't foolish enough to think that.

Jerrod smiled, all sharp lines. "Where are you headed? The Court?"

Hunter nodded, though he hadn't relaxed. He might know the other hellhound, but he didn't seem willing to let his guard down just yet.

"Are you going through Styx or taking the pass?"

Hunter's jaw twitched, as if he didn't like the question. "Styx."

"Good idea, because I've heard the pass is awfully dangerous. Creatures there will tear apart anything for a meal, and that girl looks *delicious*." Jerrod shimmered and his other face, the one of a dragon with dripping fangs, stared at me.

Hunter made a sound that was so much like the one Jerrod had, an answer but with far more aggression. "Do you need another lesson about looking at her like that?"

Jerrod shook his head, turning from me. "No. I've never bested you before, and I doubt I'll start now. I like to exploit weaknesses, and you've never had any." Jerrod lifted his eyebrow. "At least, you didn't used to…"

The speculation in Jerrod's gaze couldn't mean anything good, and a furious snarl from Troy said he'd read it for what it was.

Then again, even if Jerrod wanted to attack me, he had four ill-tempered males between us, and that made me feel far more comfortable.

"So I'll see you in Styx, right?" Jerrod tore his gaze from me and looked at Hunter again.

Hunter rolled his shoulder before he nodded. "Yeah, sure."

Jerrod offered up a smile that chilled me, one that made me try to take a step backward, before he shifted into that smoke form again and left.

And when Hunter turned back around?

Well, having him look nervous wasn't something I liked…

Chapter Three

"So that's what you really look like?"

Hunter chuckled, dressed in a pair of pants, though I wasn't sure where he'd gotten them from. I'd accepted that he had to be stealing things, and while maybe it should have bothered me, thief-Hunter was the least upsetting thing in my life. At least this time he didn't have to squeeze into a pair of my sweatpants.

We'd started to climb a mountain, though this one having a path was a nice change of pace. Troy, Kase and Grant remained at the camp we had set up at the base, since Hunter said our little trip wouldn't take long. No doubt, he'd planned for it to just be us so I could ask about what I'd seen.

"Yeah, that's me in all my glory." Even though his words held a shadow of self-deprecating humor, it was different than with Troy. Hunter seemed aware I might not love his other form, but nothing in his tone implied he hated it for any reason.

"So, you still going to let me take off your pants after seeing it?" He lifted an eyebrow and gave me one hell of a smirk.

And just like that, I remembered why he got away with so much.

Though, to be fair, he'd been the only person in my life so far who hadn't lied to me, not even once. He'd not explained what he was at first, probably so he didn't freak me out, but he hadn't ever told me something that wasn't true. He hadn't betrayed me, hadn't gone behind my back.

Boy, have my standards gotten low.

"I'm harder to scare off than that." I bumped my shoulder against his, trying for flirty-playful.

Hunter twisted, and before I had a chance to even squeak, he had my back against a rocky wall and his lips to mine.

After being in hell for…well, however long it had been already, I understood his taste. It wasn't just flames. It had a hint of the ash that coated my tongue from the air, the hellfire that moved across the landscape like living creatures, the smoke that swirled over his body, especially when he was angry or distracted. Hunter wasn't just something that came from hell—he *was* hell, all wrapped up in a body that was nothing less than sinful.

When I grabbed him behind the neck and leaned up, pressing against him, the tattoos on his skin swirled and moved beneath my palms. Then, something pinned my hands to the rock wall despite his hands being busy slipping up the front of my shirt, slowly and teasingly.

I was ready to yell at Grant—who else would do that?—when I broke the kiss and glanced up.

It wasn't the empty space I expected, the muttered words from somewhere else as Grant held me in place with his magic. Instead, it was smoke. Tendrils of black stretched from Hunter's skin and held me still. They were warm and strong and I gave myself a moment to see if I'd freak out.

Even Hunter paused, waiting.

Rather than my lust drying up, instead of letting myself worry about how this was extraordinarily weird, I went to my toes and bit softly at his full bottom lip.

It seemed my perversions were more than even I expected, because there was something unfailingly hot about this.

Maybe it was the surprise, maybe it was the fact that it showed, in no uncertain terms, that Hunter was not even close to human. I'd known it, of course, but seeing it this way made me desperate to have him.

Which was strange, since I'd spent so much of my life wanting what was normal. I'd craved the boring, human life, the human boyfriends, the whole package and yet the moment I was confronted with how *not* human Hunter was, I was smitten.

Hunter chuckled, though an edge to it said he hadn't been as confident as he'd appeared. "You know," he whispered as he moved his hand up again. "I have extraordinary dexterity with my smoke." The words didn't quite sink in, but leave it to Hunter to throw subtlety to the wind. "If you're ever feeling unsatisfied with just me, don't worry. I can fill you up all on my own."

Those words I got. When Hunter rumbled that, low and promising, I pictured it. I thought about how the smoke would heat against my skin, how it would glide along me, how helpless I'd be against anything he wanted.

I lifted one of my legs to wrap around his, to pull him closer since I couldn't move my hands still. *Yes.* He wasn't asking me for anything, but my answer was an absolute yes.

Something touched my hand, and for a moment I thought it was more of his smoke. Soft, featherlight touches, a bunch of legs.

Legs?

I jerked my gaze up to find something that looked like a spider on acid crawling on my hand.

Whether I said something or he spotted my fear, I wasn't sure, but Hunter's smoke released me. I jerked my hand, the creature flung to the ground. It reared back on a few of its legs, and large, dripping fangs bared toward me.

Why does everything here have fangs?

When it charged, Hunter brought a booted foot down on it, the squish turning my stomach.

He twisted toward me, ready to take another kiss, to get right back to it, but this time I shoved his chest. "I don't think so, buddy."

"But…it's dead."

Goo leaked from beneath Hunter's shoe, a sickly, green color, and I gagged. "Nope. Sex is not happening out here with things like *that* around."

Hunter scraped what was left of the creature from his boot on a rock. "Cock-blocker," he snarled at the body.

I shuddered, reminded that maybe hell wasn't the place for crazy outdoor sex, what with creatures after me and everything wanting to eat me.

Hunter offered me one hell of a leer. *Including one hellhound who might just succeed…*

"You said you wanted to show me something." I tried to steer the conversation back on track and ignore the way my body *still* craved his touch. "I'm assuming it wasn't just your penis."

"Well, that *is* a sight to behold, as you well know." He winked, then held his hand out to me.

I set mine in his, and he tugged me farther down the path we'd taken, the one that wound around between rock walls and opened into countless caves.

When we'd passed a few, I would have sworn I'd spotted red eyes gazing out at me from the opening. A quick glare from Hunter or, on occasion, a growl, sent whatever hid there running deeper into the darkness.

Everyone else had stayed at the camp we'd made, seeming to trust Hunter with me on his own. Then again, if anyone knew how to keep someone alive out here, it was him.

This was his home.

Each time I thought that, it weirded me out again. Hell didn't seem like a home to me at all.

Has anywhere seemed like a home?

Before the melancholy thought could burrow in too deep, Hunter stopped short. He pulled my hand until I stood beside him, and in front of us?

A huge ravine was tucked between two sprawling mountains. In the center, trees rose, and a red river sliced through the place. Things crawled along the far mountain face, though they were too far away for me to make out details.

"What's this?"

"This is the pass."

I frowned, recalling the conversation with Jerrod. "I thought you said we were going through that town."

"Jerrod was *far* too anxious to know where we were headed for me to tell him the truth."

"Why would he care?"

Hunter lowered himself to sitting, dangling his legs over the edge of the cliff. A tug to my hand got me to take a place beside him before he slid his arm around my waist, as if wanting to make sure I stayed close and didn't tumble off. "You don't belong here, shadow-girl."

"If the whole throwing up thing didn't tell me that, I'm pretty sure the spider sold the point to me. I could tell him I don't want to be here anymore than he wants me here."

Hunter shook his head, his fingers stroking my side as if an unconscious motion. "You don't understand. Hell is the antithesis of the living realm. Life exists there, corporeal form, light. Here it's the opposite — darkness, smoke, death. Just like creatures in the living realm harness the power of death and shadow because it *is* a power there, creatures from hell are drawn to the living the few times they manage to get here."

The way Jerrod had stared at me made slightly more sense, and terrified me even more. "How exactly do they *harness* it? I'm guessing it isn't a process I'd enjoy."

"You don't need to worry about that, because I won't let it happen. Jerrod is a sneaky fucker, though, and I have no doubt he's got something planned."

I wanted to argue, to remind him I needed to understand the dangers I faced, but the tight lines of his face made me listen just this once. If he found the idea this objectionable, it was probably something I was better off not knowing.

"I never figured hell for having towns. It's been all empty so far."

"That's because I've led us through the wilderness. I know every inch of this realm, so I've avoided anything with other beings. I was hoping no one would catch your trail, but Jerrod is a good tracker."

"So why lie to him if he can just follow us?"

"Because if he thought we were headed there, he'd plan based on that. Jerrod is one of the weaker hellhounds, but he's one of the cleverest. He wins by plans, by ambushes and exploitations." A hesitation in his tone made me frown.

"What aren't you telling me?"

Hunter pointed at the ravine. "Normally we'd take a path down there, cross it, then follow a cave system on the other side. It would let us bypass the cities, including Styx."

"But...?"

"You see the movement."

Even as I tried to ignore the way when I stopped forcing just a little, the entire ravine looked a bit like hands moving along the ground, I couldn't forget it.

"Jerrod said there were creatures."

"There are *always* creatures, but this is different." Hunter hopped to his feet and grabbed a large rock from behind us. He hurled it, and it took a long time to fall to the ground beneath. I lost track of it, my vision not good enough to see where it landed below, but I didn't *need* to see to know.

The floor of the ravine went wild. Things I couldn't fathom much less identify moved in the sudden chaos. Some were so small I couldn't make them out, but some had to be the size of elephants, slithering among the trees and crawling from the red river.

"Fuck," I whispered.

"This isn't an accident. For a concentration of beasts like this to happen, someone did it on purpose."

"How?"

"A lure. You can't see it, but I *smell* it. Someone placed a lure at the center of that ravine to attract all those things into such a small area. If we can't use the pass, we won't have a choice but having to go through the more populated areas. More beings cluster around the center of hell, so if we have to go that way, we can't avoid them. The pass was the easy, safer way, but someone blocked it. Someone wants us to have to go through the cities."

"Who? Jerrod?"

"Probably. He's the only one who knew where we were going. Still, he usually couldn't resist setting a lure."

I froze as I stared down, thinking about everything Hunter had said, a shiver as the pieces fell together, the thing he hadn't said. "What exactly is the lure, Hunter?"

"There is only one thing that can call that many creatures, one thing that beings from hell want more than anything else."

"Something mortal?"

He nodded, then took my hand and helped me up. "There's nothing we can do about whoever they tore apart down there to make it, but I swear, I won't let the same happen to you."

A weak laugh left me, the sort that people did when overwhelmed and without options. "How do they even get mortals here?"

"They fall this way now and again. Sometimes they're snatched by the creatures that can pass through, sometimes they are unlucky enough to slip through a crack that can occur. I'd say there are perhaps a dozen or so a year."

"Have you ever brought one?"

He shook his head. "Hellhounds can pass, but we can't bring anyone else with us. You're looking at wardens, mages, Lucifer or some of his kids. It isn't easy and the creatures that can do it aren't the ones who crave mortals, so it doesn't happen much."

I blew out a breath when there wasn't anything to say back. "So, I guess we're going to go through the cities, then?"

"It looks that way."

"And here I thought I wouldn't get to see any sights."

He didn't even bother to laugh at the stupid joke, but I couldn't blame him for that.

There was something working against us, something forcing us toward the cities, and there was no way it could be good.

If someone in hell wanted something, it was a good bet it wouldn't be something I liked.

Not that I had much of a choice…

Chapter Four

The small town looked normal in an odd way, and that made it all the more unsettling. Hell should be kind enough to make sure their towns look like shitty haunted houses from Halloween.

Hunter had given me a rundown of basic etiquette, which had amounted to "*don't tell anyone what you are, don't act weak, don't go anywhere alone, and don't look anyone in the eye.*"

In addition, he'd brought a damp and sticky cloak with a hood and wrapped it around me.

I tried to ignore the scent of it—which I could only describe as rot—but it overpowered everything else.

According to him, it should hide some of the smell of my mortality, which, after hearing about how tasty creatures in hell found me, sounded like a good idea.

Hunter had taken off an hour before to scout the town ahead of us and run some errands. I hadn't asked what errands meant in hell, but I figured it wasn't grabbing a cup of overpriced coffee and hitting up the post office.

Kase walked behind me, Troy to my left and Grant to my right.

I pulled at my cloak. "Why don't you all have to wear these?"

Grant had a casual tone but a sharp gaze as he checked our surroundings. "Because we don't smell like humans."

"You're basically human," I pointed out. "I saw you trip and fall when we had to climb that fence. I bet you *still* have a bloodied knee."

He let out a soft, low laugh. "I may be more fragile, but I'm still not human. What they're attracted to is mortality. It's that humans age and die. None of us do that, so we're useless to them."

"It seems unfair that I both have to age and die *and* creatures from hell are after me. I feel like that is the short end of the stick."

"If it makes you feel any better, they'd probably tear apart Troy too if they could. He doesn't smell as good as you do, but his blood is closer to human than the rest of us. It'd be best if he didn't bleed."

Troy snorted, something that said he hadn't found the comment funny. "I'll do my best."

"So werewolves have human blood?"

"Close enough to," Grant said when Troy didn't seem to want to discuss it. "When they're in human form, they're almost impossible to tell apart. It's why they can live in the human world so easily. Even blood tests won't show a difference. It won't give the things here any power, but they'd probably enjoy the taste."

Troy answered that with a low growl, telling me he was as testy as he'd been since we'd arrived.

And, yes, I realized that being annoyed after being dragged to hell was probably a fair reaction, but I knew damn well it had *nothing* to do with the location and everything to do with me.

Well, with his own self-hatred, at least.

"That's where Hunter told us to meet him," Kase said from behind us.

Up ahead was a large building. four stories tall, built of stone and crumbling at the corners. Everything in the town was an odd mixture of medieval and modern. Lights lines the streets, but instead of electricity they glowed with either flames or a sickly green tint that reminded me of that spider's blood.

The people that milled around — it was hard to call them people — took little notice of us and I did my best not to stare.

Some looked normal enough, though those walked with a fearful gait, quick and unsure. Others were twisted, only looking vaguely human. Some had lips that curled up and rows of fangs, eyes that were all sorts of colors but rarely ones I'd ever seen before. Yellows, orange, green, red, and all glowing. Their limbs were mishappen, often different lengths and with masses on them, and most were far taller than any human. Some had wings, hooves or claws that tipped their fingers, all things that said I needed to keep in mind what Hunter had said.

A man sat on a low fence that lined a shop, wearing nothing but a pair of ragged shorts, boils over his head that pulsed as if they might break open at any moment. His left arm was longer than it should have been, and burns covered his right side.

I tried not to stare, but we met gazes for a moment, and something sinister crept through that connection, as if whatever was inside him was powerful enough to cross the distance and threaten me.

Jayce Carter

Kase put a hand on the nape of my neck and shoved me forward, breaking the connection.

A dark laugh came from behind us, as if the man had enjoyed the little interaction.

"Don't you remember Hunter's warning? Avoid eye contact, Ava," Kase scolded.

"What was that?" I asked.

"Beings in hell like their games, and whether it's harming someone's body or tearing apart their mind, they don't much care."

I might have argued, except I still felt slime covering me from that split second of connection, and I had no desire to repeat it. I shuddered to think what might have happened if Kase hadn't kept me moving.

"*What* is he?"

Kase answered, though he kept his hand on my neck so I moved forward. "It's a spirit. Most of the beings you'll see here are spirits that were sent to hell."

"Why does he look like that then?"

"Because hell twists things here. The longer spirits are here, the worse they are, the more hell changes them into things like that."

The thought that the creatures I'd seen in the town were people—or at least had been at one time—made me grateful for Kase's grip. Hell wasn't the sort of place I wanted to go wandering alone in.

We went to the large building, a sign hanging outside I couldn't read. At least, I couldn't at first. After a moment, the foreign symbols shimmered, and after a moment, I understood it. *Skull Point Inn.*

I frowned, glancing around, finding that each other sign did the same thing. I couldn't read the words, didn't understand the letters, and yet after a moment it came to me, like some old instinct.

"Can you read that?" I asked, pointed at the sign.

Grant nodded. "I studied some of the demon languages when I was in the guild. I wouldn't want to try and write love poems, but I can get by."

"Why isn't anyone speaking the other language?"

"They are. Hell isn't entirely corporeal, which means language isn't entirely spoken. It's more fluid, like thought exchange. The language doesn't matter, because it's the meaning that is passed person to…" He hesitated, then added, "*person.*"

Troy pulled open the door to the Inn, surveying it before moving through the doorway and letting us enter.

I expected it to be more…hellish? Medieval? Instead, the inside look like a strip club, without the neon lights. Flames danced along the rafters to light the place, and tall tables and booths were set throughout. Center columns sat with people dancing on them, dressed in very little.

There were both women and men, but I didn't feel the desire to give hell credit for gender equality in this. A woman was on one closest to the door, wearing nothing, her skin a deep purple, and with black horns that went from just above her temple to curl back, like a ram's. Her nipples were black, matching her lips and nails, and a tail went from just above her ass, tipped with what looked like a black arrowhead.

She moved gracefully, reminding me of a rattlesnake—movements smooth but no doubt lethal.

Others sat around where she danced, leering, drinking, laughing.

If it weren't for the monstrous beings there, I would have thought I was in any seedy strip club or bar back home.

Not that I had been in many, but I watched TV.

"He's not here," Troy pointed out.

"Let's grab a seat and wait." Grant nodded at a booth near the back.

We piled in, with me sandwiched between Kase and Grant, Troy at the end. They offered vicious looks to anyone who risked glancing our way, but it seemed to keep anyone from coming closer.

A waitress approached, and it was funny that she had the same tired expression all servers had. It seemed service jobs were the same no matter where a person was.

Grant ordered for everyone and tossed what looked like small pieces of bone on the table, which she scooped up happily.

At my look, Grant shrugged. "I've been to hell a time or two before."

"Why?"

"There are some ingredients for spells you can't get anywhere else. Plus, come on, look around." He gestured to one of the other dancers, this one a male.

The man was lithe, his fingers longer than a human's, tipped not with black like the woman's but with flames. In fact, fire danced over his entire body like a pet, moving along his arms, down his spine, over his hips. He grasped the pole at the center of his platform and arched backward, and the sudden warmth in my cheeks outed me for never having spent much time in a strip club before.

Grant chuckled, then elbowed me. "They're pretty good at controlling those flames, and a burn or two is a very worthwhile risk."

I muttered beneath my breath, calling him a man-whore, and trying to pretend I was not at all jealous.

Food and drinks came, but before I took a sip from the cup set before me, Grant picked it up and sniffed it. He dipped a finger in, then whispered a few words. The liquid on his finger glowed blue, so he pushed it back toward me. "It's safe. Well, safe enough. It won't kill you, at least."

Somehow 'won't kill you' seemed like the best I'd get in hell.

I took a drink of whatever was in my cup and promptly coughed it back up. It felt like acid going down my throat, some strange and all together bad mixture of liquor, cinnamon and peppermint.

Grant slapped his hand against my back, helping me to expel the rest.

"What is that?" I asked once I caught my breath.

"You remember how humans used to drink so much beer because it was safer than water? Well, you've seen the rivers here…"

"That tastes like liquid fire. How can you drink it?"

Grant shrugged and took a gulp of his own. He grimaced the way one might after their first shot but kept it down. "It's not so bad after the first few gulps. They sort of burn off all the taste buds."

Troy pushed his cup away. "Is it really a good idea to drink anything that has alcohol here? We aren't exactly in friendly territory."

Grant placed his hand, palm down, then flipped it over to reveal pills that hadn't been there before. "We need to drink, and water is hard to come by, which is why all ours goes to the fragile one. Ambrosia, the drug added to this, can put an immortal or demon on their ass, but it'll also kill anything dangerous in the liquid. Don't worry, though. Just chew one of these and it'll sober you up instantly." He handed one to each of us, and I tucked mine in my pocket.

"You can just summon things?" I asked.

Grant took another drink before he shrugged. "Some things."

"So why not summon fresh water? Or anything else that is way more useful than sobering up pills?"

"To get things, I have to know exactly where they are, and it doesn't work across realms. That means I can't do it between the living and dead worlds."

"So how did you know where these were?"

"I said I've been here before. I have a stash of things here so I can have access to them when I need, including the currency we used to pay with."

I frowned, thinking back to Troy and Kase's fight. "You summoned popcorn once. Did you happen to know where it was, or do you have popcorn waiting and ready somewhere?"

"I may have a stash there as well."

The picture of Grant making popcorn every day, so it was ready in case he needed it, struck me as incredibly funny.

He offered a smile when I couldn't contain a laugh anymore, when I was struck by how absurd the situation was.

I was in *hell* because the devil wanted to have a chat with me, and to help me I had a vampire who found my blood gross, a werewolf with serious self-confidence issues, a mage who had a stash of stuff somewhere like an anxious squirrel, and some sort of smoke dragon who gave one hell of an orgasm.

I had not seen my life going like this, and if a fortune teller had tried to give me this reading, I'd have called her a hack and demanded a refund.

"Well, at least everyone is in a good mood." Hunter pulled a chair over, then sat in it backward.

I caught my breath before trying for another drink of whatever it was Grant had ordered. He was right, though this time it didn't burn nearly as bad, and I managed to actually swallow it.

"Any luck?" Kase asked.

Hunter nodded, then tossed pieces of twine onto the table. "Rooms for the night. I'd say it'll be better than sleeping on the ground, but they often rent these things by the hour."

"Let's just be glad they don't have black lights here," Grant said.

I nodded at the twine. "What's with the rope? Does the bondage come complimentary? Come for the rooms, stay for the rope play?"

"You telling me you want me to tie you up, shadow-girl?" Hunter picked one up and reached across the table to catch my wrist. He tied it on me, the feeling of his strong fingers against me enough to make me wonder if the rooms might give us a second, spider-free, shot at sex. "These are enchanted to get us into the rooms. Think of it like a keycard, hell-style. We have four rooms, and the sigil on the bead matches the one on the door of the room."

I twisted the string on my wrist. "There isn't a bead on mine."

"That's because you're approved for all the rooms."

The statement sounded nice until math caught up with me and fucked me like it always did. "That means I'm not getting my own room, doesn't it?"

Hunter didn't even *try* to look sorry. "It isn't nearly safe enough for you to sleep alone, shadow-girl. You'll bunk down with someone else."

"And let me guess—you're offering?"

Hunter offered one hell of a grin. "As much as I'd love to offer you up a spot in my bed, I have other, less pleasant obligations to deal with tonight."

"Then why did you get a room?"

"Because I want it to look like I'm there." He answered with such an *obviously* tone, I gave him a glare. So much for spider-free sex for him.

Nothing was obvious here. I didn't understand the rules, and it made me realize maybe I'd fit in before better than I'd thought.

"So what happens tomorrow?" Troy asked.

Hunter pulled his gaze from me before he reached over and stole Grant's drink. "We keep moving inward, toward the Court. After this stop, we'll sleep on the road until we reach Styx. It's the biggest city in hell and it surrounds the palace, like a large ring. Between Styx and Lucifer is a dead zone."

I laughed at the term, which I knew wasn't that funny, but it seemed whatever they'd gotten for me to drink was stronger than I'd realized.

Hunter kept going. "It isn't much fun to cross, since its entire point is to keep all the shit stuck here in hell from accessing the palace. I'm hoping Lucifer has the bridge over it for us, since he should be expecting us, but you never know with him."

"If he doesn't, can we cross it?" Kase asked.

"Sure, but it won't be much fun. We'll want to be properly supplied." At my look, he sighed. "That means weapons, shadow-girl. Think of the dead zone as a big moat, but it's not sweet crocodiles in there."

"Crocodiles aren't sweet," I pointed out.

"Compared to what's in the dead zone? Yeah, they are. You remember that warden in your living room the night I saved you?"

The memory of the darkness swirling came back to me, made me shiver. Yeah, I remembered it.

"Well, that was a glimpse of one, and there're plenty of those at full power in the dead zone."

I poured another mouthful of the drink, swallowing it before I had to taste it.

Not that I could taste much of anything anymore.

Suddenly facing all those things in the ravine sounded like a much better idea than it had before.

Kase spoke up, his tone strained. "And the Court? Should we be worried when we get there?"

"You should *always* be worried where Lucifer is concerned, but once we reach where his people are in control, I doubt we'll need to look over our shoulders. At least, Ava won't. The rest of us are disposable, but he wouldn't drag her here unless he really wanted to talk to her."

Kase nodded, then sat back. There were edges to his expression, something that hinted he wasn't entirely okay. Then again, we were in hell headed to visit the devil. Some amount of discomfort was probably expected.

I knew better than to ask him right then. Men didn't like outing their shortcomings or injuries, and Kase was every bit the sort of alpha male who lived by that.

The drink clouded my head, and before I knew it, I'd finished off the entire cup. When I reached for Troy's, Hunter snatched it away and moved it out of my reach.

"That will leave a hole in your stomach the size of my fist, so maybe stick to the weak stuff?"

"Weak?" The idea that what I'd guzzled down had been considered the fruity drink of the underworld made me shudder.

Still, the way my brain couldn't quite hold on to thoughts was rather nice. I teetered in the booth, leaning first against Grant, then against Kase. The men talked, discussed the plan, the upcoming city, the dead zone.

It all bored me. I'd never been a study-hard sort of woman, maybe because the rules had never applied to me. There hadn't ever been a 'how to survive seeing ghosts' textbook, and somehow books titled *How to Draw the Perfect Cat Eye* hadn't seemed all that useful to my problems.

So I let them talk, resting my head against Kase's shoulder when remaining upright on my own seemed like far too much effort.

The noise in the bar swirled together, and the steady collection of talking, the beat of music, the conversation of the men's rough, deep voices, all lulled me to quiet.

I never would have figured that I'd fall asleep there, in the middle of a crowded bar in hell, but I managed it.

Chapter Five

Normally, after drinking too much, I'd wake hungover but sober. I tended to sleep hard when I drank, because it was one of the few times when my nightmares didn't come. It meant I'd sleep long enough to wake to nausea and a splitting headache instead of fun drunkenness. This time, however, was different.

The spinning room had me reaching for my pocket, for the pill that Grant had given me. It tasted chalky, like mints, but almost as soon as I chewed it, my head started to clear.

I waited until the room stopped moving, giving it time to wipe away all the fuzziness before I risked sitting up and peering around. My cloak hung on a hook by the door. The room was small and dirty — everything I'd expect at a by-the-hour motel in hell. In the large bed, beside me, Kase had stretched out, his eyes closed.

It reminded me of the night he'd been naked, when he'd been in my bed back home. His lips had moved over my shoulder and even though his skin was cool, his touch had warmed me right up.

Heat stirred inside me, making me want to experience that again. The fact that I'd been angry with him, or how he'd betrayed me, or how he'd acted like my blood was the vampire version of cold, stale coffee didn't matter all of a sudden, as if even though I was sober, the ambrosia had left that need in its wake. Or maybe it was just good old-fashioned horniness and I was reaching for another explanation.

He lay still in a way entirely unlike any regular sleeping person. When humans slept, we twitched, we breathed, we shifted. Kase didn't move in the slightest. He wore his slacks and his button-up shirt—his jacket had been lost somewhere along the trip—though neither looked nearly as pristine as they had before. Between all the walking and the fight with Troy—which seemed like a lifetime ago—he was far less put together. His feet were crossed at the ankle, his black socks on and one of his hands rested on his stomach while his other was to the side next to me. Had he fallen asleep like that to touch me?

I shifted, moving slowly so I didn't wake him. I really wasn't sure how deeply vampires slept. My knees pressed into the mattress as I studied him.

His face looked younger right then, when it wasn't pinched with that self-restraint. It made me wonder against just how old he was. When awake, he had an air of control, of caution. There was always a wall I couldn't get past, like a ward around him that kept everything away.

Which was why it was odd to watch him sleep, to see him so…approachable. He didn't look like the vampire who had terrified me, the one so many were afraid of.

I reached out and traced my hand over his arm, the skin beneath the shirt hard.

I wasn't planning on molesting him, but I was drawn to how vulnerable he was. For once, I felt like I could see him, like he wasn't hiding.

I moved my fingers down over his wrist to touch his hand, to where I could brush his actual skin.

The moment it happened, however, the room spun again.

When the breath rushed from my lungs, I realized it wasn't the room spinning this time but me.

I found Kase's face above me, his lips peeled back to expose his fangs, his eyes glowing red.

All those times I'd though he looked scary before were nothing. I'd never seen *this* face. The idea he was older than Colter didn't seem so crazy anymore.

If his face wasn't enough, the hand I'd just touched was wrapped around my throat.

He could have snapped my neck right then, ended me without a second thought. It was reminding just how out-powered I was by these supernaturals. I had started to feel myself, to think I could stand toe-to-toe with them, especially after shoving that shadow from Troy, but in that moment Kase showed me how wrong I was.

His hand kept me from drawing breath—I was really tired of being choked—and even as I clutched at his wrist, I couldn't make him budge.

Kase didn't blink, but his hand tightened a hair before loosening. A split second later, he yanked backward and off me.

I rolled, then coughed hard while I fought to fill my lungs again. Suddenly the ash-laden air wasn't so bad, anymore.

"Ava, are you okay?" Kase asked but didn't touch me.

My palms pressed into the mattress, my lungs burning until I was able to stop the hacking and slow my breath.

To my left, Kase stared at me, gaze intense, his eyes that same red.

He looked like himself, that flat, expressionless face, except for the eyes. As if he'd realized it, he darted his gaze away and when he turned back, his eyes had returned to normal. "Are you okay?" he repeated.

I rubbed my fingers against my sore throat. "What was that?"

"You shouldn't wake me that way."

"I just touched your hand," I argued. "It wasn't like I was going for your pants!"

He dropped his gaze to my throat, and I thought I read a moment of regret. "I don't do well with being…touched."

The last word came after a loud silence, full of explanations he didn't give.

It forced me to think backward, to recall the times we'd touched.

Wait, no, that wasn't quite right. Each time I'd try to touch him, he'd stopped it. He'd restrained me, kept me from having any free contact.

Why hadn't I realized it? I'd chalked it up to some sort of dominance kink. Hell, I'd even gotten off on it like some game. It lost that magic, however, when I realized something sinister rested beneath in the action.

"Why not?"

He blew out a breath, then shook his head. "It doesn't matter, does it?"

I pointed at my throat. "Yes, it really sort of does. You don't get to do this then not talk to me."

He reached forward, and I couldn't help my flinch. Sure, I wasn't exactly afraid of him, but he had just strangled the shit out of me. Even if he hadn't meant it, it was entirely reasonable that I might be a little jumpy around him.

Even with my reaction, however, he only paused for a second for me to regain my confidence. He slid his fingers against the mark. "It looks like after you had that run-in with the poltergeist."

"Well, you and she have the same go-to move."

His Adam's apple bobbed as he swallowed. "I could have done far worse. I could have snapped your neck."

I wanted to reach up and touch him, but I kept the desire in check. I recalled when Troy had touched me, after I'd told him about my past, about the man who had abused me, and about how much I *didn't* want his hands on me then.

"Do you know much about vampires after they're turned?"

I shook my head.

He continued to stroke the mark, as though that were how he could distract himself from what he said. I got the sense it wasn't a story he told often, or perhaps ever. "When newly made, vampires are exceedingly weak. They're hardly stronger than a human and have far more weaknesses than one. They rely heavily on the vampire who made them."

I noticed he used *they* instead of *we*, probably to distance himself from his story. I let him have that, if it was what it took to get it out.

He pulled his hand from me, moving to cross his legs on the bed and lean forward. It made him look less like the unapproachable and extraordinarily strong vampire I knew, and more like a man who had a very long past, much of which wasn't good.

Then again, even in a short human life, how much was shit? How much of my life had been just terrible? If I extrapolated that out to however old Kase was, he had to have a lot of horrible memories locked up in that head of his.

"Old vampires are dangerous, cold. The stronger and older they are, the worse they become. My maker was amongst the oldest and strongest, and certainly the most sadistic."

That last word held a wealth of information. No one called someone sadistic without good reason. It wasn't the term used when people were jerks, when they were selfish. Sadism was about enjoying the suffering of others, and there was a level of evil there I rarely dealt with.

Still, I didn't speak, letting Kase get his entire story out.

His shoulders sagged, as if he crumbled. "I have no wish to go into any real detail, but I spent the first few centuries of my life as little more than a plaything for the vampire who made me, for him and whoever he pleased."

Even without Kase saying it, the reality bled through his words. I had always seen him as untouchable, as larger than life, so to recognize he'd come from nothing, that he'd suffered beneath those so much more powerful than him for *centuries* made my throat tight. It also explained him a little better—his need for control, his attempts to manipulate people, his aloofness.

"I'm sorry," I said, knowing damn well the words didn't mean a thing.

He didn't lift his gaze, didn't acknowledge my useless platitude. "I have had a very long time to get past it, to move forward. As I became older, stronger, it was easier to pretend it had never happened at all. However, when someone touches me, they put their hands on me, I feel the same spark of disgust I did before, and I react as in on instinct."

I folded my hands in my lap, trying to make it clear I wouldn't press his boundaries. "I didn't realize."

"Of course not. How could you? I have shared that with no one."

"No one? In"—I muttered a jumbled string of sounds since I had no idea how old he actually was— "years?"

He let out a humorless laugh. "If you know the worst of my secrets, what does my age matter? I was turned around 1800 BC."

That shocked me. I'd known he was old, but I'd thought a few hundred years. Maybe a thousand? The math quickly added up to over three thousand years old, and I wasn't sure I'd ever heard of a vampire of that age.

Most, when they reached a fraction of that, retreated from the world, found some out-of-the-way place and all but atrophied to nothing. The weight of time passing grew too much for most, which was one reason asking a vampire's age was such a taboo. It was an unwelcome conversation, a reminder that while they didn't grow old, their time was rarely unlimited.

"How..." I asked, unable to formulate a question.

He turned his head to look at me, and it reminded me of when he'd been asleep, as if he'd lowered those defenses for a moment and let me see *him.* "Not many of us make it to my age intact. We are most often killed by those we turn who want more power. I, however, have never made another vampire. Time passed, and no matter how much, I always knew I had something worth being engaged for."

"What?"

He turned away. "It doesn't matter. I understand if this is too much, Ava. After what I did, I understand if the danger is too great, or if you simply don't wish to pursue anything, especially because of…"

"Like I'd hold that against you. My life hasn't exactly been peaches, and what the vampire who made you did, that wasn't your fault."

He sighed, as if my answer was unexpected. "It isn't exactly the sort of thing one wishes for from their male partner." Before I could jump in and tell him, again, that it didn't make me think less of him, he changed the subject. "I would not hurt you, not on purpose."

"I know. Maybe bed sharing isn't such a good idea, though?" I laughed, but it held no humor.

"Perhaps," he admitted softly. "I'd hoped it would be different with you."

"So you've tried this before?"

"Not exactly. You are unique, a situation I've never found myself in before. However, yes, I have attempted to *work through* my aversions in the past."

"And?"

"And I am able to enjoy sex—*fully*—but still can't allow a female to touch me freely. I'm afraid that may be too far for me to ever expect to get." He paused, then blew out a long, unhappy breath, one that reminded me of how many years of pent-up feelings he had—especially given his revelation about his age. "I truly hoped it would be different, that I wouldn't react to you as I had in the past, so if this isn't what you want anymore—"

He was rambling. It was obvious, the way his language became impossibly more formal, as he restated the same thing over and over because he wasn't sure what to say next, that he would just keep talking until he hit a point where he ran out of words. He was caught in a loop, one where he wanted to give me an out I didn't need.

So I tried to tell him what I needed to the only way I could. I shifted so I sat front of him and pressed the insides of my wrists together, then set them in his folded hands.

He lifted his gaze to mine, his eyes the same deep brown I was used to—I might accept him, but I didn't love that red thing they did when he went all feral—and he closed his hands around my wrists.

He leaned forward and kissed me, hungry and desperate, as if he could put the unpleasant conversation behind us with that alone. I could taste the chalk of the sober-up pill on his teeth, telling me at least it wasn't ambrosia driving his actions.

He shifted my wrists behind me, held them against the small of my back, then tugged me forward and into his lap.

No matter how I shifted, his grip didn't loosen at all.

And yes I *wanted* to touch him. The need to run my hands along his hard flesh, to explore his body fully consumed me, but I'd rather have what he was willing to give than nothing at all.

His fangs were sharp, but he was careful, even when he deepened the kiss. I kept my tongue away, not wanting to slice myself, especially after his last reaction to my blood.

I might have been offended by that again if it wasn't for how his hard cock pressed against his slacks—and against me.

It was difficult to care about him not fancying my blood when he clearly wanted my body.

He slid his free hand into my hair, holding me still as he took my lips until I was mindless with want.

He wasn't old as fuck, we weren't in danger, we weren't even in hell. It was two bodies driven by something they'd wanted and been denied.

He broke the kiss to meet my gaze. "Can you keep your hands there?"

I nodded. If it meant he'd have *two* hands to use on me? I was pretty sure I could do anything.

Kase undid the fastening on my pants and worked them off, one leg at a time, and while it would have been difficult to do so normally, given my lack of help, his strength and speed meant he had me bottomless in seconds.

Next, he hiked my shirt up, taking a long look at my chest as if enchanted by the sight. He slid down the cups of my bra, then brushed his thumbs over my nipples. "Beautiful," he whispered, then leaned forward to take the left between his lips.

His mouth wasn't as warm as a human's, but his tongue was talented enough for me to not care. He teased my nipple with his lips, his tongue, even his fangs, as if each were a tool he had to drive me mad. Meanwhile, his hand slid down my stomach before reaching my cunt. His groan against my breast was deep when he found my drenched sex, when he glided his finger along my slit and teased my hardened clit. Because my legs rested around his hips, my cunt was spread out for him, and he took full advantage.

When he plunged his agile fingers into me the first time, I cried out. I wondered for a moment if the rooms were soundproofed as well, but the thought left as quickly as it came.

It was hard to pretend to be shy or modest, especially as he twisted those fingers inside me, as he fucked up into me with purposeful and strong thrusts.

Before long, I moved with him, rolling my hips as I rose and lowered myself, wanting more from him.

"Please," I asked him, lacing my fingers together to keep me from reaching out.

He pulled away from my breast, leaving the nipple shiny from his saliva, like a reminder of what he'd been doing. "We don't have to rush—"

Stupid man, thinking he needed to take it slow, that I was fragile. I licked across his bottom lip, the only way I felt comfortable to touch him. "I want you, Kase. I want all of you."

"Even after..." His hesitation spoke volumes. Even after he'd accidently hurt me, even after his story, after admitting his past, his hang-ups, his failings. He was asking how I could still want him after knowing it all.

It reminded me of his secrecy, of the way I was never sure if he was honest or not, and it all made so much sense. From the start, he'd been hiding because he never thought for a moment that I could still want him if I knew it all.

I pressed my forehead against his, my hands safely tucked behind me. "Yes. It doesn't matter what you tell me, what you've been through, it doesn't change how I feel. I want you."

His breath held that copper tinge it always did when he exhaled, when it blew across my lips. He hadn't fed in…I had no idea how long, so him smelling of blood was odd.

And far more arousing than it should have been…

Clearly my perversions were an ever-developing issue.

I thought, for a moment, he might turn me down. Maybe he'd decide it was too fast for him, or not the right place.

Maybe he was, under it all, a romantic who didn't want to screw me for the first time in a by-the-hour motel in the afterworld.

Those thoughts went away when he moved, the way he did when it was faster than I could follow, and I found myself on my back, his strong, lean body above me. He stretched my hands out above me and pressed them against the headboard, the meaning clear.

I grasped the iron of the headboard, the designs twisting around like plants, giving me plenty of good spots to wrap my fingers around.

When I did, he dragged his hand down my arm, his other unfastening his slacks. He didn't bother to remove them entirely, as if he were too afraid to lose the moment, that if he left me for even as long as it took to shuck his pants, he'd lose it all.

I spread my thighs, wrapping a leg up and around his hip, offering myself to him entirely.

He leaned his forehead against mine a moment before the blunt head of his cock seated against my cunt. I'd seen him naked, of course, but *feeling* him was a whole different matter. Again, it was strange that he wasn't as warm as other men, but that didn't matter. His cock was harder, the skin having that smooth, almost marble quality to it. It almost reminded me of a glass dildo, yet that couldn't come close to just how amazing this felt, or just how anxious I was to have him fill me.

He let out a low, wild groan as he sank his thick cock into me, my body more than wet enough to allow him to glide easily.

I lifted my hips when he slowed. I didn't want careful. I didn't want him thinking or worrying. I just wanted *him*.

His hips jerked forward when I tightened my leg around him, stealing another inch of his hard cock, before he seemed to understand.

"My brave Ava," he all but growled into my ear. "I never expected you to want me, not really, but I swear I'll give you all you can take." The words were sweet, but his actions were anything but.

He shifted backward, then plunged deep into me in one hard thrust. The way my body stretched and how deliciously full I felt made my hands tighten on the headboard.

I planted one foot against the bed and met him thrust for thrust. Funny how he could seem so wild in that moment, yet I'd *felt* his strength when he'd wrapped his hand around my throat, knew what he was capable of if he actually lost control.

Even as he took me hard, he was careful, because he could have easily hurt me if he'd wanted to.

He whispered, his voice strained, but I didn't know the words. They were in a language I didn't understand, as if he'd reverted to his native tongue, yet the tone gave away the meaning.

They were oddly sweet, said earnestly as if he'd meant nothing more. The words not translating must have had to do with him not being from hell, either.

He grasped my thigh in one hand, his hand tight, keeping me against him as he sank as deep into me as he could, as if he couldn't get enough.

Neither could I.

It was like, in these moments, in the times when I could let everything go with another person, I had a reprieve. I didn't have to worry about anything.

Kase took my worries from me, leaving no room for them inside me. I kept my hands on the headboard but leaned up, wanting his lips.

He obliged, and I had to admit, kissing someone with fangs wasn't as awkward as I had expected. Then again, I was careful. I would *not* risk ruining the moment with a stray drop of blood.

He growled, a sound that sounded so odd from him. He'd always been controlled, the epitome of sophistication, so seeing this side of him thrilled me. His fingers tightened almost painfully around my thigh, and each time he plunged deep into me, he caught my clit, a spark of pleasure but not quite enough.

As if he noticed, Kase leaned up, breaking the kiss and bracing his weight on his hand to put space between our bodies. "Let go of the headboard," he demanded, the order in his voice the biggest turn-on. "Touch yourself, Ava."

My name was like a prayer on his lips, his accent heavier than I was used to, as if during the heat of the moment he couldn't hide it anymore.

I did as he said, letting go with one hand so I could reach down—careful not to brush him—and slide my fingers against my needy clit. The first touch was shocking in its intensity. I hadn't realized how wound up I was, how much I needed this.

The new position made Kase's cock stroke against my cunt differently, angling him up and it worked for me. I didn't tease myself, didn't do gentle, feather-light touches. Instead, I parted my fingers into a V so I could stroke both sides of my hard clit in time with his rough, deep thrusts.

The strain on his face said he was close, that he wanted me to come apart first, and I was *so* ready for it. He peeled his lips backward like an instinct he couldn't help, but instead of giving in to fear, I let the sight send me over.

This was Kase. It wasn't the careful face he offered to the world, the one of an untouchable and controlled vampire. It wasn't the one he'd given me at first when he'd been afraid that I couldn't handle the real him. He was wild, passionate, and if I couldn't accept this part of him, then I couldn't accept any of him.

The orgasm took me over, but I didn't stop, prolonging it with how I stroked my nub.

Kase let go of my thigh — probably for the best, since he'd against cranked down his grasp just before — and threw his head back.

It was beautiful in an odd way, the sight of him entirely lost to pleasure. I had a feeling Kase wasn't someone who was ever lost, someone who was ever without control, so when the cords of his neck stood out, when he plunged deep and stilled as my cunt tightened around him, drawing out both our orgasms, I savored the moment.

A minute later, he shuddered and withdrew, his cock softening, though even that was enough to pull a whine from me.

He stretched out behind me, then rolled me so my back was to him and tucked me against his chest. He wrapped an arm around me, enveloping me.

I frowned at the lack of stickiness on my thighs. Condoms weren't needed due to the sterility, but had he not…

"Kase," I started, though I knew there wasn't a good way to ask if a man had actually come…

He shushed me. "Vampires don't ejaculate," he explained as if he knew what I'd ask.

I guess that made sense… They didn't have the same bodily functions.

After a moment, the other worry wouldn't be ignored, especially when I swallowed and remembered what had happened the last time.

He pulled me tighter against him with a sigh, as though I were being all together annoying and ruining his afterglow. "Sleep, Ava. I will stay awake. I just want…"

He paused, like he wasn't sure what to say. Saying he wanted to cuddle was probably too far. He'd already given in a *lot* so I supposed I could offer him that one reprieve.

"Get some rest," he finished with instead.

Sleep cuddled up with the vampire equivalent of my very own guard dog after amazing, long-overdue sex?

That sounded like exactly what I needed.

Chapter Six

The next morning, I woke alone, though that didn't shock me. Kase didn't strike me as a "hang around and have breakfast together" sort of man, especially after his revelations the night before.

After donning my cloak, I crossed the hallway to Grant's room to find Kase there as well. We ate, and by the time we left the inn, I finally felt ready for another leg of the trip.

The ability to sleep in a bed, to stop and rest, to see something other than spanning wilderness had done wonders for my stamina.

It certainly wasn't Kase I had to thank for that, given the slight ache in my body. He'd used up stamina if anything. *Worth it.*

This time we took a road, which made the trip much easier. I was over the whole climbing thing, where we made our own trail. Instead, we followed a beaten path with trees and farms lining the way.

"Where were you last night?" I asked Hunter.

He was still shirtless — not that I minded. "Checking the roads ahead. I wanted to make sure there weren't any traps or ambushes."

I frowned, glancing to my side. "Was it a smart idea to go out there by yourself?"

"You worried about me?" The smile he flashed me said the idea amused him.

Instead of saying anything about it — he'd be far too pleased by that — I tugged at the cloak I wore. "Can I take this thing off, yet? No one else is around."

"What if you take off everything under it instead?" He lifted an eyebrow as if that were the best compromise he'd ever heard.

"Well, my normal clothing doesn't smell like rotten sludge, so I'm pretty sure I know which I'd prefer."

Hunter huffed a soft laugh. "You can take the hood down but keep the rest on. It'll help hide your scent."

"No one in the bar even looked twice at me. I think you're being overly dramatic about this."

"Yeah, you say that now because you haven't faced anything around here that wants to devour all that delicious mortality you have. Trust me, you'd be less confident if you had."

I wanted to tell him that wasn't true, but then I recalled how Kase had thrown me around, how Jerrod had charged, how the dancers in the bar had moved.

So, okay, maybe I was out of my league.

I took down the hood as he'd said but didn't complain about leaving the cloak fastened at my throat.

Hell seemed stranger the more time I spent there, and just as soon as I thought I had a feel for it, it changed.

I'd gotten used to the wilderness, to the dim sky and the freaky, spiky trees. Climbing over the sharp rocks hadn't been fun, but I'd accepted it.

Then we'd ended up in an honest-to-God town, complete with strippers and a no-tell-motel. That had been weird, but again, I'd adjusted.

My night with Kase helped that…

And now? Now we walked down a road, a red mist hanging on the ground like fog, with fields that stretched out growing something I couldn't identify. Houses were set in each huge space, but they didn't look like the cute, southern-type houses. These held a sinister edge, which I could understand because I doubted good-ole-boy farmers ended up in hell. *Well, maybe the racists ones.*

"What are these farms?" I asked.

Hunter nodded at one of the houses that sat in the middle of a large field of spindly plants, ones that looked dead despite growing in perfect rows. The mist was so thick, I couldn't see the ground. "Nothing much grows here, at least nothing usable. I'm sure you've noticed all the trees are bare."

"Yeah, it occurred to me when I had to pee behind a shrub and there wasn't much cover."

He snorted softly. "These farms grow ambrosia, which is what is ground up to make alcohol, along with other mind-altering substances that work on demons, spirits and immortals."

I frowned before going over to where the fencing separated the plants from the road. When I peered closer, the mist shifted without breaking apart. "Why does it grow?"

"There are some things you don't want to know," Hunter said.

"I find people tell me that when they don't want to tell me something. It doesn't seem to have much to do with what's best for me."

The mist swirled, moving from the way I approached. It parted, but Hunter caught my chin and brought my gaze to his.

"Trust me, shadow-girl, there are things in hell you don't want to see. You'll leave here, go back to your regular life and you don't want those images in your head. Some things, once they get in there, you can't get them out." His gaze was so serious, it made me pause. Though, beneath that there was something more.

Instead of pressing, I pulled away. I'd had *enough* of men with hang-ups. I didn't need to unravel anything else.

"So this is where that alcohol came from?"

Hunter nodded, keeping up with me as I started back down the path. "Yep. The ambrosia plants are harvested and ground up. They're about the most valuable thing in hell, at least outside of mortals."

"And they use a flimsy wooden fence to keep it safe?"

Hunter bent down and picked up a rock from the edge of the road, rolling in his palm for a moment before tossing it over the fence into one of the fields.

Plants near the house moved, from at least three separate spots. The tall branches shifted as whatever it was barreled through us, and those small moments of bravery fled entirely. Something dark, angry, and with flames struck the fence, bouncing off it.

Not a fence, but a ward of some sort.

My ass hit the ground after I stumbled backward. Even though I didn't see any real details, I'd spotted more than enough to make it clear I should avoid the fields.

Hunter reached out for my hands, then tugged me to my feet. "They keep those things in the fields to discourage anyone who thinks about stealing. Not that it stops them. I'd say a few a day still try it."

The idea of that made my stomach uneasy. "What happens to them?"

Hunter glanced to his side, his gaze hitting the mist that swirled over the field and near the ground.

He didn't need to say it. It seemed I'd gotten good enough at understanding hell to hear it loud and clear.

The thin mist, the red that coated the dirt...

Blood, the particles thin enough to float like fog.

I tried not to think about the dampness of my ankles.

In fact, I didn't say another word to Hunter. He was right—there were things I didn't want to know, facts I just didn't want to have. I would have happily gone to sleep every night for the rest of my life without knowing that fields of blood fog existed, that they were watered by the death of things that ventured into the yards patrolled by monsters.

Hunter didn't try to coax me into conversation after that. We traveled the path, and he said we only had a day's walk before we reached Styx.

The odd thing was that despite how much we'd traveled, I wasn't as sore as I'd have figured. It wasn't like I was overly athletic before, since my exercise usually went as far as paying for a monthly gym membership and swearing weekly I'd go.

Grant walked just ahead of me, fiddling with something in his hands.

Hunter had taken off again, always quick to check the space ahead of us, while Troy hunched forward, hands tucked in his jacket pockets, as surly as ever, taking up the rear with Kase.

I jogged up the few feet to stay beside Grant. "Why aren't I more tired?"

He didn't lift his gaze, focused instead on what appeared to be a necklace made of string. "Because Kase probably isn't that good in bed."

His words took a moment for me to understand, and when they did, my cheeks burned. Apparently, I hadn't been all that quiet…

Grant's lips pulled into a smirk, telling me he enjoyed rattling me far too much.

"You aren't as funny as you think you are."

"Of course I am," he said without a speck of uncertainty. "You aren't tired after the walking because you aren't in the living realm. You don't expend energy the same way here you would back home, especially because you're mortal."

"That makes no sense."

Grant continued to work, his hands sliding along the string, braiding and tying it as he spoke. "You're mortal, so let's say you're an electric car. Hell, it runs on gas."

"Wouldn't that mean I'd get tired faster? Since I couldn't recharge?"

"No, because the only way you move here is essentially hitching a ride on a gas truck. You're using very little of your own power. That's why we have to hide your scent, because others here would love to get a look at your…battery." He chuckled softly at his own joke.

I nodded at the string. "What's that?"

Grant held his arm out, the mark he'd had on the small bare area of his forearm gone. "When we're here, my tracking spell doesn't work. Spells don't transfer because they use power from the living realm."

"So stalking me becomes harder? Poor man."

He added another knot to the string, whispering a few words beneath his breath. "The keys for the rooms gave me an idea."

"To give up magic and become a jeweler? Not sure there's a market in hell, but I appreciate the hustle."

Grant stopped and reached toward me. He fastened the string around my throat, so it fit like a choker, whispering a few more words as he did before explaining, "Magic doesn't work quite like it does in the living realm, but this connects here." He held up another string with a bone tied to the end, one that didn't hang down but arced toward me. When I shifted side to side, it followed. "I'll be able to follow you. It isn't quite as nice as my old one, but it'll work."

I frowned as I thought about something else. "The guy outside the bar noticed me. Jerrod did, but he followed the scent. Shouldn't my tattoos have made it so the guy ignored me?"

"Those tattoos weren't done in hell. They were made to work in the living world, to keep you hidden from things there. It's like having desert camouflage and going into the jungle."

I blew out a breath. "Just great. I finally accept that my parents put something useful on me and it stops working."

"I doubt they'll even blast someone anymore. Sorry, you're as visible and vulnerable as the next person now. Unfortunate, since you ended up in so much trouble even *with* the spell before."

I offered him a half-hearted glare before kicking a rock from the road. It sailed to the side, into a field, and the same response as the last time happened.

At least this time it wasn't as scary.

"So you really think we can make it to the Court?"

He lifted his dark eyebrow, as if the question surprised him. "You having doubts now?"

"It just seems like everything I see, everything that happens, all just ups the ante. I feel like we're betting too much."

"Maybe," he agreed, "but we don't have much of a choice. I wouldn't have suggested hell as a vacation spot for you, but as long as Lucifer's markers are on you, we're stuck." When I huffed, unconvinced, he kicked a rock as I had before. "I learned something when I was young, a lesson I've never forgotten. It's easy to obsess about options and choices when you have them, right? If you have cake and brownies, you can spend forever deciding which one is best. If all you have is cake, however, the fact that cake isn't your favorite doesn't matter. Worrying about it, hating it, none of that changes what is. One you get pushed out of an airplane, the time to wonder if you should jump is over."

I cast a side eye at him, the words strange from him. He was the 'I can do anything' man. He was the one who could create things from nothing, manipulate the laws of physics, and he was lecturing me on what a person could and couldn't do?

"What do you know about that? It seems like you can do about anything." Then his story about the council also hit me. "Besides, your father was the Magistrate, wasn't he? Doesn't that make you some sort of legacy? I doubt you know much about not getting what you want."

Grant's demeanor changed, just the barest tensing as if the conversation had turned into dangerous territory. "Not exactly," he said, but didn't elaborate. "I'm just saying that we've got one choice, Ava. Forward.

Wasting energy wondering if we can climb this cliff isn't going to change that we have to."

The advice made sense, in the way good advice always did. It sounded so easy and yet was rarely simple to apply.

Still, arguing with good advice never got anyone anywhere, either, so I curled my shoulders in and kept moving forward.

I was tired of getting answers that didn't help. It wasn't like before, when I didn't want to know. I asked questions, and I understood what I was told. Vampires died when someone stabbed them. Werewolves didn't like silver. Poltergeists liked to strangle the shit out of me. Those were basics that I knew.

Now, however, every question I asked had some open-ended answer that meant nothing to me, that left me no better off after hearing. *You're mortal so you don't get tired for some complicated reason that makes no sense.*

My foot caught something, pitching me forward when I was too distracted by my frustration to notice the rock buried in the road.

Wait… It wasn't a rock.

A skull stared up at me, buried partly in the road and cracked at the top, as if heavy things had stepped on it for years. The eye sockets were large and empty, and it mocked me.

"There's a skull," I said, voice flat.

Kase came up beside me, as though he'd spotted my pause and wanted to check in. When he saw the skull, he frowned. "And?"

"Nope." I shook my head, crossing my arms.

"Nope?" Troy walked up alongside the others until all of us stood in a circle, even Hunter, who usually disappeared for long periods of time.

"That's right. Nope. Not doing it."

"Doing what?" Grant asked.

"There is a skull in the road like it's nothing. It's too much. This is stupid, all of it." I gestured at the skull, then around us. "There shouldn't be random skulls just chilling in the middle of the road. I don't care that this is hell, I don't care what is normal here, this is ridiculous."

The men all looked at me as if I had lost my mind, which annoyed me even *more*. How was I the unreasonable one when my complaint was corpse parts just hanging around. That was a basic boundary for most people, right?

Hunter answered carefully. "You've seen plenty of bodies before."

"Yes, but they're not *in the middle of the road.* They're in shallow-dug graves like decent dead bodies should be. This thing has been run over for years and no one cares. Do you not understand how fucked-up that is? What sort of place do you have to be in for people to just ignore the skull in the middle of the path?"

"Ava," Kase started to say, but I lifted my hand toward him.

"No. I'm done."

"You can't be *done*," Grant said. "We're stuck here until we see Lucifer, in case you've forgotten. It isn't the sort of thing you get to be done with just because you feel like it."

I walked away and yelled over my shoulder, "Done!"

Okay, so I wasn't done forever, but I needed a moment. I needed a chance to reset again, to take back my own sense of normalcy. Damn it, I needed to feel like I was in control, even if it was just of this hissy fit.

"Ava," Troy called out, his *let's be reasonable* voice. It seemed that my hissy fit was enough for him to talk to me.

I turned and stomped my foot on the ground. "No more. No more blood mist, no more weird drugs, no brimstone or wardens or anything else."

The men stared at me, their eyes widening, and for a moment I thought they'd taken me seriously.

Then their gaze moved up, above my head, and I realized…*shit.*

I turned to find a large, misshapen figure behind me. He was huge, easily eight feet tall, with fangs that dropped below his chin and skin covered in burn scars.

So I shouldn't have walked away from the men. I remembered one of my foster mothers telling me that having tantrums never made anything better.

One point for her…

The man lifted an orb, then slammed it down, the ground disappearing beneath me as I fell into a darkness that swallowed me up, and the sounds of familiar roars distanced, grew fainter, until everything went black.

C h a p t e r S e v e n

My head pounded when I came to, but my eyes wouldn't open. It was as if my entire body refused to come to get with the program of being conscious.

Eventually, I shifted, rolling to my side, then pushing up to sitting. When my eyes finally opened, I didn't recognize anything around me. I was inside, but it didn't seem like a house. Plank walls and a dirt floor made me suspect some sort of shed.

On my wrist sat a steel manacle that hooked to a large metal bolt in the floor.

Which was a really bad sign.

No one woke up cuffed and thought, *Yes, this is a positive turn of events. Everything is going according to plan.*

I yanked at the chain, grasping it with both hands and planting my feet against the ground for leverage.

It didn't even budge, though the metal groaned.

As my head cleared, I realized more things, and each one painted a worse picture. None of the men were around—I couldn't remember anything after that sinking sensation—something sniffed around outside the wooden walls and the ground beneath me had big splotches of red which could only be blood.

Or someone was really aggressive with their finger painting...

Whatever stalked outside was large, and when its shadow played against the wall, it gave me a glimpse of black and red.

Why was *everything* black and red? It was like hell had no other colors to use.

Then again, maybe obsessing over a small color palate wasn't the right thing to focus on at the moment, especially when something chuffed right next to the door, as if it knew I was in there.

Which made me realize yet another bad thing. My cloak was gone. I never figured I'd miss that smelly, damp piece of cloth, but I sure did.

I reached for my throat, and at least the string still rested there.

If Grant's even still alive...

The thought made me swallow hard. The idea that anything could have happened to Grant, to any of them, felt like something entirely impossible. They were bigger than life. Nothing could take them out.

Except...I'd also learned that life wasn't so easy.

Heavy steps thudded against the packed dirt outside, something a lot larger than the creature who sniffed around the door. When the new figure approached, the creature let out a loud yelp after a thud of flesh on flesh.

Anything that could send that thing running wasn't something I wanted to see.

Not that I had a say in the matter. The hinges of the door squeaked as it opened, and I got a better look at the same being who had stopped me in the middle of the road.

And he was even worse this time, when I had the chance to study him. His skin was not just burned but melted. Worse, it was shiny, as if it leaked some sort of slime. His fangs made Kase's look like nothing. They were so long, they passed his chin, like a saber-tooth tiger's. Huge black horns curled back and over his head. His hair was stringy, thin and didn't quite cover his entire scalp.

He left the door open, and through it I spotted the rows of ambrosia plants and the flash of a creature running through them.

Which meant what had sniffed around and been kicked by this guy was one of the protectors of the fields.

I couldn't stand, the chain around my wrist too short. Still, I scooted as far away as I could.

He didn't look toward me, and somehow, him not even looking my way was worse, like I wasn't important.

The man dropped a large bag that had been slung over his shoulder. Dust kicked up when it hit the ground, and the clatter of metal made my eyes widen. Never in the history of time was a big, heavy bag full of pieces of metal ever the start of something good.

"So, if you just open the cuff up, I'll get going." My voice came out high and panicked even though I tried to act controlled, like I was abducted on the daily and it was no big deal.

He didn't respond, though he did reach into the bag and pull out something that resembled a machete.

It had a longer handle, but, really, the blade was the important part of a machete, right?

He set it down and went to pick up something else.

I did *not* need to see what it was. I yanked at the chain again. "You don't want to do this."

Still he didn't answer. I thought about how a goat might feel as someone prepared the room to butcher it. Suddenly, going vegetarian sounded much better.

Too bad Grant's little mark didn't work anymore—I was pretty sure his entire arm would be in flames because of my fear.

The man turned, finally looking directly at me. His lips curled into a sickening smile, though something about the fangs made it not *quite* as scary. It was like someone with fake vampire teeth trying to smirk. "I haven't seen a full mortal this far into hell in a while."

"A mortal? Me? That's crazy."

He made a chiding sound, as if scolding a kid. "I can *smell* you, human. You reek of mortality, of life. Even with the cloak, my nose is good enough to spot it." He took a step toward me.

"Okay, fine, I'm mortal, but I am a *terrible* one. Whatever you want, I won't be helpful with it. Did you know a vampire *spat out* my blood? See? You should save us both the trouble and just let me go."

He neared me, thankfully without his weapons, but didn't seem to be listening to me at all. He caught my hand, the one without the shackle.

I kicked. Okay, so I'd only taken like two of those cardio kickboxing classes, and it wasn't like I had much power behind the kick, but I was without options.

My foot struck his leg, and it sank in as if his body was made of not quite solid flesh, but he didn't react.

He lifted my hand, having to lean down in the end because the chain kept me from standing fully and he was a *lot* taller than I was. He ran his fang over my palm in a quick jerk, the sharp tip slicing it open.

I cried out. Sure, it would have been nice if I'd been stoic, but he'd just opened a gash in my palm that made Grant's seem like a paper cut.

He released me, then went to a cabinet. "My crops need to expand," he said, his tone civil, as if we were discussing basic gardening and not my eminent demise.

"I've heard fertilizer does wonders."

"The blood mist keeps them growing, but new plants must have roots. I take clippings of the old ones, the strong ones, and plant them into their new home when I can, but roots are hard to come by."

I had a sinking suspicion *roots* had something to do with me.

He took out an empty pot—no, wait, it had dirt in it—and another pot with a large plant, setting both on the ground beside me. "This is my oldest, my best crop. I don't harvest it for product anymore—it's too valuable for that. Instead, it creates new plants, fathering some of the best crops in this area."

"Proud papa, I'm sure." I yanked again at the manacle, my wrist aching.

"Let us see how much it likes your blood."

"Let's not."

Even as I spoke, he snatched my bleeding hand and held it above the plant. Fat droplets of red fell from my palm and over the grayish leaves, the long, stalk-like trunk.

When he let go, I pulled away, cradling my hand to my stomach, swallowing to keep my food down.

Something about feeding that plant felt wrong in a way few things did to me, sickening, like something that twisted nature in a way that should never happen.

"See, the blood mist, made by the creatures that live in hell, will nourish them to grow, to stay alive, but we need living material to create new plants. You could be mother to so many new ones."

"Not really the mothering type."

"You don't have a say. You shouldn't have come here, and a hellhound of *all* people should have known better. That one was a fool who should have known better."

Hunter. That gave me another idea… "Lucifer summoned me. I bet he'd be pretty angry if you killed me before he got to talk to me…"

Sure, name dropping the devil wasn't my normal go-to plan, but one worked with what they had.

Which for me, right then, was fuck-all.

The man laughed, something that sounded like spiders skittering across a tile floor. "Well, in that case, it'd be best if I made sure I buried you deep, wouldn't it? If Lucifer cares at all about you, I'd imagine he'd already be angry with me. Besides, you're worth the risk. I haven't grown my crop in *years.*" His eyes took on a red tint, one that reminded me of Kase's, but where I didn't fear Kase, I feared this man.

A high-pitched sound filled the shed, something I wasn't sure I even heard rather than felt.

The man turned toward his plant, rising to his full height. The plant *moved,* shivering, and more of that sound came again. Leaves curled in on themselves, like a bug sprayed with poison.

"What did you do to it?" the man roared.

"Nothing," I swore, again trying the chains.

The plant continued, and from outside the shed, a similar sound echoed up, as if the rest of the crops felt the pain of that one.

The sound died down just as the plant wilted, collapsing on itself, until crumbled, dried pieces were caught on a breeze from outside and blown into the air like crushed leaves.

Which was probably not something the man was going to be happy about.

He turned toward me, his face not even remotely human anymore. His lips curled up showing that all his teeth were sharp, not just the two fangs. "You killed it! What are you?"

He gave me no chance to answer — not that I had an answer — before he charged.

Fear like I'd never felt before went through me, consumed me. I was going to die. Sure, he was going to kill me before, it had been a necessity in the man's eyes. Now?

Now it would be painful — now he would make sure it lasted.

His huge, claw tipped hand swung for me, but instead of making contact…

A coldness went through me that sank right to my bones, something terrifying and familiar and instinctual.

It consumed me, and the man's hand went *through* my body.

His eyes widened, and I look down to find the manacle had fallen free, that my hands were almost invisible.

I was pretty sure I wasn't supposed to see *through* my own body.

When he reached again, his hand again passed through me, like I wasn't there.

It was the sort of thing that probably deserved some study. Going incorporeal wasn't *normal*. However, since it meant I wasn't being torn apart by this psychotic resident of hell who wanted to use me as some sort of plant fertilizer, well, I wasn't going to question it.

Instead, I took off, out through the doorway, through the plants. As I ran through the field, I couldn't feel the ground beneath my feet or the plants exactly. A small current skirted over my skin, like touching the surface of water, but I could pass through without issue.

Plants moved around me, telling me I wasn't the only thing running through the field. Sure enough, one of those creatures sailed through my body, snapping its teeth but unable to actually get hold of me.

The edge of the fence line was ahead. The man could follow me—he'd been on the road the first time—but I didn't think the beasts could.

A flickering sensation in my hand—like when an arm falls asleep and it starts to wake up—came a moment before it spread through me.

Which, I had to assume, was not a good thing.

My foot caught a root and I pitched forward, into the dirt, into the red mist. I dug my fingers into the ground to shove myself to my feet, but they encountered something warm.

When I shifted, it moved dirt from the base of a plant and down there—the roots the man had said—was a hand... It shifted, the fingers twitching as if still alive, the plant growing right from its palm.

Sickness swamped me, but I relegated that for later. I could find a good therapist when I got back home, could spend years pouring this all out to her and unpack it then.

For now, escaping was all that mattered. I didn't want to become another root in that farm.

"You ruined everything," spat the voice of the man.

I rolled to my back, finding him towering above me, the machete in his hand and murder in his gaze.

A flash of something too quick for me to track slammed into him.

When they paused, however, I recognized the other person.

I wasn't sure I'd *ever* been so happy to see Kase.

Kase was far smaller than the man, but that hadn't stopped him from plowing into him as if the man weighed nothing.

I'd seen Kase take on a shifted Troy, yet it still shocked me to witness his speed and strength. Maybe it was because he acted so civilized the rest time, because he hid that side of himself in a way no one else did, because he was unfailingly careful around me. Even Troy, with all his hang-ups, had the look of a rough country boy.

Kase looked like an aristocrat who never got his hands dirty.

At least, he normally did. When going toe-to-toe with a resident of hell, he lost that pristine image.

Kase was faster, but the man hit harder. Worse, the claws that tipped the man's fingers tore into Kase's body despite his hardened skin.

The fight was bloody in a way I wasn't used to, and all I could do was scoot backward.

I wasn't any help here, couldn't do a damn thing but stay out of their way.

To my left, the plants parted and one of those guard creatures lumbered through. It was my first good look at it, and I wished it had stayed hidden.

They looked less like dogs than I'd thought and more like a cross between a Komodo dragon and a spider. Eight legs came from its body, flames sparking from its eyes, and large, sharp teeth lined its jaws. The thing was from a nightmare, and in that moment, I swore I'd seen it before, like some memory from something I'd spotted in a vision.

It crept forward, slowly, which seemed rude. I'd seen how fast they were, so this one approached slowly for the fun of it…

It ignored its master, didn't try to intervene in the fight. Then again, I doubted it gave a damn about its master. This wasn't a beloved pet—it was a guard, and it had no care for the one who imprisoned it.

It leapt forward, and I rolled to avoid it. Teeth dug in, but caught the ankle of my shoe so I didn't lose my foot. I used my other to kick it—hard.

It let go, and I got to my feet. The fence line was only about ten feet away…

"Go," Kase snapped, as if he'd known what I was thinking.

The beast leapt, but Kase was faster. Somehow, he got between the thing and me, took the hit himself, let it dig its teeth into his shoulder instead of mine. He grabbed its throat and threw it to the side.

Worse, the distraction let the man close in land another vicious slash to Kase's ribs.

My feet wouldn't move. I couldn't run...Kase was obviously overwhelmed, and I couldn't leave him like that.

A thought came to me, one that made little sense, but then again, I was in hell. Things hadn't made sense since I'd arrived.

I opened my hand, the one still smeared in blood, and let it drip on the plants to my side.

That same high-pitched scream from before came again, but I didn't stop. I bled on the ones close by, and the man jerked his gaze toward me.

Suddenly, Kase didn't matter as much to him.

Though, I didn't care for having his attention, either.

The beast left Kase alone, as well. While it might not love its master, it had been trained to protect the plants.

Kase didn't move, collapsing to the ground as his opponents moved away.

The beast jumped toward me, and I flung my hand out to try and catch it before it got its jaws around my face. The action sent drops of my blood flying toward it.

When they landed, the thing yelped as if my blood burned it. The beast shook its head and bolted in the other direction, a whimper following as if it had just realized *to hell with this*.

"What are you?" the man repeated, his hands open, his claws spread, his voice low and furious.

He walked toward me, each step slow and lumbering. It was then I realized all the wounds that covered him.

It seemed Kase had done his share of damage, even if it didn't show as openly...

I brought my arms together, a last-ditch effort, but nothing happened, just as Grant had said.

The man was so close, I could see the glistening of that slime-like substance on his skin. I could smell the rot on his breath.

However, before he could do anything else, a familiar roar filled the space, one that had terrified me before.

Troy—fully shifted and looking every bit as large and monstrous as the man—flew past me, and with one swing of his claw-tipped hand, decapitated him.

I charged forward, past the still falling body, past Troy, and dropped to my knees beside Kase.

Please let him be okay…

I hadn't thought about losing him before. Vampires were immortal, so it wasn't the sort of thing I *had* to worry about.

Fear gripped my chest, made it hard to pull in air, especially when I stared down at Kase's battered form, his chest not rising since he didn't need to breathe.

Finally, he blinked, eyes that same red that I used to hate, and I drew in a shaky breath.

Thank fuck.

Chapter Eight

Filth covered the house, but I lacked the energy to complain about the accommodations.

Staying in the home of the man who had been ready to carve me up and *plant* me wasn't my idea of a good time, but one good look at Kase had reminded me that there were bigger issues than my comfort.

He looked...horrible. His skin was even more pale, dark red blood covering so much of him, his shirt in tatters that helped expose his damaged body.

It made the fight with Troy seem like nothing, and I couldn't shake the memory of him taking blows meant for me.

Troy had reminded me that the creatures that guarded the fields hadn't been interested in coming anywhere near me after the whole flinging-blood thing, and with the master himself dead...the house was probably the safest place around.

So Troy had helped Kase inside and gotten him settled in a bed upstairs, before heading down to check the rest of the house, and probably to shift back to human.

"Are you going to be okay?" My voice wavered at the question.

Kase leaned against the headboard, red covering so much of his clothing. "I'll be fine."

"But—"

"I will be fine," he repeated. "I just need to rest."

"And feed?" I held my arm out. "I know my blood isn't to your liking, but if it keeps you alive, maybe your delicate sensibilities can deal with it."

He shook his head. "After seeing what it did to the things here, I'm going to guess that the taste is the only warning I would get. I don't want to know what it might do to me if I swallowed it."

I opened my mouth, but he held up his hand to end the conversation.

I sat on the bed beside him, hunching forward. "I wish I could have helped more."

His eyebrows drew toward each other like I wasn't making any sense. "Ava, even after I told you to run, you stayed there. I'd be dead—more dead than normal, as you would say—if you hadn't come up with that blood trick. Also, I did happen to see you running through the field like a ghost," he said. "I wasn't sure if I was supposed to mention that or not."

"What does that *mean?*"

He shifted, a grimace before he stilled as if realizing no amount of moving around was going to resolve his pain. "I don't know."

"You're old as shit," I pointed out. "How can you not know?"

His laugh was strained and rare. In fact, I'd bet it was only his horrible condition that meant he laughed at all instead of suppressing it. "Because I suspect whatever you are isn't supposed to happen."

"Why now, though? I've been whatever I am for thirty-five years, and all I've had to show for it before was bad dreams and talking ghosts. Why am I changing now? Why am I finding all these new skills?"

"Probably because you hadn't needed them before." He gestured for me to come closer, to sit beside him.

I moved slowly, trying not to jostle the bed. Though I was sure I did, he didn't react.

Once I leaned against the headboard, he went on. "We do things when we need to. The saying, necessity is the mother of invention comes into play, here. You stayed in your safe little world for a long time, Ava, and in doing that you never needed these skills. They atrophied, perhaps, but now that you've needed them, that instinct has kicked in and you aren't suppressing them. I wonder what else you may be hiding."

"I've recently learned my blood is toxic, I can rip invading spirits from bodies and occasionally turn into some sort of ghost. I feel like I've reached the end of my ability to deal with new things."

Kase made a soft sound, one that said what he didn't need to. Whether I wanted to know more about me or not, it would probably happen.

"How did you even find me?" Another question struck me. "Also, where am I?"

"That *thing* that took you" — *thing* was clearly a far worse word he was substituting for — "created a portal. He also decided to pull in a few of those creatures you scared off when he took you."

My mouth went dry. "Is everyone okay?"

"I assume so. They aren't anything Hunter and Grant couldn't handle. However, other than Hunter,

I'm the fastest since Troy has to shift, so Grant gave me the tracker to follow you while they dealt with the creatures."

Which explained why Kase had shown up before Troy.

"How will they find us now, though?" The thought of them chasing nothing and getting lost in hell made me frown. It was true, Hunter and Grant tended to have plenty of fun on their own, but I suspected even they'd get sick of each other eventually.

"Hunter is an exceptional tracker. Don't worry, he can find you without Grant's spell. I'd guess they'll be here in a few hours. You were transported a very long way from where we were, and they can only move as fast as Grant can walk."

"Please tell me it was at least in the direction we were going. I really don't want to add any more time to this ordeal."

"You are always one to find those silver linings, aren't you? Yes, it was in the direction of Styx. In fact, we are only a few miles away."

That let me breathe in, until I took another look at him. "You can't walk a few miles, Kase. You can barely move…"

"There isn't much of a choice. Don't worry, Ava, I'm tougher than my current state would suggest."

I recalled how he'd fought that man, how he'd taken the beast on, how he'd accepted the wounds meant for me. I had no doubts of his toughness…

"There is one choice." Troy leaned against the doorframe, having approached so quietly that I hadn't noticed him.

Kase shook his head, his voice hard. "No."

"What choice?"

Jayce Carter

Troy lifted an eyebrow as if it were obvious. It took a moment for me to catch up.

"Wait, you can drink from werewolves? I thought they had to be human?"

"Ideally, yes, human is the best source. There are…complications when it comes to feeding from werewolves."

I shook my head. "You said you needed a *mortal* because it is the life force you drink. He isn't mortal."

"I'm not mortal, but I'm as close as we can get. Grant gives up his immortality to turn into a mage, and it corrupts all his cells. Werewolves, on the other hand, are largely human when in their human form. My blood will work."

I sat up, crossing my legs. "You both seem like this is a bad idea…why?"

Neither answered at first, but eventually Kase spoke. "Werewolf blood is forbidden because it can cause addiction for vampires. Should a vampire become reliant enough on werewolf blood, withdrawal could kill it."

"How much does it take to become addicted?"

Kase shrugged. "There is no exact answer to that. The older the vampire, the stronger the werewolf, the quicker it could happen. It could occur in as little as one feeding."

Troy had his gaze down, and the tension didn't break. I doubt he cared much about Kase becoming addicted, so what was it?

Then I remembered my reaction to being fed from…

That all-consuming lust, that need. Troy didn't even like Kase let alone have any attraction to him.

"And the other thing you don't want to say is that the reaction to being fed from would be less than ideal..."

Troy huffed, an unhappy sound. "That's putting it mildly. Werewolves respond even more strongly than humans."

"Which is yet another reason it is a horrible idea. Believe what you want of me, I've done my share of horrible things, but I'm not a rapist who would put someone in that position." Kase's voice had dropped, an undercurrent of anger there.

Then I recalled his story about the one who had turned him, about how he'd been used.

I guess I could understand it being a sticking point for him.

"Just because you feed doesn't mean — "

Kase nailed me with a hard look, one with more edges than I was used to from him. "I bit you for a split second, Ava, and you had a tiny taste of what my saliva could do. Even then, you would have slept with me no matter what you wanted. I could end things because I'm older, because I have control. Werewolf blood is a different matter. It's like a drug, and it would steal that control of mine as well." He shivered, as if picturing something wanted *so* bad. "I can promise you that things neither of us want to happen would happen if I fed from him."

"What about if he just bled into a cup? No biting or saliva needed?"

Kase shook his head. "It doesn't work like that. The saliva that is produced during feeding is part of what preserves the blood and allows me to use it. There's a reason that vampires don't just used bagged blood — that is essentially rotten to us. There is no way to feed without the bite, and there is no way to bite him without the reactions that come with it."

An ache started inside me at how I'd never know, that because of whatever I was, because of however fucked-up I was, he'd never have that with me and neither would I.

Then I stilled as the picture shifted, adjusting to the reality we were in.

I bit my bottom lip as an entirely forbidden idea came to me. "What if I took care of you both?"

The heat in the room went up a few degrees, and a near-identical groan left them both.

"The saliva, the blood, it causes lust, but that doesn't mean you two have to spend it on one another, right? What if you used me instead?"

Kase was the first to speak, and everything in his tone said he hated his answer. "It is still an unfair thing to ask of either of you."

Troy let out an unhappy snarl before yanking his shirt over his head. "Let's get this over with."

"Why?" Kase gave Troy a hard look that screamed of stubbornness.

Nothing was happening until Troy answered.

He snorted softly before lowering himself on the foot of the bed. "Because we aren't even at Lucifer's Court yet, and the reality is that we need every last one of us at our best to keep Ava safe. If that means I open a vein for you, well, I'd do a lot worse for her benefit."

Kase stared, as if looking for the truth of Troy's words. I could see the fight in his eyes, the war between how badly he needed to feed and his worry about taking advantage of Troy.

Funny, given exactly how little Kase seemed to care about most things, had killed no shortage of people, *this* was his line.

And yet, it endeared me to him more than anything else could have. After what had happened to me, after how my foster father had abused me, the fact that Kase had *that* line mattered.

Finally, Kase nodded after letting out a long breath.

Suddenly, it became real. I sat on the bed with Kase and Troy, and I was about to have sex with the two of them.

My time in hell was starting to look up…

Chapter Nine

As it turned out, having sex with a werewolf and a vampire caused more anxiety in me than I expected. It was far scarier than it had been with Hunter and Grant.

Maybe because Grant and Hunter hadn't let me think straight enough to worry about the reality or consequences of what I was doing. We'd gotten right into it without this moment of stillness.

This time, in the quiet room, my nerves ran amok.

What if I was making a fool of myself? What if I realized this was a horrible idea? What if I somehow screwed the entire thing up and one or both blamed me later?

I mean, Troy had barely *looked* at me since the issue at the house, since he'd shifted and nearly killed, well, all of us.

A part of me was amazed he was allowing this at all.

Then again, as he'd made clear, we didn't have much of a choice. We needed to get to Lucifer's Court and this was the only way it was happening.

Troy sat at the foot of the bed, and Kase moved behind him, energized as if the upcoming meal had given him strength. I hadn't watched this before, had only felt the strike of Kase's fangs into my throat.

A memory of my reaction, of the sensation drew a shiver from me. Sure, I wasn't going to get a dose of that aphrodisiac, but I didn't think I needed it, either.

Kase moved with a sureness that was staggering, looking every bit the predator. It was probably for the best that I hadn't seen it before. It was as though he transformed again, from the man I knew to the creature that needed sustenance.

Troy swallowed and the bob of his Adam's apple betrayed his nerves.

I slid from the bed and took a spot in front of him, then leaned in for a kiss. He hesitated for only a heartbeat, as if that were all it took for him to throw caution and worry aside. He pulled me closer, crushing me against his solid chest.

He broke the kiss, then blew out a slow breath that slid teasingly over my lips before he tilted his head, exposing his neck.

Kase had taken a spot to his side, then had him lean farther. It was *far* less intimate than it had been when he'd tried it on me, where I'd been pressed against him as much as possible.

Then again, I doubted Troy wanted Kase's cock grinding into his back, so I guess there was some wisdom in a different position.

Even still, Kase didn't restrain Troy.

"Are you ready?" Kase asked the question, but the other question was there between the words. *Are you sure?*

Troy offered one quick jerk of his head before it happened.

Kase peeled his lips back to expose those sharp, white fangs of his then struck, sinking them into Troy's neck. It was so fast it was almost a blur.

Troy hissed softly, his only reaction, and Kase's eyes lost that deep brown I so loved, taking on the primal red they did when he went full-vampire.

And, even though I wasn't being bitten, even though I didn't have Kase's saliva affecting me, I couldn't help the way my body heated at the sight.

Kase's lips pressed against Troy's neck, a small trail of red escaping, Kase's hand now wrapped around the front of Troy's neck to keep him still as he fed.

It was erotic in a way I'd never have expected, and my body sizzled with need. It crawled through me, making me heat, making me desperate to have a taste of that.

The moment Kase's saliva started to work, though, was obvious. Troy's white-knuckled attempt to stay still drifted away, and his muscles went lax.

Well, not *all* of them.

His jeans tented, the outline of his swelling cock telling me how quickly the saliva worked. He let out a groan, heavy and masculine, before curling his fingers in the blanket as though to try and keep still.

And *boy* did I remember that feeling, the way Kase's saliva had made my skin overly sensitive, made me want to rub against anything and everything.

I lowered myself after pressing Troy's knees wide. I left a trail of kisses across his chiseled abs, enjoying the way they twitched beneath the touch. I traced each line with my lips, my tongue, then undid the button at his waist.

He *whined.*

I never figured I'd be much for men making noises like that, as if I'd enjoy them being so needy, and yet I did. It felt powerful in a way I couldn't believe, especially over someone like Troy, someone so carefully controlled.

I grasped the waist of his jeans, and he lifted his hips so I could work them down. I left his shoes on, which meant when I took the jeans to his ankles, they made a shackle, one I placed my knee on to farther hobble him.

He let his legs drop open more, a plea and a surrender.

A glance up his body let me catch his silver eyes, see the want there, the drunken lust. Kase's worries made sense as I saw it, as I witnessed how the aphrodisiac effect could make a person beg for *anything.*

But Troy had agreed before he'd been affected, which meant I didn't need to feel guilty about enjoy it.

I ran my tongue up Troy's desperately hard cock with one hard, long lick.

He cried out, forcing Kase to strengthen his hold to keep the werewolf still.

Troy's cock was thick enough that when I wrapped my hand around it, my fingers didn't meet. All the filthy ideas I had came to me, about how badly I wanted to have him, how easy it would be to crawl into his lap and sink down on his perfect cock.

I shook that off, though, instead focusing on my first plan. I traced the veins on the side of his shaft, teasing them, prolonging the game. Kase wouldn't feed quickly, and this was one of the few times Troy was entirely open with me.

I wouldn't waste it.

A growl left Kase, and when he readjusted, when he sank his fangs in again, Troy jerked his hips up, thrusting against nothing, a pathetic whimper leaving him.

Which pushed me over the edge. I leaned up and wrapped my lips around his cock, savoring the salty taste and the heat of him. He kept his hands to the side, grasping the blankets in tight fists.

Which worked for me.

Troy was *so* strong in real life, so alpha, that him giving in for me was a huge turn-on. My cunt was drenched, but I focused all I could on him.

I ran my tongue along the flared head of his cock, then slid my lips down his shaft. I worked the base with my hand, though it made me frown. The very bottom of his cock felt odd, not quite as hard as the rest.

Not that I was going to ask about it. For one, because questioning how someone's goods worked in the middle of sex was universally considered rude and, also, because my mouth was currently full.

So I filed it away for later as I slid my lips along his length, taking him as deep as I could, ignoring the way it stretched my jaw in a wonderful way.

His hips twitched but he didn't thrust up. Instead, he seemed to give himself more to the moment, letting Kase keep him sitting upright.

Another growl came, and I lifted my gaze to Kase, to where his red eyes watched me with an insatiable hunger.

I reached out with my free hand, undoing his slacks with my nimble fingers before pulling down the zipper. He didn't help, too busy keeping Troy still. I also think he enjoyed the game, enjoyed watching what he'd started as I wrapped my hand around his shaft.

He wasn't warm, not like Troy was, but that didn't stop me from moaning when I felt how hard Kase was.

I stroked Kase, my grip solid, as I worshipped Troy's length with my mouth.

My cunt felt empty, desperate and forgotten, and the sight of the two of them was more than I could resist.

I pulled from Troy with a noisy *pop*, rewarded with another of those needy whines, then toed my shoes off and shed my pants and underwear.

I crawled into Troy's lap, and his hands found my hips with ease, so I wouldn't topple backward.

I reached between us, grasped his damp cock and slid down his hard length.

And *yeah*, he was thick. I hissed, the stretch hot and painful and wonderful all at once. Kase released him, letting Troy sit up straighter, but moved behind him again.

A small smear of blood sat on Kase's lips, on his white fangs. I leaned in, over Troy's shoulder, and licked a drop from his fang. It was like copper, but tinged with something almost cinnamon. That same rush from before happened, though not quite as strong, just a tiny taste of the aphrodisiac in his saliva.

I rode Troy, aided by his grip, as Kase bit once more into his Troy's exposed neck. Given he was a werewolf, Troy would likely hold no scars afterward, which mean Kase didn't have to be as careful with where he bit.

I reached down, behind Troy, having to tilt to reach Kase's cock. Still, a little acrobatics was worth it. Troy kept me upright and moving, pulling me down harder, as I focused on stroking Kase.

It was insane and magical and passionate in a way I never would have expected from *these* two. They were both so careful, so self-controlled, and yet they'd thrown that to the wind. I took every inch of Troy, a soft cry on my lips each time he plunged deep into my tight cunt, and Kase rocked his dick into my fist.

I came first. I'd love to say I outlasted everyone, but who could blame me? Troy's pelvis ground against my clit and Kase's saliva shoved me over the edge. I clenched around Troy, my body so overwhelmed I could hardly breathe.

Kase let out a snarl that was worthy of the best nightmares before his cock twitched in my palm, before he released Troy's neck and shuddered.

Troy's grip tightened on my hips, a wild look in his silver eyes, drunk on the aphrodisiac, on the moment, on me? He fucked me with such hard thrusts that I let my head fall back, a whine with each time he bottomed out.

He didn't snarl when he came. He didn't groan or growl.

Instead, he *roared*. It was a sound that rattled windows, that came not from him but his wolf. Sure enough, when I met his gaze, it wasn't the silver I knew. It was that bright light that said his beast was staring back at me.

Just as I was ready to pull off him, however, his cock jerked inside me and something changed. A fullness was there, another stretch so much like when he'd first plunged into me.

When I shifted, he yanked me against him, pressing deeper into me. It didn't hurt, and in fact it set off another aftershock to my orgasm, made me grasp his shoulders and arch my back.

"I thought as much," Kase said.

I met Kase's gaze over Troy's shoulder. "What—" I didn't get any more out before Troy lifted his hips, trying to get even deeper, that pressure increasing.

"I thought you were his mate, but I wasn't sure. However, werewolves only knot their mates."

"*Knot*?" The word came out on a gasped whimper as whatever his cock was doing wrung more pleasure from me, made me twist against the sensation.

"Shh," he said softly and ran his fingers through my hair. "You'll be fine. Werewolves just tend to go a bit wolf when they take their mates."

Again, I met Troy's eyes, saw little of the man I knew. Even still, it wasn't the scary beast from the house, either. *That* had been what the shadow turned it into. This was different, and even though the feeling was overwhelming, even though clearly shifted claws dug into my hips, I wasn't afraid.

Kase moved over beside me and pressed his forehead to mine. "He'll come back to himself in a few minutes, but you're stuck for a bit."

Troy chuffed at Kase, an annoyed sound but without real aggression.

Kase pressed his lips to mine for a quick kiss before pulling away. "All yours," he said to Troy — or to Troy's wolf? "I'm going to go get cleaned up and wait for Grant and Hunter."

With that, Kase was gone, leaving me stuck to Troy, overwhelming and nerve-wracking with more little aftershocks from each time his knot pulsed.

Knot?

Why hadn't anyone told me about that? It felt like it should be somewhere in werewolf 101. A *what to expect when you're going to bang a werewolf* sort of thing.

Troy wrapped an arm around me, keeping me pinned to him, before he rolled. Again, I was reminded how strong he was, when he was able to move me as if I were nothing. He stretched me out beside him, my leg curled around his hip, his cock still deep inside me and showing no signs of vacating…

He leaned forward and nuzzled my throat, the action odd and sweet.

He paused for a moment, then in a slow and somewhat strained voice, he spoke. "Sorry." The voice wasn't his, not exactly. It was as if it were squeezed through someone else's throat.

I pillowed one arm beneath my head to get comfortable. It turned out it wasn't easy to do when stuck to someone else. "About not telling me about *this*? What's a few secrets among lovers?" I kept my tone light, playful.

He pulled back so he could look at me. "Mine," he said, a deeper, rougher tone that sounded more like the roar than the man. He narrowed his eyes as if glaring at someone else, then shook his head. "I didn't think I'd lose myself," he said softly.

The struggle was etched into the lines of his face, the way he tried to rein in the other part of himself, the wolf.

I slid my fingers over his side, then curled them against his back. "Don't worry. Your wolf and I, we get along just fine."

A chuff, a very *wolf*-like sound, then he rocked his hips forward, making his thick knot stroke against me, setting off another gasping orgasm through me.

When I could breathe again, I caught him smirking.

The smug wolf was trying to tell me that *just fine* wasn't a good enough response.

Instead of scolding him — old dogs and new tricks and all that… — I snuggled in closer against his chest. "How long does *that* stay?"

"Thirty minutes or so," he said, voice stronger as if the wolf was retreating.

Thirty minutes of forced cuddling?

Well, I'd suffered through worse....

Chapter Ten

Why was it that men walked out of quickies like some sort of victory lap, but women felt like we had *whore* tattooed across our foreheads?

Troy had already headed downstairs after dressing. He hadn't said a lot, had regained a little of that distance he'd had before. I chalked that up to the awkwardness of the moment.

Besides, I had needed a moment to get myself ready. I'd cleaned up as best I could, using a tiny bit of the water Kase had left for me. No one wanted to walk while still sticky...

Still, as I went down the stairs, as all four sets of eyes swung toward me, I felt like each of them could see what I'd done.

They've all seen you naked. They've all been inside you. There isn't much mystery.

My cheeks burned as I tucked my hair behind my ear and tried to look as if I didn't care.

Men could screw everything that walked. Why not me?

No one spoke at first, and I had a moment of thinking everyone would pretend nothing happened. We didn't need to address anything, right?

"So what did you think of a knot, shadow-girl? Always wanted to try it myself, but I'm a chicken." Hunter paired the words with a grin so wide, he looked like some sort of jester.

So much for pretending...

Troy twisted and let out a low snarl, to which Hunter raised his hands. "Just curious."

Hunter didn't look all the worried — or sorry — but the comment broke the tension in the room.

Grant chuckled beneath his breath before shaking his head. "Okay, so, we're all alive. That's good. Kase filled us in on what happened."

Hunter snorted, no doubt in reference to *filled in,* but had the good sense not to actually say anything. Troy might usually have pretty good control over his wolf, but he'd still hit Hunter if he went too far.

"Kase said Styx was only a few miles away," I said.

Hunter nodded. "We'll be there in just a couple hours. I scouted ahead, and we should be fine."

I felt the need to point out he'd thought that before and look what had happened, but I let it go. No need to pour salt in the wounds, and we'd all survived.

"Styx surrounds the dead zone and the Court. We'll get some rooms near the inner edge, then head to the bridge after some sleep. I'm not sure what we'll face, so we should be rested up and ready for anything."

"Did you hear about my blood?" I asked.

Grant froze at that, his expression darkening. "Yeah. I also head about your little turning incorporeal trick."

"And?"

"And nothing."

The words were a lie. It was loud and clear that he had come up with *something*.

"Tell me, Grant. I deserve to know."

He tucked his hands into his pockets. "I don't know anything for sure, and I don't like making wild guesses."

"But you think you know?"

He cut his gaze away without answering at first. The set of his lips said I wasn't swaying him. "I have a guess, but it isn't possible. Look, we can deal more with this after we get *out* of hell. Don't we have more pressing issues?"

I wanted to argue with him, but somehow his unwillingness to tell me what he thought cut. It was like Kase and the coven all over again. More secrets.

I told myself he didn't know shit. He'd tested my blood and hadn't come up with a single thing, so the odds that he knew anything *now* were next to nil.

I didn't really believe that, but it was easier to tell myself that then to think he had answers he wasn't sharing.

The one thing he was right about was that we had bigger problems.

Like a hell city and the devil.

* * * *

Styx was set up like a bustling city, made up of all bad areas.

Hunter had retrieved my cloak, and it was once again smelly and damp. After finding out about the plants, I didn't complain about the garment.

There were a lot worse things than sticky clothes.

Hunter disappeared, again, and Kase and Troy hardly looked at each other. They were going overboard trying to pretend nothing had happened.

Which, nothing really had between them, but apparently two naked and erect penises in the same room created a problem for some men.

Grant stood just to my side, and during the walk toward the city, he'd created another three of those charms, so each of the men could find me.

Except Hunter, who it seemed could track me without problem — no magic needed.

"How often are you here?"

Grant shrugged. "I visit hell every few months."

"Do all mages come here?"

"No. Not many have the power to create the portals. It means I also make a good sum selling the things I pick up here."

"Why can you if others can't?"

He pressed his lips together, as if deciding how to explain it. "I told you magic was finite for a mage, right?"

"The bowl theory. Yeah, I remember, you refused to magic away vampire dust from my cleavage."

He didn't look sorry. "Exactly. Different spells take different amounts of magic, so if you have a mage with a very small bowl, they simply don't have enough to create a portal."

"But you do?"

"What can I say? My equipment is quite impressive."

I ignored his crude joke. "But why? What determines a mage's *bowl*? Are they born like that, or do they get more powerful as they grow?"

A slight tension started in Grant's cheek, despite his smile, as if the conversation veered down a path he'd rather not go, the secretive bastard. "A little of both. A mage is born with a certain amount of magic available, but all of it won't be accessible until they become immortal. Mages get better at using their magic as they age and learn, but they're mostly stuck by that central size issue."

"Mostly?"

"There are ways to change it, but they're forbidden."

"Forbidden?" I drew out the word to point out how odd it was to hear it from *him*. "You never struck me as the kind to care about what's allowed."

He cast a withering look my way. "The only way to increase a mage's innate power is to steal it from another mage, preferably a child, since they have a lesser hold on their magic. The process kills the person if they're lucky."

His words chilled me, though I suppose, in some strange way, it was good to know he did have lines.

I would have kept asking questions—it wasn't like I had anything better to do and I *was* curious—but someone stumbled in front of us before I could.

A kid flinched, as if I'd kick him for getting in my way. He had a round face, darkened with dirt and bruises, and stood no taller than my waist. I doubted he was older than six.

It was the first child I'd seen, and after the conversation with Grant, it shook me all the more.

The kid lifted his arm to ward off a hit. "Sorry."

"It's okay," I said, reaching down to help him to his feet. "You okay?"

He brushed off his legs, as if that did anything about the layers of filth caked to him. "Fine. I didn't mean to get in your way, though. Really sorry." His gaze flited to the side.

"What's wrong?"

"Nothing. Nothing at all." He went to take off, but I shifted into his way.

"Wait a minute. Are you running from something?"

The kid paused, trading his weight from one foot to the other. "See…"

Grant caught my arm and leaned in. "He isn't a kid, Ava."

"Look at him. He's scared."

Grant shook his head. "You don't know what hell is like."

I remembered that man who had nearly killed me, the way he'd held that machete. "I'm a quick learner, and I've had a few lessons taught to me."

"Nothing here is what it looks like."

"So you'll just turn your back on a child?"

"If he's *here*, then he isn't as innocent as he looks."

I stared back at the boy, but try as I might, I couldn't see any evil in him.

He looked back, then cowered when Grant met his gaze. "I don't want any trouble," he swore. "I'll go."

Before I could stop him, he scurried off, leaving me facing Grant, my hands on my hips. "How do you know he didn't need help?"

"Because kids don't get sent to hell, Ava."

"And spirits look like they do when they die." I thought about the twisted forms I'd seen and amended my statement. "Except when they're here in hell, where they look worse after a while. They don't turn into sweet-looking kids, though."

"Ava," he started to say, but I shrugged off his hand.

"We should get to the rooms."

He let out a long sigh, one that said he didn't appreciate my dodging of the conversation, but I didn't care. Turnabout was fair play, and Grant had kept *plenty* from me.

I didn't owe him anything.

The hotel this time was a far cry from the small inn we'd stayed at before. It reminded me of something that would fit in in the living world, a tall building that stretched up into the sky with flat glass windows across the front. Still, without regular electricity, it held the same orange and green glow that lit everything else.

Hunter waved us over from the counter, and I pushed past Grant, eager to put him out of my mind. Funny that these men could annoy me so much one moment, and I could worry about them the next.

It infuriated me.

"Rooms will be ready in an hour or two," Hunter said.

"That long?"

"Do you really want them to skimp when it comes to cleaning rooms *here*?"

Fair point.

"What are we supposed to do until then?"

"Take your friend to a show," the woman behind the desk said, her gaze locked on Hunter like she might cross the barrier and mount him there.

Hunter snorted. "I don't think that's really her speed."

"Well, the ballroom is open. It's early, so there isn't much activity, but maybe that's more her style."

The way she said *style* irked me, as if I couldn't hang with them. I was tempted to tell her I'd escaped a man who wanted to use me as plant fertilizer, that I'd scared off those beasts that guarded the fields.

A sharp pain to my side had me turning to find that Hunter had pinched me to keep me quiet.

Probably for the best. No need to be advertising that I'd been a target, or they might decide to figure out why.

"Sounds good. I'll just head in there," Hunter said.

"Mella is serving," the woman called as Hunter ushered me away. "And I'll be off in a few hours if you want both of us to help you christen your room."

I turned, ready to give that woman a piece of my mind — her sharp teeth and claws be damned — but Hunter pulled at me to keep me moving.

"I like your jealousy, shadow-girl, but maybe keep it in your pants?"

"Why? Because I'll get my ass kicked by her?"

"Hardly. I wouldn't let her lay a finger on you." The declaration was oddly sweet. Sure, I didn't want to be a damsel in distress, but the protective nature charmed me.

At least, until he added, "Because then I'd have to fight a shit load of people."

"You like fighting," I reminded him.

"I do, but see, I want to strip you down and enjoy every last inch of your sexy little body, and I'd really prefer not to have to waste energy on anyone else before then."

His words seared me, made my breath short. I'd had sex with Kase and Troy not that long before, and yet I felt entirely up for his plan.

Then again, I usually felt up for whatever Hunter suggested. He was easy and safe in a strange way. He didn't have that many hang-ups, didn't want me to be anything I wasn't. It was refreshing and relaxing and easy.

The ballroom was large and spacious, with a stage at the back, tables set in the middle and booths at the sides. The red flames flickered over chandeliers, casting the entire room in an orange glow. A few of the tables and booths were occupied, but most of the room was empty.

"I never figured there'd be ballrooms in hell." I sat in the booth Hunter pushed me toward.

"Trust me, *all* men knew there'd be ball dancing in hell," Troy answered, his face pinched into tight lines. No doubt he was thinking back to some traumatic time he'd been forced into the activity by a woman.

"Hell is as boring a place as any. Worse, really, because there aren't ever any *big* changes. In the living world, things move, they grow, the change. People have dying to look forward to. Here? It's always status quo. Hell, especially the bottom level of it here, is like a prison, so it follows the rules and sticks with what works. Because of that, we make our own fun."

"What were the shows she was talking about?"

"Oh, are you going to a show?" a new voice, sultry and smoky, asked.

I twisted to find another woman there, small black wings from her back, hooved feet and furred legs up to her thighs and hardly any fabric to cover up the rest of her. She had blonde hair and one hell of a smile for Hunter.

"Lucifer is holding more of them lately. He had an elder demon a week ago! Have you ever seen one of them?" She leaned in, setting a hand on the table and bending so her breasts became more of a centerpiece to the table.

"Yeah, I've seen one," Hunter said with a soft laugh. "Last time he brought one of those, I backed the hell out of the competition."

I sat straighter. "Backed out? Wait, you *participated* in these things?"

Hunter turned his gaze to me. "Sure, shadow-girl. There isn't a lot to do here, and whoever hosts the competition sets the prize. Lucifer usually just offers a favor, but a favor from him is worth it." He chuckled. "Well, it is when the opponent isn't an elder demon, at least. The second I heard he'd gathered up one of those, I withdrew."

"Lucifer lets you just back out?"

"Only before a round starts. Once it's going, everyone is stuck until the end."

Just when I felt like I had a handle on things, they changed.

Hunter tore his gaze from mine and looked back to the woman. "Sorry, Mella, but no shows for me."

"But I haven't seen you in one for *years*." She stuck out her bottom lip in a pout, before exchanging it for a salacious grin. "Of course, we could have our own show, couldn't we? You could put those skills of yours to other, more fun uses."

Oh, I was going to give her a piece of my mind. How *dare* she try to pick up my... well, whatever Hunter was — right in front of me!

Before I could, though, Hunter answered. "Sorry, Mella, but I don't do those shows either, anymore." He cut a glance my way, a loaded look there.

She sighed but nodded, then took the orders.

Once she'd left, I glared at Hunter.

"What?" he asked as if he had *no* idea why I might be annoyed.

"Have you screwed everyone here?"

"Not everyone," he said, then pointed at a man at another table. "Not him. Wait, never mind." He turned his head as if getting a better view. "From this angle, I think maybe I have."

I sat back in the booth, the ease of my relationship with Hunter suddenly not quite so easy.

"Come on, you can't be mad I'm turning people *down*."

I was pretty sure I could be annoyed, at least, so I didn't answer.

Mella brought the drinks a few minutes later and gave the entire table one hell of a show as she leaned over.

Though, from my glance around the table, it seemed I was the only one who noticed.

She left, probably since she didn't seem to be getting anything she wanted and tried at another table.

"I don't think I should drink anymore of that alcohol," I said, recalling how I'd passed out against Kase the last time.

Hunter nodded. "This close to the palace, it isn't smart. Lucky for you, this is one of the few places where I could get you safe water, so enjoy it."

I hesitated as I took a sip, glad to see it was in an actual glass but not sure I entirely trusted him. I didn't think he'd give me something that would hurt me, I just wasn't sure he knew what water actually was. I recalled whatever he'd put into the waterskin for me, and while that had worked in a pinch, it certainly wasn't what I'd consider water.

Yet, when it hit my lips from the large cup, I could have cried with joy. It was not just *water* but cold and entirely pure-tasting. I sent out an apology to water for all the times I'd passed on it before, the times I'd thought I'd rather have coffee or something else.

I took big gulps, finally able to fully quench my thirst.

The men drank their items, though none of them ordered water. Then again, supernatural metabolism meant they didn't get hit hard with alcohol like I did.

Plus, Grant handed out more tablets.

"Do you really think Lucifer will just have the bridge ready?" Grant asked.

"Well, he's the one who sent for her." Troy leaned back in his seat. "Why send for her and make it more difficult for her to get there?"

"Why have her arrive all the way out at the boundary anyway?" Grant asked. "When I come here, I portal directly to where I'm headed. Only an idiot would go to the boundary then walk." He cut a look toward Hunter, then grinned. "Well, I mean, you do that."

Hunter blew a kiss back. "I do it because I can't make random portals like a lazy mage. I can only cross the boundary line."

"How do you end up where you want, then?" I asked.

"The space between the realms, the boundary, is like this nil space. It connects to the living realm anywhere, really. I follow the trail I want, and it takes me to where that being is, or at least pretty close to it." He shrugged. "Travel like that is always iffy."

The conversation went on, back and forth, but I wasn't sure how useful any of it was. In the end, it was really just guessing. Guessing what Lucifer had meant to do, how we'd get across the dead zone if there was no bridge, how to deal with Lucifer.

So I drank glass after glass of the water, since each time I neared the bottom, Hunter ordered another from Mella.

Eventually, though, the water won.

"I need to use the restroom," I said when squirming stopped working.

Hunter slid out of the booth, making room for me. He walked me back toward a door.

I opened the door and he tried to follow me in. I turned to block his way. "I don't think so."

Hunter looked past me, as if surveying the empty bathroom. "Modesty is useless if you end up dead."

"But if I can't pee in peace, is it even worth living?"

He lifted an eyebrow then studied the room once more, drawing in a breath as if to sniff. I could have told him trying to smell a public restroom in hell was probably a really bad choice, but I just wanted him gone.

Finally, he nodded. "You have five minutes before I'm coming back in, privacy be damned. I'll be right here."

I shut the door, thankful to have a moment to myself. I thought about how moms always talked about sitting in the bathroom for far longer than it took to actually pee because they needed the break, the quiet, the time to get off their feet and just sit in silence.

After I did my business, squat-style over the seat because I was *not* going to be sitting on that—who knew what sort of diseases one could get in hell—I washed my hands, ignoring the red-tinged liquid that left the faucet.

We were close. It was strange, since I couldn't feel magic, yet there was an odd sensation that ran over my skin. It wasn't a pull, not something I felt connected to, but rather an awareness. The closer we'd gotten to the Court, to the center of hell, the stronger it became.

Why?

Why any of it? I sighed, drying my hands on my pants when there wasn't anything else to use.

Whys weren't all that useful, really, since they hadn't given me any answers.

Something moved in my peripheral vision, and I turned to catch sight of someone through the back window.

The boy I'd seen earlier. Where he'd had an edge of anxiety before, he was in a full panic, now.

He backed away, hands up, tears running down his dirty cheeks. The window was behind the row of toilets, up high enough to give bathroom goers privacy.

I moved without thinking. It was stupid, yes, but all I could think about was how I'd felt as a kid. I thought about the times I'd had no one looking out for me, the times I'd moved to some new group home or foster family with nothing. The fear on the kid's face was so familiar that the only thing I could think of was doing *something*.

The reach wasn't easy, but I pulled myself through the window, using the toilet as a stepstool, and shimmied out.

I planned to grab the kid, to get him to follow me back into the bathroom. Grant had to be wrong about him because he was *just* a kid.

I followed where he'd gone, just around the corner, to find him cowering in the shadows.

"Hey there," I said, using my best '*I'm a friend*' voice. "Come on, why don't you come with me? We'll get you somewhere safe."

He sniffled, then ran the back of his hand across his nose. "I can't."

I crouched down just in front of him. "Yes, you can. My friends look scary, but they're really not."

Okay, so they really *were* scary, but that wasn't the sort of thing that would reassure the kid, so I kept it to myself.

He lifted his face, and it shifted before my eyes. That fear was gone, disappearing as if it'd never been there at all.

It was in that moment I realized Grant had been right, that I'd been stupid.

I'd left the protection of people who could keep me safe and for what?

I was as bad as every stupid woman in a movie, making dumb choices.

"You are so fucked," the kid said, the words coming from his young voice and yet tinged in so much blood. "Never should have come out alone."

I scrambled backward but ran into a solid body.

Please let it be Hunter.

I wasn't so lucky, though, because when I twisted, it was Jerrod's face I found. His unnaturally pale skin, his yellow eyes—they weren't the sort of thing I'd forget.

I went to scream, to try to alert Hunter or the others, but he wrapped his hand around my mouth.

It was so similar to that first night with Hunter, but where Hunter had been saving me, I was pretty sure Jerrod had no such good things in mind.

The curl of his lips into a blood-freezing smile assured me of that.

Chapter Eleven

The frayed edges of the string tied at my throat were the only thing that kept me from panicking. I kept telling myself that the men would come looking for me, that they'd find me because of those strings, because of Hunter's tracking.

All I had to do was buy time.

But why *hadn't* they found me yet?

It didn't seem like we'd gone far, though the streets all ran together so I wasn't sure. Hunter had said he'd give me five minutes, and it had been far longer than that.

Jerrod had tugged me through the city, then to a building near the inner edge, I was pretty sure. Few had looked out way, and the only ones who had had scurried away at the first good snarl from Jerrod.

The closer to the center we got, the more deserted and run-down things became, and the place we stopped at was no different.

It looked like it had been a shop at one time, with a large counter like a register, but the glass front had been broken then boarded up.

Jerrod hadn't bothered to bind me, just tossed me to the ground when we reached the building as if I weren't a real concern to him.

The kid came, too, though his language had further deteriorated.

Hearing him talk like an angry, vulgar eighty-year-old man was at best disconcerting.

"Come on, you don't even want a *taste* of her first?" the kid asked.

"I'm not into mortals. It's like sleeping with farm animals," Jerrod snapped. "Besides, Raylor, we don't have much time."

"This place is too close to the wardens for anyone to pick up a scent. You worry too much." Raylor knelt beside me. He caught my chin to force me to look into his eyes, ones that glowed green. "Whores cost a pretty penny, and it'd be a fucking waste to put her down without getting some use of her."

I shuddered at the threat, swallowing down the sickness churning in my stomach.

Jerrod let out a low growl, one that sounded so much like Hunter's. "I said *no*. You were paid for your help already. I suggest you leave before I take away your option to do so."

Raylor released me, then took off as if he couldn't get out of there fast enough. It told me who exactly was in charge.

Then again, most beings in hell had given Hunter a very wide berth. It seemed Jerrod had earned a similar level of fear.

"What do you want with me?" I scooted backward until I could lean against the wall. Nothing being able to sneak up on me helped me focus. "Because someone already tried to plant me. Turns out I'm toxic to those things."

He lifted his eyebrow. "Really? That is unusual. However, no. Planting you for ambrosia would be a waste. I'm not some farmer, mortal." He paused, then came over to sit in front of me, one of his knees bent, his arm there. "Hunter sure had a tight grip on you, though. I have to wonder why."

"Why don't you ask him?"

"Because you saw when we fought. Hunter has *always* been stronger than me, just not as smart. It wasn't hard to set the lure, to remove the pass as an option and drive you into town instead. I didn't really think you'd be dumb enough to fall for Raylor's trick, figured I'd have to snag you another way, but you managed to prove me wrong."

He sounded like Grant, scolding me for my stupidity. I'd loved to have argued, but given my current predicament, it felt hollow.

"If he's that much stronger, is it really smart to screw with me?"

"The secret about us immortals, especially those of us on the higher end of the food chain, is that we don't hold grudges. Forever is a long time. He'll be mad for a few centuries, but he'll get over it."

The reminder of how long forever was hit me, at how brief my life was in the scope of things. Some people found comfort in that big picture, in the fact that there was so much else going on. Not me—it made me feel even more insignificant than I had before.

Stay on topic. "None of that says why you went through this trouble, though."

"How much has Hunter told you about what he is?"

"A hellhound. A tracker who catches things that escape from hell, that sends them back."

Jerrod nodded. "We are one of the few things that can pass into the living realm at will, who can pass the boundary. Do you know what allows us to do so? What makes us more powerful than the other things in hell?"

I figured magic was a bad answer, so I kept quiet.

"The dragon, the beast of smoke and fire, that's our true form. At the heart of it, however, we carry a spark of the living. When we were created, a drop of mortal blood was added to allow us passage into the living realm. We are of hell, but our strength comes from that tiny drop, that spark. It's what gives us an edge over things wholly from hell."

"Still not getting your point."

He tilted his head, as if waiting for me to get it.

He had to be overestimating my intelligence because nothing came to mind.

He blew out a slow breath. "That spark isn't just blood—it's the life force of a mortal, and *you* have one of those."

"But you can go to the living world. Why not just pick up a mortal there?"

"Because hellhounds are made in hell, but with a spark of life. That means, to us, there isn't anything more delicious than a mortal who has spent time in hell. It appeals to every side of our being. Nothing better."

Delicious.

There was no worse word to hear as a descriptor, and it made it clear that while rape was beneath him, eating people wasn't.

"I'm super gamy. I don't exercise either, so my fat content is really high. Also, I eat a *lot* of sweets, so expect a sugar spike and crash," I rambled. There was no way to pretend the words coming from my lips weren't random, but I wasn't sure what else to do or say.

I'd *seen* Hunter in action, and even if Jerrod wasn't as powerful, he was far higher up the evolutionary ladder than I was.

"I never understood why Hunter abstains. He used to revel in what he was, but now? Now he pretends he doesn't even want it anymore, which I knew is a lie. No one ever loses that craving."

Now?

"Hunter never *ate* people."

Jerrod laughed as he rose to his feet. "You see who he wants you to see, who he pretends he is now. Everyone has a past and that past is who they really are. Trust me, Hunter and I tracked and slaughtered *plenty* of mortals side by side, the unlucky ones who ended up down here. There is nothing quite like that. Killing and consuming humans in the living realm? Boring. When they cross that barrier, though, *that's* when they're good, as if that cooks them, makes them ready. You've been here in hell for *days,* basically marinating. How he's resisted this long, I have no idea."

He came forward and leaned in, drawing a slow breath as if savoring a steak fresh off the barbeque.

I kicked him, but he didn't even budge. Instead, he slid his fingers into my hair and inhaled again, burying his face against my throat. "I wonder if I started, if Hunter would join in. He couldn't possibly turn down a meal like you, not after I've unwrapped you."

Unwrapped had one hell of a bad connotation then.

He shifted, his hand turning to smoke before his body transformed into that huge beast. He barely fit in the room, his scales dark without any real light to reflect off them. His muzzle was large enough that he could have bitten down on my head in a single bite.

That gaping maw of his opened, teeth sharp and long, breath like fire, before he was slammed backward, regaining his human form in the blink of an eye as his body fell to the ground.

"You failed to invite me to dinner? That's just rude."

I turned and scooted away when a new man stood in the small room, someone I hadn't seen enter. He wore a black suit with pin stripes and a red tie. His hair was black and smoothed backward, with large horns that left his temples and curled back.

He looked like another other citizen but…better, as if hell hadn't shifted him into a monster but somehow only made him more handsome. His eye were red, like Kase's when he lost control, but this man showed no lack of control.

Jerrod pushed himself up weakly, and with one look at who was there, dropped to his knees. "I didn't mean to—"

Again the man flicked his fingers and Jerrod slammed against the wall. Blood leaked from the corner of his mouth when he hit the ground.

"I have few rules here, and even fewer for beasts like yourself. My one consistent, however, is to not meddle in my affairs."

"I didn't—" Again, his explanation was cut short, this time when the man lifted his hand and Jerrod's body hovered as if held aloft by some invisible grip. His toes brushed the dirt as he was pulled closer to the man.

"You did. You hoped I wouldn't notice, believed yourself too smart, but you chose to insert yourself into something you had no business in. I have few rules and even fewer consequences."

Jerrod's eyes widened, and he kicked his feet. Nothing could shake whatever held him, though, and the tattoos that wound around his body, just like Hunter's, pulsed. They shifted, until the black gave way to red, until the smoke marks turned to flames.

Seconds later, he combusted, all that pale skin turning black and charred until ash rained down into a small pile, all that was left of the hellhound.

The man brushed his hands against each other as if to clear the dust despite not having touched Jerrod directly. He turned toward me, and I struggled to my feet beneath his gaze.

The enemy of my enemy had never been my favorite saying, probably because I'd had too many enemies for it to make sense.

"You're late," he said, censure in his tone.

"I'm...*sorry?*"

"No, you're not. Still, when you failed to show, I had to venture out. You should be appreciative—I don't do that for many."

I had a sinking suspicion, but I asked the question anyway. "Who are you?"

He straightened his suit jacket, then the cuffs of his shirt. "Introductions, then? Very well. Welcome to hell, Ms. Harlin. I'm Lucifer."

Yep. Never should have followed that kid...

* * * *

The palace made the rest of hell look like… well…hell, I guess.

While it kept that creepy tone and the green and red lighting, it was spotless and modern.

I didn't follow Lucifer so much as he snapped his fingers, and we were suddenly somewhere else. A moment of panic struck me, but there wasn't much to be done.

I brushed my fingers against the strings at my throat and could only hope they were still able to follow.

"You haven't told me why you called me here," I said as I walked beside Lucifer.

His words were careful and polite to an almost uncomfortable point. He folded his hands at the small of his back. "That will come in time."

In *his* time, he meant.

"I was here with others," I said. "They won't know where I am."

"They are of no importance to me. I summoned you, not a rag-tag team of misfits."

"Well, that team of misfits is the only reason I reached here, since someone dropped me off at the boundary."

"You seem to confound good travel magic. The mix-up was hardly my fault. And them keeping you alive is why I won't kill them. However, I have learned that when men with designs are involved, plans tend not to go so smoothly."

"Are you talking about them or yourself?"

He stopped in the center of the hallway and turned toward me, his eyebrow lifted. "Few speak to me that way."

"I'm new here. I don't know the rules, yet." I tried to pair the words with a confident smile I was sure I missed the mark on.

"Perhaps you will prove yourself useful," he said.

"Useful for *what?*"

"All in good time, my darling." He waved his hand toward a door that opened without him touching it. "This room is yours for your stay. There will be guards posted at the doors, but you are safe."

"Are the guards to keep me here or to keep me safe?"

"Yes."

I sighed before walking into the room, him on my heels. "Are you going to remove the tracers on me?"

"Not until our business is concluded. It would be foolish to give you a way to escape before then." He gestured around the room.

A large balcony sat at the other side of the massive space, and it overlooked an open courtyard. In the center of the courtyard towered a tree with an archway in the center. "The bridge," he said from so close behind me, I jumped.

"It's a tree, not a bridge. They're not that similar, you know?"

He shook his head and pointed toward it. "That is the point where this level of the afterlife connects with the others. It is the passageway between levels, and the center of the power here."

I thought back to what Hunter had said. "I was told souls could move between the realms, to wherever they belonged."

He nodded. "Wardens, the creatures who fill the dead zone, can pass through that bridge with spirits who do not belong in the area they are in. That can mean moving them to a better or worse level. However, they still use that bridge."

"If it's there, why do you need wardens?"

"Because the path between is treacherous and difficult to navigate. Wardens are one of the few who can find their way. Most who venture in without a warden never make it out again."

I recalled the creature that I had seen the night I had met Hunter, which felt like a lifetime ago. "One showed up in my house…"

He turned to stare down at me, a calculation in his eyes that made me more than a little hesitant. "Wardens are drawn to things that do not belong where they are. You, mortal, seem to consistently be somewhere you do not belong."

Truer words were never spoken. Still, I kept that to myself and turned to survey the room. It had a sitting area, a large bed, a dining table that sat eight, a bathroom through an open doorway. On the balcony, which didn't appear to close or have drapes, were more places to sit. It reminded me of some penthouse room in a fancy hotel where diplomats and princes might go to stay.

Then again, what was hell if not some horrible travel destination that always sounded better in theory than person?

"Does the room meet your needs?"

His words were so careful, so polite. It set off alarm bells in my head. This man was, by all accounts, the most powerful being in hell, and yet he spoke to me as if he were an errand boy.

"Tell me what you want," I said again, his careful demeanor enough to make me risk it. "You drew me here, so clearly you need something. Just come out with it."

"That will come in time," he answered. "For now, rest easy knowing I do not wish you dead. I have questions I hope you have answers to, but such things must be approached in the right way. Tonight, we will have a get-together to welcome you. There is clothing in the closet through that doorway, but if you require anything else, simply let the guard at the door know. There is also water on those shelves—I know how much you mortals need your liquids." He stepped away with a slight bow, something old world and strange.

"I want to know if the people I came with are safe," I blurted out as he turned away.

He paused, then glanced over his shoulder. "We want many things, mortal. What you will discover here is that they are all possible…for the right price."

With that, he was gone, leaving me alone in the room, cut off from the people I relied on, and more confused than ever.

Chapter Twelve

I couldn't take my eyes off myself. I had never been the dressy type of girl, maybe because no one noticed me even when I tried, and yet something about my reflection in the large mirror on the wall drew me in.

I wore a black dress that fit snug at my hips but flowed looser to my ankles, giving me room to move comfortably. The top had thick straps and didn't sit too low, so I didn't feel like that waitress at the ballroom, the one who nearly fell out of her shirt each time she bent forward.

My hair wasn't greasy despite not having been able to wash it, but the black of it had been lightened by the ash. It was like a natural and gross dry shampoo.

My first look at the dresses had made me want to complain, but then I'd thought…what the hell?

When was the next chance I'd get to wear something like that, where I got to *be* the sort of girl who wear it?

So I'd thrown caution to the wind and tried on a few of the pieces, all of them fitting me to a suspicious degree. There was no way they hadn't been put there specifically for me to wear.

Worse, the amount of clothing made me wonder just how long Lucifer expected me to be staying.

Instead of dwelling on that, I finished getting ready and drank more of the delicious water.

The bottles were glass, but somehow the water inside was cold despite no source of refrigeration that I could see. I had to guess it was magic, since everything else in hell had been stiflingly hot.

The room was no different, and even though it was immaculately decorated, the heat was worse than it had been farther away from the palace.

A knock on the door came, one that had me pulling away from the mirror and standing straight.

The knock came again, and I realized I'd never said to come in. Then again, I was pretty sure I was a prisoner, so I didn't think manners counted for much. "Come in," I called out.

The door opened, no creak to the hinges, but instead of Lucifer, it was a woman with long green hair and silver eyes. She was tall, thin and looked like lightness to the darkness of hell.

Her smile was wide and honest, and she walked around in her flowy yellow gown as if it were the most natural thing in the world.

That was the sort of comfort in dresses I'd always wanted and never managed.

"Ava?" she asked.

I managed to close my gaping mouth and nod.

"I'm Persephone. I told Lucifer he could handle the other guests and I would see to you. He can be dreadfully overwhelming with all that glowering he does."

It took a moment to hear anything past her name, because the Greek mythology I had taken started repeating in my head.

"Wait, wouldn't that make Lucifer Hades?"

She paused, her smile widening even more. "Yes. Well, sort of. Everyone gets parts of the stories wrong, or they take one tiny bit of truth and make it into a tale that becomes more fantasy than reality."

"But those are two entirely different sets of myths."

"And there are a hundred others, all with a speck of the truth."

I frowned at the entirely unsatisfying answer, though I'd grown used to that. "Are you his wife, then?"

"Heavens, no. I was smitten with him—who wouldn't be?—but I got over that. Still, because of the entire pomegranate seed thing, I spend half my time here. We all do crazy things when we're young." She stopped just in front of me, then looked me over head-to-toe. "I'm not a fan of such gothic looks, but I can't deny you'll fit right in. We haven't had such a large party in"—she bit her bottom lip—"years, at least. Lucifer has been in such a mood."

She slid her arm through the crook of mine, standing taller than me by a good foot like some goddess.

Wait, she is a goddess…

The whole thing made my head spin, but I didn't dwell. Sometimes there was too much change, too much new information, and trying to make sense of it all at once would drive a person crazy.

"What does he want with me?" I asked.

"What does Lucifer ever want?"

"I don't know," I snapped. "I'm new, remember?"

She waved off the guards when we exited the room. "No one ever knows—that's my point. I have known him longer than almost anyone else, known him better, and I still have no idea why he does anything that he does. I have found it's best to not try and figure it out. When he's ready, he'll come out with whatever he needs to say."

"Easy for you to say. You weren't kidnapped."

"Perhaps not, but I do spend half my life here, away from my family and my friends and my *life*, so I do understand loss and loneliness." Even as she spoke, her steps never faltered. A slight quiver in her voice betrayed her, but that light she had didn't dim in the least, as if she refused to allow the reality to get her down.

Did I ever have that sort of optimism? Probably not...

"At least tell me what sort of party this is."

"Lucifer loves to throw parties—at least, he used to. The wardens help bring people from other areas of the afterlife, allowing us to mingle in a way we normally wouldn't be able to. We even get people from the living realm, such as important immortals, some of the elder ones, things like that. Oh, I love to hear how earth is doing. I've never been, you know? Maybe we could sit down sometime, and you could tell me everything." Her expression turned dreamy, as if she were thinking about earth, about how badly she wanted to see it.

I could have told her it wasn't all it was cracked up to be, but dashing her dreams felt rude.

"I'm sure we'll have entertainment," she went on. "Lucifer has been hosting more competitions lately, but fewer parties. No real ones for a long time. This is the first time I've seen him out from his room in months."

I recalled Hunter talking about the shows. "Is that where people fight demons?"

"It's barbaric," she said. "I personally miss them whenever I can. However, he likes to make them a central part. I suspect he'll have the competitors at the party tonight, before the first round. He likes to host those competing, to show them off like toys, to let people get their bets in."

"First round? How long is the party supposed to be?"

"A few nights, at least. Don't worry, we rest during the day. Given he hasn't hosted any real parties in years, this one will be one to write home about. *Everyone* will be here."

"Any chance I can get a few invites of my own, then?"

"Oh, I wish I could, but Lucifer said specifically that you were not allowed a plus one. I found it rather rude, but he outranks me here. Don't worry, though, I'll make sure you have fun without it."

I blew out a breath, ready to face the disaster of surviving a few *days* long party in hell all on my own.

Just when I'd convinced myself I could manage it, a large set of doubt doors opened in front of Persephone and me, and the large courtyard I'd spotted through my balcony was there, *full* of people, who all turned to stare at me.

I am so not ready for this…

* * * *

Persephone, the cheery women who was difficult to hate, had abandoned me within thirty seconds of arriving at the party when she spotted someone she hadn't seen in months.

It left me standing awkwardly by what was either a morbid display of body parts or a buffet table.

Or both.

Being in parties had never been my thing, but it turned out there was nothing quite as uncomfortable as doing that in hell. I didn't know anyone and starting up a conversation with people who sometimes had hooves, horns and occasionally actual flames on them was outside of my realm of knowledge.

"So what do you think, Ava?"

The familiar voice was like a hug I hadn't known I'd needed. I turned to find Gran standing there, beside the table of bloody bits, and before I had the time to even think about it, I threw my arms around her.

It felt like it had been so long since I'd seen her, since I'd been anywhere I understood, that she was a connection back to my real life, to the normal world. Funny that I never thought I'd miss my old life so much.

She was my past, the only true constant for me. I'd spent so much of my time in her occult shop, the one place I'd had where I felt as though I truly belonged. During a life of being unnoticed and unwanted, Gran was the person who had always seen me, always made time for me.

She huffed a soft laugh before hugging me back. "I take it you're not doing so well?"

I pulled back and wiped my thumbs beneath my eyes for any stray tears that dared to escape. "It's *horrible*, Gran."

"Really? I rather like hell."

I gave her a look that said exactly how stupid I thought that was. "What are you even doing here?"

"I'm always on the party list and given Lucifer hasn't had a real one in ages, I had to assume you were at the root of this one. Whenever things become chaotic, I know you're at the center."

"What does he want with me?"

"Believe it or not, I don't know everything."

I crossed my arms and blew out a long breath. "I just want to go *home*, Gran. I'm tired of this game. Do you know I almost got chopped into little pieces and buried as plant food? I got kidnapped by a hellhound —"

"Oh, but Hunter is cute. I'd let him kidnap me."

"It wasn't him."

"Pity." Gran offered me an indulgent grin. "But you're here, and you're fine."

"Fine seems like a very generous word. I'm stuck in hell, by myself, and am a prisoner of the devil."

"You're not alone," she said.

"I don't even know if Kase, Troy, Grant and Hunter are okay."

"They're fine. Even if they weren't, you'd be okay."

"You like to say that, but I'm not so sure, especially after all this." I pressed my lips together, then asked her, my voice low, "What *am* I? I went incorporeal, like a ghost, and my blood is dangerous to creatures here. I know you said it doesn't matter, but I need to understand."

Gran's eyes did that thing when they went white, when she stopped focusing on me and went *somewhere* else. Her voice took on a distanced quality, as if distracted. "You are something unique, Ava, something that isn't supposed to be."

"I don't find being cryptic cute right now."

"I'm not being cryptic. You are something that has never been, something that may never be again. How does someone explain something that hasn't existed? I told you before, when you're ready, you'll know. And when you do..." She shook her head, the white clearing away like fog rolling out. "You will have choices to make, ones that will reach far and wide."

I wanted to ask more, but the conversation was cut short when Lucifer walked up, his back straight, his hands folded behind him as before.

"Gran," he said, nodding politely. "I see you have met our guest of honor."

"I've known Ava here since she was a baby."

Lucifer showed no surprise, but I couldn't tell if that was because he'd already known or if his poker face was just that good. "Of course you have. Foolish of me to think such a thing could have gone unnoticed by you." He focused on me. "I assume you are enjoying yourself? I see Persephone abandoned you. My apologies, but she is easily distracted."

"Bloody chunks of meat, demons, the wails of the damned—what's not to like?"

He offered a half smile, as if to humor me. "Exactly. Now, the competitors for the show will arrive shortly, and as the guest of honor, Ms. Harlin is expected to greet them. It was..." Lucifer paused, as if searching for a word. "*Nice* to see you, Gran. Please, enjoy yourself."

"I always do," Gran said and offered me a wink before Lucifer gestured to follow him.

He paused and leaned in to speak to a guard. "Please keep an eye on Gran. Do not get in her way but watch her very carefully."

I frowned when he started to walk again. "Really? With all the people and *things* you have here, you're worried about one little old lady?"

Lucifer huffed, the least regal thing I'd heard from him. "There has yet to be a party she has attended where she did not kill, banish, blackmail or sleep with someone she shouldn't have. There is only one other person who has managed to give me more headaches."

"This is hell. I didn't think you had 'shouldn't' here."

"We don't, unless they end up causing me problems. Do you not recall what I told that hellhound?"

"I doubt Gran caused you that much trouble…"

"She turned one of my head generals into a goat a few years ago."

"Yeah, the goat thing seems like her go-to move."

He shook his head. "I would simply not invite her if that were possible. Unfortunately, she is one of the few who could attend all on her own, thus I send an official invite and she rarely shows. If I left her off the list, she would come to spite me. Somehow it does not shock me that she would come for *you*. You seem to have your hand in many places it does not belong."

"To be fair, I wouldn't even be here if *you* hadn't abducted me."

"I didn't abduct you. I simply invited you."

"Your letter transported me here without my permission. What would you call that?"

"An aggressive invitation."

I cut him a sharp glare, and I swore I almost saw his cheek crease. That didn't feel possible, however, since he hadn't shown signs of having any sort of emotion.

We wound through the party, though it was an easy path since people parted for him. Near the large tree were a row of seats that reminded me of the coven's throne room. Sure enough, at the center, a chair made of skulls. Beside it was another, smaller one, though I would have sworn it was made of other bones as well.

Lucifer pointed at the chair beside the large throne.

"I don't sit on bones," I said.

"It is customary for the guest of honor to sit beside me. In fact, it is a great honor that many have fought and died for."

"Well, let them use it, because dead bodies are not for furniture or eating utensils." I thought back to the cup at the inn.

Lucifer's eyes narrowed, which told me not to push my luck.

I reached out and plucked the pocket square from his jacket—if he wanted to kill me, he could have already, and I doubted stealing his handkerchief would push him over the edge—unfolded it and placed it on the seat. I was not going to get bone germs on my pretty new dress.

He shook his head, an almost imperceivable gesture, before taking his seat in the large throne.

The other chairs were quickly filled as well, the room falling silent as if his presence signaled something important.

To his other side was a chair that remained empty, a throne much like his, and to my other side sat Persephone.

"Sorry, Ava," she whispered. "I hadn't seen my friends in months. I won't leave you again." Almost immediately, she leaned to the other side and starting to talk to whoever sat there, despite being the only person talking in an otherwise silent room.

And despite Lucifer's sharp look.

It seemed she wasn't afraid of him at all.

"Thank you for coming," Lucifer said from his throne. "It has been too long since we have done this. Now, let us see our brave competitors for tonight."

Someone walked in, a woman who reminded me of the waitress at the ballroom, though this woman was better dressed. She wore a suit with a skintight skirt that showed off her hooved feet. "We have six teams for tonight," she announced. "The first team are local favorites."

As she listed the people, they came from a door off to the side, and each one she named made me want to shift closer to Lucifer.

Which was dumb, as I'd bet he was far more dangerous to me.

The creatures—I couldn't even call them people— were worse than the man who had almost killed me. They were large, muscled bodies scarred and twisted. Each gave me no doubt about just how lethal they were.

The woman went through the groups, one by one, while Lucifer sat impassively and Persephone chimed in to anyone who would listen about the rumors surrounding the people.

It seemed everyone ignored her breaches of protocol.

"And the last team," the woman said, "is new. We have witnessed one fight before, a fan favorite, undefeated."

The rest of her words disappeared as I watched Hunter, Kase, Troy and Grant walk into the center of the courtyard.

This wasn't the reunion I'd planned on…

Chapter Thirteen

I shifted in my seat, wanting nothing more than to rush forward.

Unfortunately, Lucifer must have guessed it, because he reached over and set a hand on my shoulder, keeping me in place with what seemed like zero effort.

As soon as the woman finished her introduction, Lucifer spoke, his voice booming across the courtyard. "I welcome the competitors. Enjoy yourselves, because in one hour, there will be fewer of you." When he'd finished addressing the others, he lowered his voice just for me. "I take it these are the ones you asked about."

"Yes. Would you let me go, now?"

"You test my patience, *mortal*." His use of the word mortal felt like the threat he probably meant it to be, a reminder that I was far weaker and at risk. It was enough to make me settle down as he gestured for the men to approach.

Hunter strolled up at the front, looking entirely at ease with the situation. "Lucifer, nice to see you."

"I doubt that. I rarely let creatures into my palace."

"Which is why these competitions are so useful. How else will I get to drink all your booze?"

Lucifer made a disgruntled sound. "I take it you four are here because of Ava?"

Grant had his hands tucked into his pockets. "Of course not. I'm just really interested in fighting to the death for the entertainment of others. I'm a giver, you know."

Troy didn't look at Lucifer at all, his gaze locked on me. I could see his wolf peek through, as if they both needed to reassure themselves I was okay.

Even without him asking, I nodded, letting him know I was fine.

Kase remained silent, though I got the sense he was absorbing everything. The man was too smart to not already have a few plans on how to handle the situation.

And, oddly enough, I felt better. I didn't feel so alone, so lost.

"As a competitor, I don't think I'd be out of line to ask for a moment with the guest of honor," Hunter said.

"Last request? At least you're realistic about your odds," Lucifer said, his hand still on my shoulder.

"I recall being undefeated," Hunter said.

Lucifer snorted softly. "And I recall you backing out when facing an elder demon."

"The prize wasn't worth it."

"My favors are worth *everything*."

"Not always."

Lucifer shook his head, then stood. "Very well. Enjoy your time, *competitors*. It will likely be your last."

With that, Lucifer left, giving me the chance to bolt from my seat and throw myself against Hunter.

His lips were familiar and warm and *perfect.* He grabbed my ass as I wrapped my legs around him, desperate for that moment of connection.

Silence from around us made me pause and break the kiss.

With Lucifer gone, everyone was staring at *us,* including Persephone, her mouth hanging open.

I frowned, then whispered to Hunter, "We're in hell — public displays of affection can't be that taboo. I saw two people screwing by the snack table earlier."

Hunter lowered me to my feet, making sure I rubbed against his front on the way down. "You, shadow-girl, were seated beside Lucifer. That is the top of the food chain here. We are competitors, who are allowed in the party so people can place bets, mostly. We're at the bottom. This little show was the equivalent of the princess rushing off a throne to kiss a bellboy. You're breaking quite a few unspoken rules."

In for a penny…

I turned to offer a searing kiss to Grant, who smiled softly as if thrilled by my lack of proper etiquette. Kase didn't lose himself, choosing instead for a quick, light kiss. No doubt he was too busy studying the room and potential threats to give in.

Troy pressed his lips to my head, as he'd done before, the chaste way he liked to give me affection but didn't care to do so in public.

Except with Kase…

"Want to share what you're thinking?" Grant asked, that quirk to his lips that said even if he hadn't been reading my mind, he probably didn't need to.

"Maybe now isn't the time," Troy said, coming to my rescue.

"Right." I frowned, then pointed my finger at Grant. "There are *much* bigger things at hand. What are you even doing here?"

Hunter gestured at me. "You're here."

"I mean why are you in the competition? Nowhere in our plan did it include become a gladiator."

"The bridge was down and the path through the dead zone would have taken too long," Grant explained.

Hunter continued the answer. "Quickest way to get here was to enter. The second I saw the announcement about the competition and the party, I figured Lucifer was doing it for your benefit."

"But you could get hurt," I said as I leaned in.

"Small risk," Hunter whispered back with a smile. "Besides, when we win, we get a favor from Lucifer. Pretty sure that might just come in handy."

The fact that Hunter didn't appear worried in the least helped, but I doubted he'd admit even if he were concerned. He was the sort to fake it even if he knew he was fucked.

"You do like to make a stir, don't you?" Persephone came up, a big smile across her lips. "I haven't seen everyone quiet like that in..." She paused, as if her history were a very long one.

Then again...it was at least as old as Greek mythology.

"Well, in a very long time." She stuck her hand out to Hunter. "I'm Persephone. I remember watching you fight that monstrosity, the one with the acid breath." When Hunter shook hands with her, she came up closer, looking like a fangirl with a celebrity. "That was amazing."

Hunter chuckled, turning a charming smile on Persephone that was like the one he'd given Mella. Not the same one he gave me, though.

There was a tension in this smile, one that said he was playing a part.

Some of the jealousy lessened when I realized that, when I saw how the smile didn't reach his eyes, how the heat in his gaze was absent. I guess this was just the part he played… Looking back, it seemed familiar. He sure turned that charm on when he needed to.

"I remember that one. Took a hit to my shoulder."

She touched his shoulder. "Oh, I saw that! I was sure you were out of the game then. I don't think I've ever seen someone came back from something like that."

He smirked. "I'm tougher than I look."

I snorted at the display. Knowing it wasn't real didn't quite soothe all my annoyance at Persephone fawning over Hunter, and him puffing up his chest like it was the best thing he'd ever experienced.

Bastard.

Kase gave me a chiding look, but I rolled my eyes in response.

Like he would act any differently if I were flirting with random men.

In fact, I recalled how he and Troy had gotten into an actual fight because of jealousy.

"So, do you have any hints for me?" Hunter asked.

"Oh, I couldn't say. That wouldn't be fair." Even as she said it, she smirked and set a hand on his bare chest.

"Certainly, you could," Hunter argued. "Just a little something? I'd hate to die in round one and not get to see you tomorrow night."

Persephone giggled—actually giggled, which I wasn't sure women really did after ten years old—before leaning in until her lips were almost on his ear. She whispered so quietly, I couldn't catch it, but Hunter lifted an eyebrow.

"Thank you, sweet," Hunter told her.

Someone called her name, and she stuck her bottom lip out in a pout. "I have to go. Do try to stay alive."

When she left and Hunter turned toward me, he was met with one hell of a glare.

He opened his mouth, but I cut him off before he could speak. "Don't you *shadow-girl* me."

"Well, at least if we're killed in round one, I won't have to worry about her castrating me in my sleep," Hunter said.

Kase shook his head before turning toward me. "Has Lucifer told you anything? Given you any idea as to why he summoned you?"

"Nothing. He said everything in good time and made it clear he didn't appreciate me asking."

"How did he even grab you?" Troy asked.

"Well, technically he didn't. I saw that kid—"

"Please tell me you didn't ignore me and follow him?" Grant rubbed at the bridge of his nose.

"I can tell you that or I can tell you the truth but not both." After he sighed, I went on. "The kid was working with Jerrod, who decided I looked too tasty to ignore. Before Jerrod could do anything to me, though, Lucifer showed up."

"I never thought I'd be thankful to Lucifer," Grant said, his annoyance from earlier gone.

Hunter reached for me, but I pulled away. It was a reaction I couldn't help, but it was one born from Jerrod's words, from recalling what he'd told me about what Hunter and he had done. Seeing him had surprised me enough for me to forget, but after mentioning Jerrod and what he'd tried to do to me, what he'd said about Hunter came back to me.

Hunter let his hand drop, a question in his eyes he didn't voice.

And one I didn't want to give life to.

"So you're going to fight in some stupid competition? Then what?"

"We win," Grant said with a shrug. "I mean, we discussed losing, but since that would mean we were dead, it seemed counter-productive."

"This is one of those you-win-or-you-die things?" My stomach sank.

"Pretty much," Hunter answered, thought his voice had lost some of its humor. "They drop in a big bad beast of some sort — or a bunch of smaller ones — and see who's standing once the critter is dead. Teams usually take one another out, as well. Rounds keep going until there's one team left and they face whatever Lucifer has up his sleeve for the ending. People can back out between rounds, like if they lose too much of their team and don't want to keep going. Winner takes all, or in this case, one open-ended favor from Lucifer. Anything he has the power to grant, he will give."

"A favor can't be *that* useful."

"I'm sure you've heard about a deal with the devil, haven't you?" Grant gestured toward Lucifer, who stood across the courtyard talking to someone I didn't recognize.

Not that I recognized many people…

"Well, Lucifer has a lot of sway. He can make life *very* comfortable for someone here and could even orchestrate a ride out of this level, to somewhere else, to a better area of the afterlife. People have been lining up to fight and die for these favors forever."

"So what would you ask for?"

Before anyone could answer, a loud, low sound reverberated through the courtyard. It rattled up through the floor, into my feet. I covered my ears, the sound so deep it felt as if it could throw off the steady rhythm of my heart.

When it stopped, I turned to find Lucifer looking directly at me, at all of us.

"That's our sign," Grant said.

I caught Troy's hand, the fear becoming real. "Don't go. "

"Don't really have a choice," he said, turning his hand over so he could grasp my wrist in return. "We'll be fine."

"You better be," I responded.

Grant snorted. "We'd better do as she says. Normally women can only make our lives miserable as long as we're alive, but with this one? Well, death doesn't seem to have much on her. Pretty sure she'll make eternity a bitch."

Hunter chuckled, and despite the seriousness of the moment, I could have *sworn* even Kase and Troy grinned as they followed Grant.

"What if that's the last thing you ever say to me?" I called after them.

Grant turned back toward me and held his arms out. "Then you'll know what a pain in the ass you are. I'm good with that."

All I could do was watch them walk away, and hope Grant's stupid joke didn't come true.

Chapter Fourteen

I'd assumed the competition would occur elsewhere, but when all the partygoers moved to the outer edge of the courtyard, creating an empty space at the center, I realized nothing would be as simple as I'd thought.

Lucifer waved his hand and the area in front of us shimmered, then cracked through the ground and space. It seemed to open on itself until it showed somewhere else.

I shifted side to side, and the view changed as if inside that small area—a cylinder only about ten feet across—there were hundreds of feet inside. Even with that, however, I could somehow see all the details of the large, open, desert space.

"What is that?" I asked out loud.

Lucifer didn't turn to look at me as he answered. "I attempted live competitions before, but cleaning blood stains from my stone floors became tiresome. We open this small tear to a pocket universe within hell for these, now. It enables us to see the events while at a safe distance."

I peered past the space to see a few people meandering near the food tables. "Safe distance meaning near the snacks?"

He made a noncommittal sound before placing his elbow on the arm rest between us. "You seem rather attached to those immortals."

"Surviving hell on my own wasn't all that likely. I get attached to the people who keep me alive." Saying the lie chafed, but it was better he thought they were simply a means to an end for me. Giving the devil any leverage to use screamed of a bad idea.

"Of course." The slightest curl of his lip said he didn't buy my story. "Well, now that you are here, and under my protection, you won't need them anymore, will you?"

I swallowed hard, wanting to tell him to shove it but knowing it was a piss-poor idea. Instead, I leaned forward, narrowing my eyes to try and see more of wherever the men were.

The teams were spread out on the edge of a large circle with tall stone walls surrounding it. There didn't seem a direct light source, like a sun, but it was brighter than where we were. The sand was a light brown, but huge splotches dyed it red all across the obvious battlefield.

Finding *my* competitors wasn't all that difficult. The other groups were made of hell creatures, ones that didn't look close to human. There, at the far side, were the men I was looking for.

They wore different clothing, as if they'd been given things for the competition. Each group was color-coordinated in a jumpsuit, and my team wore black.

It seemed oddly fitting. They faced off against yellow, red, blue, green and purple, but at least it would make it easier to tell them apart amidst the chaos.

"Why did they change?" I asked.

"To make it easier to see who is on what team, and to prevent advantages for creatures such as shifters, who could impersonate another team. Also, I prefer combatants stand on their own abilities, so we strip them of their weapons. I like a fair fight."

I doubted that. Lucifer struck me as the sort of man who considered a fair fight one he could win. He judged everything by his own power, skewing the rules to help him.

There was no reason to say that out loud, though, so I kept it to myself.

My stomach grumbled, not out of hunger but anxiety. I knew my men were dangerous, but *this* was different. There was run of the mill lethal, then there was competing in hell lethal.

"Are you hungry?" Lucifer asked.

"No."

"Then would you cease that *noise* you're making?" He nodded at my stomach, as if I could have a chat and make it settle down.

"Sorry, but it isn't something I can control."

"You mortals are so complicated. It is a wonder you manage surviving even your short lives."

"Yes, because planting body parts so you all can get high is a *much* less complicated way of life."

I knew I kept going back to that, but it felt like a sticking point, like the thing I couldn't get past.

I was sitting on a chair made of bone, there were demons with hooves and horns around and people happily masticated bloody chunks of raw meet.

I didn't feel much like being told how odd *I* was.

"I have questions for you, Ms. Harlin," Lucifer said as a large bell rang. The sound didn't come from the courtyard, though. It filtered through the barrier between the pocket realm and this one, so it was less abrasive.

"Is this really the time?"

A spark of light came up in the center of the dirt, so blinding I had to place my hand in front of it to shield my eyes.

On the edges of that, though, a figure moved so fast it was little more than a blur of yellow. In its path one of the red fell, then a green and finally a purple.

I leaned forward and my breath caught as the flash of light dissipated and that one person felled combatant after combatant.

"He can't do that," I said. "He isn't even focusing on the actual enemy!"

Lucifer didn't lean forward, didn't seem interested in the battle at all. "Of course he can. That's part of the game. It is about the last team standing, and nothing in the rules says a team can't remove another team."

My heart pounded as I watched that yellow blur approached the black team, my fingers digging into the arm rests of the chair.

It closed in on Kase, and I barely stifled a gasp when it slammed into him. I expected Kase to fall, as all the others had done, a scream already in my throat.

Instead, the yellow came to a complete stop, held in place by nothing more than Kase's grip around its neck. He jerked to the side—I felt a sickening crack more than I heard it—before the yellow team member fell limp to the ground.

"You see, you worry too much," Lucifer said. "I may not care for *your* team, but there is no chance any would fall in round one. Hunter alone has taken on teams such as these in the past."

His reassurance didn't help much. Somehow knowing they *could* wasn't the same as knowing they would. I'd learned plenty of times in my life that could didn't matter.

I *could* have lived a perfectly normal life, but I didn't. Things *could* have gone right, but they never did.

Could could bite my ass as far as I was concerned.

"You seem to find yourself in the wrong place a lot, Ms. Harlin."

Dust cleared from the center of the space, where the light had shone, and I got my first look at the thing they faced.

It wasn't that big—which was funny, because weeks ago I would have said it was huge. It was the size of a horse, but after having seen things *much* larger, I breathed a sigh of relief.

It looked like some strange cross between a tiger and a buffalo. It had teeth and claws, but also had horns and the large, stocky build of a buffalo. Black fur covered it, and smoke escaped its nostrils when it breathed.

Not that anyone seemed to pay it any attention.

Where I'd assumed the battle would be between the beast and the competitors, the teams were more focused on one another.

Hunter had shifted, his huge dragon form incredibly fast. He charged though the field, much like yellow had before, leaving carnage in his wake.

Troy had shifted as well, his body now taller and wider than before, his claw-tipped hands swiping. When he moved, it wasn't like a man. He'd drop to all fours for a quick burst of speed, looking every bit the monster he thought he was.

Kase remained near Grant—probably for the best since Grant was the most at risk—while Grant shifted his hands and his lips in quick succession. Flames erupted, consuming the entire red team in a blink. He lifted his left hand, made a fist then drew it down. A boulder the side of a car came crashing into what was left of the purple team just as Hunter moved out of the way.

The battlefield was bloody and terrifying and vicious beyond anything I had expected.

And why was that?

The men had never been shy about their abilities, about their natures, and yet seeing them in action was different. It wasn't a case when I was in danger, when it was kill or be killed.

It was for *sport,* and they seemed to enjoy it far too much.

"You know," Lucifer said in a conversational tone, "I declare a winner at the end of this round."

"I thought the winner happened at the end?"

"The main one, yes. However, each round also has a winning team. They don't get a favor, but there is a benefit."

"What? Bragging rights?"

"No." His tone was incredulous, like that of an adult who knows exactly what game a kid is trying to play. "Competitors normally spend the night in an area just outside the palace. There isn't much in the way of benefits. However, the winning team stays in the palace. That grants them better food, access to healers for wounds, donors for vampires, willing companionship and a safer place to sleep since teams often lose one or two during the night."

I thought back to Kase, to how well blood healed him and the risk of feeding from Troy. There were going to be more rounds after tonight, and the men would fare *much* better if they had access to what Lucifer was suggesting. "You aren't mentioning that as a random fun fact. What do you want?"

"Tonight, after the round concludes, you will come to my room."

"What for?"

"In exchange for me declaring Team Black the winner, you will answer ten questions of mine, honestly."

"One, and you remove the *companionship* bullshit."

"Eight, and that is nonnegotiable as they handle all service."

I pressed my lips together. "Two, and make sure they're ugly at least."

He let out a sigh. "Four. One for each person I will be saving, and very well, they'll be homely. I suggest you don't try to push your luck any further, because if we remove another question, I will remove one of your precious team."

The hard tone of his voice reminded me that he wasn't just anyone. He was *the devil* and maybe I should be a bit more careful.

The beast in the center of the field charged Grant drawing my attention back, but Kase stepped in front of him. He grabbed the creature by the horn and twisted, sending the thing rolling into the large rock wall where it didn't move again.

Lucifer lifted his hand and another low sound echoed through the chamber.

The contestants froze inside the other realm, turning toward us as if they could see us. A moment later, the vision shimmered away and Lucifer stood, the room falling silent as it did for him always. "Team red, yellow and purple lost all members. Green lost one, orange lost two, while blue and black remain at full strength." Lucifer turned to look at me. There was no question in his eyes—he *knew* what I would say, what I had to say.

I nodded.

"I declare Team Black the winners for the evening. Tomorrow, we will resume with the teams who still wish to participate, and as winners, Team Black will have additional privileges tonight in the winner's quarters. Rest up, because tomorrow will not be so easy."

I swallowed hard when Lucifer turned and gave me a chilling smile.

What was that they said about deals with the devil?

Chapter Fifteen

The party wrapped up rather quickly after the competition. Then again, it had been going on for hours before Persephone had come to get me. The main event was the battle, and once that was over, people were ready to retire.

They rarely left alone. It seemed get-togethers in hell had more sex than teenage house parties.

Lucifer had said he would send someone to retrieve me in a few hours, but that in the meantime, food would be delivered to my room and I should rest, clean up, stop my stomach from making noises and get more *comfortable.*

Anytime a man told a woman to get more comfortable, they inevitably meant less clothing.

I was tempted to wear the dress again, but I didn't want to send the wrong message. Amazingly, when I looked inside the closet, the dresses had changed. There were the same general number of them, but now they resembled what I'd worn already, as if someone had waited to see what I liked then curated a more specific closet.

The bathroom had a huge clawfoot tub but no shower. I filled the water, amazed to see it run clear from the faucet.

There was no way I would have bathed in whatever red stuff they normally had…

Undressing in hell seemed stupid, but I hadn't gotten a proper wash since I'd arrived, and I shuddered to think of what exactly coated my skin.

Sinking into the water was like a baptism — though, given it was in hell, that probably wasn't the best analogy.

A moan left my lips at the warmth of the water when I lowered myself into the large tub.

My eyes slid closed, savoring it, letting myself pretend I was back in my safe tub at home.

"Don't you look cozy?"

I opened one eye at Hunter's voice, and I couldn't even find it in me to be surprised at his appearance. "I thought you'd be enjoying your special suite."

He crouched beside the tub and rested an arm on the edge. "I've been there before. It's nothing new."

"Well, you better enjoy it, because I'm going to pay a pretty penny for it, I suspect."

He tilted his head. "I wondered why Lucifer declared us the winners. I mean, we did well, but he never does something without reason. What did he want from you?" The last words held an edge that reminded me of how he'd moved across that field, of what Jerrod had said.

I swallowed away the thoughts, trying to stay on task. "He wanted to see me tonight, for me to *honestly* answer any four questions he asked."

"Four?"

"One for each of you," I explained.

He huffed before resting his chin on his arm, reminding me a bit of a puppy, especially with those brown eyes of his.

A puppy that turns into a dragon smoke creature and has killed mortals to eat.

"You need to be careful around him," Hunter said. "Lucifer is a master at manipulating people and making them think they're in the lead when they're just playing right to his tune. He doesn't lie, but don't take anything he says at face value, either." He reached for my arm.

I jerked backward. It was another thing I didn't think about, just a reaction I couldn't control.

He stilled, as he had the last time, then pulled his hand back. "I'm going to guess that before Lucifer finished off Jerrod, he had stories to tell."

I swallowed hard, tucking my arm under the water as if that would wash away the tense moment. "Yeah, he did."

"And now you're afraid of me?"

"Can you blame me?"

Hunter shrugged, reminding me that he was back in just the pants, no shirt, and the tattoos moved on his body. They did that more here in hell, I'd noticed, as if they were more alive here.

"I don't blame you, but we *all* have a past."

"My past doesn't include eating mortals."

He blew out a sharp breath, as if he didn't even like *hearing* the words.

Yeah, well, neither had I. It felt fair for *both* of us to suffer.

"I told you I wasn't born, that I was made, and that happened back at the very start. Do you have any idea how long I've been alive, Ava?"

Hearing my name on his tongue felt wrong, and it kept me silent.

"I wasn't always what I am now. Most hellhounds stay in hell. It's more comfortable, easier, more fun. The more time we spend in hell, though, the less we connect with that spark inside us that is mortal. For a long time I avoided the living realm. I relished in this side of me, in what I am, and yes, I did horrible things during that time. I protected the borders, slaughtered anything that dared to go near it, and anything that got past me? I let it go."

I didn't understand where the story was going, so I let him tell it, listening in silence.

"Jerrod and I hunted together. Two sadistic peas in a pod. And, yes, we *crave* mortal life force. It is this driving desire, and when we would find it here? When a mortal ended up here?" His eyes took on an odd light, something between desire and disgust. He closed his eyes and breathed through his nose slowly. "I'm not proud of what I was, of what I did, but I'm not that *thing* anymore."

"Why not? What changed?"

"I was wounded by a creature that got past me and made it through the barrier. Normally I would have let it go but I was enraged by it managing to actually hurt me. I followed it, tracked it for days, watched the carnage it left in its wake. When I finally caught up, it had cornered this girl, only ten at the most. It had already killed her family, and in her eyes, she *knew* she'd die. She was sure of it. She didn't cry, though. She stood there with this tiny little dagger, ready to do whatever she could. It was then I saw her little sister, just an infant, in a basket behind her." He went silent, his gaze on the far wall as if played out before him.

"What happened?"

He jerked slightly, as though I'd woken him. "I killed the creature before it could harm them, but when I turned toward her, she buried that knife in my side. In her eyes I saw the same fear, the same hatred. I realized that while I guarded the boundary, I wasn't any different from the things that got through." He sighed. "I wanted to be different, though. I didn't go back to hell right away. I stayed in that town, stealing food and money for that girl and her sister, leaving it for them but staying out of sight. Time doesn't pass for me like it does for others—a result of having lived so long, I guess—and before I knew it, the girl was a mother herself. I watched over her for her entire life."

"Did she ever see you again?"

He nodded. "She'd catch glimpses of me, but never acknowledge me, never speak to me. At least not until she became very sick. Her children were around her, her grandchildren. She was this frail old woman, and it was strange, because it reminded me of her as a child. Fragile yet strong. She called for me, yelling out 'come in here, beast.'"

I sat up, the story drawing me in.

He licked his lips, as if they'd become parched, but I suspected it was nerves. I doubted he'd ever told this story before.

"I gave her the knife, the one she'd stuck in my side, like some sort of parting gift. She asked me why—why had I saved her? why had I helped her?—and I told her. I said, 'I didn't want to be what you saw. I wanted to be more.'"

"What did she say?"

Hunter sighed and met my gaze. "I've learned we don't get the things we want, that good stories don't happen. I want to say she forgave me, that she looked at me like I was suddenly good, that there was some wonderful epiphany that I had earned. In reality, she coughed up blood and told me, 'You have darkness inside you. It doesn't matter how much good you do, that darkness won't go away.'"

I wanted to slap the woman, to shake some sense into her. What a *horrible* thing to say to someone who had spent decades looking out for her.

He met my gaze finally, the sorrow there and for once not hidden behind a joke. "She wasn't wrong. I am what she said. I am darkness and evil and it took a very long time for me to understand what she meant. It wasn't a reprimand—it was a warning. I am those things, but they don't mean I have to *do* those things. A tiger can kill, and nothing changes that, but they don't *have* to kill. I am darkness, but that doesn't mean I have to *do* those things." His hand moved, as if he wanted to reach out but stopped himself. "You used to look at me the way I wanted *her* to, like I wasn't that thing she said I was. Now you know, though, you've seen it, and it sticks with you. Still, if I have to do as I did before, if I have to spend all your years protecting you, I'll do it happily again, because what I am isn't what I *choose* to be." He spoke with so much confidence, as if it were a sacred oath he gave me, that he gave himself. A commitment to what he wanted to be rather than what he'd been born.

I reached out and slid a hand behind his neck as I sat up, taking his lips in a passionate kiss.

He groaned, the sound honest and surprised and thankful, as if he'd expected rejection and couldn't believe his luck.

His words stuck with me, though. How could I blame him for his nature? For what he was before he knew better?

And besides, hadn't he shown me over and over again who he was now?

"Can I have you, shadow-girl?" My nickname on his lips felt like home, and I tugged at him as my yes.

Hunter undid his pants, sliding them off so he was gloriously naked. He moved into the warm water with me, making the waves lick at my skin.

His body was solid against mine, and he fell into the cradle of my thighs.

That first time, when he'd licked me through more orgasms than I even tried to keep track of, it had been slow. It had been passionate and crazy for me, but he'd been methodical. Later, with Grant, it had been about quenching some need.

Now? This time? It was a hunger deeper than breathing. When he kissed me, he did it with such abandon, as if he needed nothing more.

He growled low in his chest as he grabbed my thigh, hiked it up around his waist and buried his hard cock inside my waiting cunt.

It was sudden and almost shocking, and yet somehow perfect. He plunged in deep, my body taking him in that one thrust as if I were made for him.

I gasped at the way he filled me, and he swallowed the sound, stealing it from me.

He wrapped his arm behind me, holding me to him as he rolled his hips, his chest rubbing against my nipples, teasing them.

Jayce Carter

He bit down on my bottom lip, tugging at it, fucking into me with a staggering amount of strength.

"I'm *not* who I was," he swore when he let go of my lip, the words whispered and solemn. "I swear it, shadow-girl. I am more now."

He said each word with the weight of a person who needed me to believe him. He caught my chin with his other hand, forcing my face to his.

His eyes, whiskey colored, so light they were almost melted honey, bore into mine, a question there, a demand.

"You need to know that. I *need* to know you believe it." He still above me, *inside* me, holding me so tightly, as if he were afraid I'd slip away.

I fell into those eyes, into the way he asked, the way he waited for an answer. He deserved my honesty, deserved me taking the moment to know my answer.

Did I believe him? Did I believe that whoever he was in the past, that the monster Jerrod was, the monster Jerrod had said Hunter was, was really gone? That he'd changed, that he wouldn't ever go back?

And could I look past it?

I would have said no at any other time, but somehow seeing his eyes, seeing how he stilled, how he held his breath even as his heart pounded hard forced me to believe him.

"I know," I whispered before closing my teeth on his lip then returning his kiss. I carded my fingers through his hair to hold him to me, which worked fine because Hunter was more than strong enough to handle fucking me without any help from me.

My back pressed into the tub, the water warm and like its own sensual touch as it licked across my skin.

Hunter breathed hard—funny since I'd just seen him face off against five teams of other supernaturals and he hadn't broken a sweat—but even so he kept me close.

My body wound tighter as he took me hard and fast, the sensation of his cock slamming into me like a revelation. He was wild, unconstrained, focusing only on the moment between us.

I stole his breath, savoring the bite of fire in it, breathing in the smoke that had escaped around him as if he couldn't keep it contained anymore, as if he were too consumed by our twisted bodies to care about appearing human.

He tightened his arm, tilting my hips so his pelvic bone ground against my clit with every thrust.

The orgasm hit me hard, just as wild as our sex. I tightened around his cock, but it didn't stop him from thrusting, from taking me roughly and stretching out the waves of pleasure that overcame me.

He made a low, hungry sound before he buried his face in the crook of my neck, then plunged as deep as he could and stilled. He came, a swear on his lips, before he went limp against me. With the water, he wasn't so heavy, and after a moment, he pulled free of me but didn't move away for another moment.

"You probably have to get ready," he said as he withdrew, an unhappy grumble as he left the warmth of the bath. He pulled his pants back on, seeming not to care that he was still wet.

I sat up and took his hand when he offered it. He tugged me to my feet, then wrapped the towel that had sat on a table beside the tub around me.

"How is everyone?" I asked. "Is anyone hurt?"

He shook his head before he helped me out of the tub. "A couple scratches, but Lucifer's healers got us all up and ready." He patted his hands over my sides. "I did notice that the caliber of service was down a bit."

"Oh really?" I played dumb as I pulled away from him, heading toward the closet for an outfit. "Lucifer must be running low on young, nubile women to service you, I guess."

"You are adorable when you're jealous, you know that? Never figured I'd have a thing for that, but I do." He chuckled, crossing his arms and leaning against the doorway. "Who knows, though. Maybe I just like you."

I opened the closet and pulled out what I'd planned to wear. I wasn't going sultry—it had never been my style anyway—and went with comfortable and powerful, instead.

I saw no reason to act shy now—Hunter had just been *inside* me—so I dropped the towel to pull on the clothing. A pair of basic slacks and a white button-up top that still managed to drop low in the front. I added a vest to it, which I had to admit made me look like one bad bitch.

"Well don't you look ready for battle?" Hunter's eyebrow hiked, the ends of his long, reddish hair curling more than usual since they'd gotten wet.

I smoothed my hands down the front of the vest, and even I couldn't deny that it accentuated me in a way that made me feel more in control. "So what are you doing for the rest of the night?"

"I can move around a bit easier than the others because of the whole smoke thing. Well, and because I know the palace. I wanted to check in on your first, so now I'm going to go off a few of our competitors."

The words took a moment to process as I braided my hair back. "Wait, what? That's horrible."

"It's the way the games work. Anyone who waits around for someone to show up and kill them is foolish."

"What about being fair?" The moment I said it, I realized how stupid that was. We were in hell. *Nothing* was fair. Beyond that, if it really came down to it…I was pretty sure I'd throw fair out the window for their safety.

I had bargained with Lucifer in order to get them a win, so what did fair matter?

"Fair didn't mean much to the member of green who snuck into our room and tried to decapitate Grant." When I stood up straighter, he grinned. "That mage is tougher than you think. The man who tried to get the jump of him is nothing but a scorch mark on the floor, now. So, I figured I'd repay the favor."

"I don't like this," I admitted. When he looked at me, I went on. "It feels like I'm waiting, like I'm just having to sit back and see what happens. I hate it."

Hunter came up and caught my chin. "Last I checked, you're dressed in a ball-buster suit and getting ready to go interrogate the devil. Doesn't seem like sitting back and doing nothing." His fingers were strong against my chin.

"I promised to answer his questions, so I think I'm the one being interrogated, not the other way around."

He chuckled and shook his head. "You know, every damned time I deal with you, I think I'm in charge. Kase sure as hell thought that, too, yet somehow you keep turning things around on us. I've got no doubt you can pull that on Lucifer himself, shadow-girl." He dropped his gaze down my body, his lips pulling into a smirk. "And looking like this? He won't know what the fuck hit him."

Chapter Sixteen

Lucifer's quarters were a stereotype. Dark, full of silvers, black, reds and expensive-looking furniture.

It was similar to the room I'd been given, in terms of layout and size, though it had no bed in the main room and had an additional door to the side that probably led to a sleeping area. Instead, it had more seating, set up like a living room rather than a hotel.

Lucifer still wore the slacks from before but had lost the jacket and tie. It didn't stop the way he appeared entirely in control. "Are you pleased with your team's treatment?"

"How would I know?" My heels clicked against the floor, and I prayed I didn't fall. Somehow, I was pretty sure my tough chick act would go by the wayside if I took a tumble.

"Because the hellhound came to see you. Do you really believe I don't know what is going on in my own palace?"

I pressed my lips together, choosing to look around the room instead of at him. "They're fine. Well, I mean, someone tried to kill them."

"If that ever didn't happen, I'd worry about people working together against me." He stopped by a large bar against the wall. "Would you like a real drink or water?"

I thought back to how those *drinks* were made and shuddered. "I am never going to touch that stuff again. It's like seeing sausage made. It ruins it."

Lucifer shrugged as he poured himself a drink from a large silver bottle with intricate designs engraved. "Your loss. Also mine, since in hell, clean water is far more expensive than any other drink." He grabbed another bottle from the shelf, one that looked just like the ones in my room.

When he handed it to me, the bottle chilled my palm. While I could have worried about being drugged, the truth was that he could have done that at any time. He could have killed me whenever he wanted, so I sipped the water without worry.

Lucifer took a drink of what he'd poured himself, then strolled over to another large cabinet. It was strange how much different he seemed.

Then again, he was the king of hell. I suppose out there, in the center of a party like that, it made sense that he might have to play a part.

Not that it made me trust him. Just because someone acted differently in public and private didn't mean either were good.

When he turned from the cabinet, he held a bracelet in his hand.

"I'm not a jewelry sort of girl," I said.

"You promised me four truthful answers. I've lived far too long to take anyone at their word."

"Is it true you can't lie?"

He nodded as he gestured toward the couch. "That is correct—I cannot lie."

"Aren't you the father of lies?"

"The stories are quite often twisted. What I suggest to people is to never believe a story, because the real ones are rarely interesting enough to last." He set his drink on the table in front of the couch as I sat down beside him. "Hold out your arm."

I let out a long sigh before giving him my wrist. His fingers were strong but thin, and he opened the hinged bracelet, then clasped it around my wrist.

A quick burn happened, one that made me hiss and jerk backward.

Lucifer released me right away, his hand up. "Try to relax and breathe slowly."

"What the hell is this? Why does it hurt?"

"It is enchanted and will cause pain when you lie."

"I'm not doing anything so why does it feel like my arm is on fire?"

Lucifer shrugged before picking up his drink again as if my issue wasn't his problem. "Sometimes it can react that way when people are particularly conflicted."

I clawed at it, though the longer it was on, the more the pain evened out. It didn't go away, but it wasn't so localized or intense. "You could have mentioned this first."

"I saw no reason to. Besides, this doesn't usually happen. You must be extraordinarily at odds with yourself for such a reaction. I wonder what exactly is going on in that head to cause this."

I hissed at the burn when I went to tell him he was wrong. It was like a warning not to let the lie leave my lips. So, instead, I swallowed then clenched my fist. "What are your questions?"

"Right to it, then?" He leaned back on the couch and put his arm not holding the drink over the back of the couch. "What are you?"

I didn't answer right away, the burning of the bracelet enough to make me wary. "What if I don't know the answer?"

"Then say you don't know, and so long as that is truthful, it still takes one of my questions." When I didn't speak, he lifted an eyebrow. "I play these games better than you do, mortal. You didn't actually answer."

That was when I realized that Hunter hadn't been kidding. Lucifer might just be more difficult to deal with than I'd thought.

I went to tell him I didn't know what I was, but a burning in my wrist said that wasn't an honest answer. So it seemed time for the entire truth… "I don't know what I am, exactly. My parents abandoned me when I was a kid, and I don't who they were. I've never met anyone quite like me, and no one has been able to tell me what I am." The burn remained at that low level, telling me the answer was acceptable.

Lucifer took a sip of his drink, staring at me carefully. "That was less helpful than I had hoped."

"I'm so sorry." The words flew from my mouth at the speed of sass, and right away, a stabbing pain burrowed into my arm, making me feel as if flames licked across the skin, as if it seared down to the bone.

I bent forward, gasping at the pain until it finally faded, leaving me sweating and shaking.

The entire time, Lucifer hadn't moved, watching impassively. "The bracelet doesn't speak sarcasm."

I kept myself from speaking again, from adding anything else because I wasn't sure what would come out of my mouth. Instead, I narrowed my eyes. "Three more questions."

Lucifer quirked his lips into a smile, as if that charmed him. "Question two—where are the spirits that haven't arrived in hell?"

The memory of the pain, the way my hand still felt as if an electrical charge ran through it, made me answer carefully. "I don't know where they are, only that they aren't in the afterworld, and that they were torn free of the tether that connected them to the body."

The liquid in Lucifer's glass swirled as he twisted his wrist. "So the spirits are taken before they would naturally move on. Interesting." He crossed one ankle over the opposite knee, making me notice just how shiny his black shoes were. "Question three. Who is behind it?"

"A shadow."

He gestured for me to go on. "That is not a full answer."

"Well, it is all I have for you. I don't know who or what the shadow is. I don't know how it is doing any of it." I blew out a breath, still shaky from the last shock, and leaned forward. "Someone was driving immortals crazy, making them kill. I felt the presence of this shadow. It attacked me once in a dream of mine." I lifted my arm to show the scar that still sat there. "It also showed up in a pocket universe with the elder ones, when they were looking for the spirits."

"But no idea who that shadow actually is?"

I shook my head. "It smelled of brimstone, so honestly, I thought it was you…"

He made a soft sound but didn't say it wasn't.

"You get one more question," I told him.

He didn't ask it right away, pausing as if reading me while he decided. Finally, he leaned forward. "What is it you really want?"

I frowned. "What sort of question is that?"

"An important one. There is no better way to size up an enemy than to understand what they truly want. That truth is at the core of everything they do. If all I get is one last question, that will tell me more than anything else could."

"What do *you* really want?" I asked with a snarky tone.

"I am wise enough to know better than to answer that one, at least not without a price, and I doubt it is one you would care to pay. You, however, owe me the answer."

I procrastinated by taking a drink of water, holding it in my mouth for a long moment before swallowing. What did I really want?

I wanted to find the missing spirits. I wanted to know who was behind this. I wanted to keep Troy, Kase, Hunter and Grunt safe. I wanted to be normal.

My arm burned, a warning that perhaps that last one wasn't true.

But wasn't that what I'd always wanted? To be normal, to fit in, to be like everyone else?

I set the glass down, afraid if I didn't answer it right, I'd end up in pain again. "I want to feel like I belong somewhere."

No pain seared through me, letting me blow out the breath I'd been holding. It seemed I'd been truthful, even if not entirely sure about it.

"A romantic, are you?" Lucifer shook his head as if disappointed. "I had hoped for so much more from you when I heard of the mortal who seemed to be at the center of this."

"Are we done?"

Lucifer nodded. "For now. We do have a few more rounds of competition left, so I suspect we will have plenty to bargain with later."

I took a large gulp to finish off the water, then rose.

"Hell is a very dangerous place, Ms. Harlin, and you seem to want to keep your team alive."

I pointed my finger at him, narrowing my eyes. "Don't you threaten them."

"It was an observation, not a threat. I am curious, though—how far would you go? What would you do to keep them safe?"

The answer came from me without having to think about it, without question. "Anything."

His gaze dropped to my wrist, to the bracelet still there, and I realized he'd gotten more answers from me without me realizing it.

Sneaky bastard.

Lucifer reached out and unclasped the bracelet. "Well, finally you show some backbone. Maybe you aren't quite as dull as I'd assumed."

Instead of arguing with him—what was the point?—I crossed my arms. "Can I go?"

He waved me off. "Go and get some sleep, Ms. Harlin, because I suspect tomorrow's competition will be even more taxing. And, Ms. Harlin?"

I faced him once more.

"I will give you a piece of good advice. Do not think about betraying me, plotting against me or otherwise working against me. People who cross me do not last long — especially mortals."

I thought back to the shadow, to the man who had tried to chop me into pieces, to Jerrod and Olin and the poltergeist. I met Lucifer's gaze head-on, met his not-so-subtle threat without flinching with a fact of my own. "And you should know, I'm a lot harder to kill than I look."

* * * *

I woke, jerking upright. The mist stuck in my throat and lungs from the dream wasn't easy to forget, to push away even if it hadn't been real.

The dreams felt worse in hell, more real, more all-consuming. It made me miss the ambrosia, that short burst of blissful, easy sleep I'd managed after drinking myself into a stupor.

I rolled over, trying to pull real air in, to reassure me that I wasn't in that damned dream. Funny that I'd be happier to find myself in hell.

"No wonder you never had a long-term boyfriend. I don't think anyone is sticking around if they wake up to *that*."

I wiped my mouth before turning to find Gran standing beside the bed, two cups in her hands. "Why are the dreams worse here?"

"Because you're closer to death here." She sat on the edge of the bed, then held one of the cups out to me. "Drink that. Don't just hold it."

The heat seeped into my palms, and I forced myself to sip the bitter tea. After I swallowed it, I shifted to get more comfortable. "What are you doing here?"

"You slept late, and I got tired of waiting around. Hell is far more boring than you'd expect."

"I never would have expected that."

"I've complained to Lucifer about it before, but he never does anything. He is one stubborn man. He used to be more fun, though. He's gotten worse the last few years."

"I can't imagine him ever being fun."

"Maybe you're right," Gran said, frowning as if trying to remember. "We're down to two teams."

Fear gripped my chest at that.

Gran patted my leg. "Unclench, dear. Your boy toys are just fine. Green and orange lost their last members, leaving only blue and black, both at full strength.

A pride that was probably totally inappropriate hit me at the fact that my boys had done so well. Maybe I didn't need to worry quite so much, but I couldn't help it. My words to Lucifer were true.

I'd do whatever it took.

This whole thing might have started out with me caring only about the shadow, about the spirits, but somewhere along the way those idiot men had become just as important.

Which was beyond stupid, because none of them had proven they wouldn't break my heart just as soon as it was in their best interest.

"Lucifer isn't behind this, is he?" When she looked at me with her eyebrow lifted, I took another drink. "Why would he call me, then?"

"Despite what Lucifer might claim, he isn't all powerful. His lines of communication are a little thin, these days."

"These days?"

Gran smiled, one that spoke volumes about what she didn't say. "Let's just say he has a little less movement than he used to. I wouldn't suggest you ask him, though. He's touchy about his shortcomings."

I didn't bother to ask her how she knew. Gran rarely offered real information to me, but she was always right. "So we have another party?"

"Given there are so few teams left, I'm going to guess we only have another two. Tonight, blue or black will be taken out, leaving tomorrow for the big event."

"Any idea what they're up against?"

Gran shrugged. "The first few rounds are usually boring. Normally there are more of them, but your team didn't seem like they wanted to drag this out. In fact, I don't know if I've ever seen it so short."

"You know, this tea isn't that bad." I frowned, staring down at it. "Please tell me this doesn't have any of that weird plant in it?"

"Ambrosia?" Gran shuddered. "No, never. Have you seen that stuff being grown?"

Thank fuck.

"So why is it better than usual?"

"Probably because you miss it. A week in hell will do that to a person. I was stuck here for a few weeks years ago, and by the end of it, black gas station coffee was orgasmic. Sort of like how after a few centuries of abstinence, even a lousy lay is great." She offered me a smile. "Not that I think *you* have that problem."

I thought back to Hunter, to how he'd taken me the night before, and took another drink of my tea to hide my reaction.

I might be willing to kiss Hunter and the others in front of an entire party, but actually talking about sex was too far.

A sound from the courtyard rang through the room, something like a bell.

Gran turned to peer that way. "That means we have about two hours before the party starts."

"Will they be there?"

I didn't need to specify who they were.

"Oh, I suspect your boys will be the belles of the ball. It's been a while since we've had a show as good as they put on. In fact, I bet we'll have a few extra people who didn't feel the first night was worth attending. Then again, Hunter *always* draws a good crowd."

I could see that. Hunter was nice to look at, and he sure managed to make things interesting.

"He's a show," I agreed.

"It's not just him. While folks down here don't always get a lot of information, Kase and Grant are fairly well known. Your little team there is like straight out of a who's who in the supernatural world. The only one who isn't already famous is Troy, but one look at that man without his shirt and trust me, he's got fans." She fanned herself, and if it had been anyone else, I'd have probably felt jealous.

It was hard to feel like that with Gran, especially because she still looked like an old woman.

Not that I believed that act for a moment.

Though, the quiet moment gave me a pause. "What do you really look like?"

"You saw a glimpse."

"So why look like *this?*"

Gran took a sip of her tea, then rested it on her leg. "I learned a long time ago that a pretty face was a detriment."

"I'd think it was helpful. Men get stupid around pretty faces."

"Men want to *own* pretty faces. They get obsessive, determined, and it makes life far more difficult. I prefer to move without that complication."

The way Kase had noticed me, how Troy had distracted me even as just my neighbor, how Grant and Hunter had entangled themselves in my life made me unable to argue with her point.

It wasn't that I acted as if I were beautiful, and honestly because of the spell my parents had put on me, I was usually ignored.

Hadn't the men made my life more difficult in many ways?

Hadn't they helped, too?

I tried to think about what my life would have been like if I hadn't met them, if I'd had to face this all on my own.

And all the times I would have probably been dead.

"Is it worth pretending to be something you're not?"

She laughed. "You're asking me that? You, who has spent your entire life trying to pretend to be normal?"

The jab landed. It was true…

Still, it also felt like an odd moment with Gran. She normally felt so…different. She felt wise and unreachable. Sure, she was my friend, but it had always been borne of a different level.

Sitting across from her made me look at her differently.

Maybe it was my time in hell, my experiences. I didn't feel like the girl who didn't know where she belonged, the one who felt unprepared for life, hiding behind her skirts.

Instead, I felt like an equal.

Okay, so I wasn't quite an equal — no one feared me the way they feared her — but I wasn't a girl afraid of life, either.

And I finally saw that she wasn't quite as together as she pretended to be. She wore a different face just to hide a part of herself she didn't like.

"Maybe neither of us needs to hide so much," I said.

"Maybe," she said, and for a moment the real vision of her shimmered, showing me a glimpse of the woman she was beneath that. "Get yourself ready, dear. No doubt that green-haired woman stuffed with far too much cheer will be here to escort you when it is time."

With that, she got off the bed, leaving my cup with me. When she got to the door and opened it, a guard stepping in front of her for a moment.

Then the guard took another look at her and stepped backward faster than I'd seen them do with anyone else.

She offered one more smile before leaving me be to get ready.

Chapter Seventeen

Gran was right—the party was *much* larger than the day before.

Beyond that, they were more dressed up, too, as if the event had become a big deal all of a sudden.

There were more groups of people milling around. Elder ones stood in the corner, their pointed ears and green eyes a sure giveaway. There were even men, which I hadn't seen before. They were lithe, just like the women, and wore suits that were fitted beautifully and embroidered along the lapels of the jacket and down the side of the legs.

Others, who at first passed as humans stood in groups. With a closer look, I noted the tips of fangs. Across the room, Fredrick, the pack alpha, stood with a few others.

Persephone left me, again. She'd come to my room to escort me to the party in an even fancier dress that dipped far lower in the front. Somehow it didn't look slutty on her, though. She looked regal, instead.

We had made it all of thirty seconds into the party before something else caught her attention and she floated off in distraction.

I hadn't run into Lucifer yet, but the bodies were packed in so tightly that didn't shock me. Besides, the longer I could avoid him, the better.

"Don't you look like a treat?" The voice was one I didn't recognize, and I turned to find a woman with long, straight black hair behind me.

She was beautiful in a way very different than Persephone. Where the goddess was all cheer and innocence, this woman was darkness, power and lust. She wore a red suit that appeared even brighter against her black hair and matched her lips.

"Do I know you?"

"No, but I know of you." The words felt oddly sinister, especially with her smirk. "Word travels fast, and I've heard about the mortal who sits beside my father. It's something uncommon enough for even me to venture home and see."

Father?

"Lilith." Hunter walked up from my side, his voice careful. "I didn't expect you to show."

"As I was telling your pet, here, even I couldn't resist the invitation when I heard Father had made a mortal his guest of honor."

"And here I thought it was to watch me."

She lifted her nails—black and filed to sharp points—and studied them. "If you believe I haven't seen better competitors than you, you're foolish."

"Ouch." Hunter set a hand on my lower back. "I'd love to hear more about how little you care about me, but I think there are others who want to meet the mortal of the hour." With that, he steered me away from the scary woman.

"Was that *the* Lilith? From the stories?"

"You find that harder to believe than Lucifer?" I gave him a sharp look, and he sighed. "Yes, that's her."

"I thought she was Adam's first wife? Not Lucifer's daughter?"

"Haven't I told you not to believe stories?"

"Come on, you can't just leave it at that."

"It's too long a story for right now, and even I don't know all of it. I promise, when we have a free moment, you can pick my brain about every last myth you want."

I sighed, but he wasn't wrong. Story time wasn't a priority.

"She was right, though. You do look like a treat." He slid his fingers along my spine, his words low and smooth and tempting. Somehow, after our talk, that word didn't freak me out like it probably should have.

I'd gone with a dress that was more flowy than the last. It was still black and red—somehow those felt like they fit—and it dipped low in the chest, then ran down from that point to drift around my ankles. I'd skipped heels—my feet hurt from dealing with them—and had gone with flats.

"How did last night go?" I asked to distract myself.

"Fine."

"Where is everyone else?"

"Word spread about our little team, so there are people here. Colter showed up, Fredrick is over there, and someone from the mage's guild, I think. I'm sure they'd rather be here with you, but business calls." He peered to the side, then sighed. "And it's my turn to go on and make nice, as well. I just wanted to save you from Lilith." He leaned in and pressed a quick kiss before backing away. "Be careful, shadow-girl. People are taking notice of you."

With that, he left, and I had to admit...he might have been correct. When I peered around the room, eyes would shift away from me and back to their conversation, as if whoever they were talking to was just there as cover.

After a lifetime of no one really seeing me, I felt *far* too on display.

As I moved through the room, I spotted Kase first. Sure enough, he stood beside Colter, and again I struggled to believe he was older than the coven leader. Kase was many things, but he wasn't the monster that Colter was. Why not? What made Kase different?

It didn't matter at the moment since there was no way I was going anywhere near Colter. The last time I'd had to see him, he'd threatened me, and sure, I'd been threatened a *lot* since then, but there was something special about a person's first one that made me want to stay the hell away from them.

Troy was beside Fredrick, though Sarah was nowhere around. Then again, who really wanted to bring their mate to hell?

No one ever takes me anywhere nice.

I was going to avoid them as well, but Troy turned to lock eyes with me, giving me no real out.

Instead, I trudged over, not bothering to look excited.

"Ms. Harlin," Fredrick said, a smile to his lips that looked honest, but I couldn't figure out why.

He'd also threatened me, though in a much nicer way than Colter, into doing a job for him.

A job I didn't really do all that well.

"Fredrick."

Troy wrapped an arm around my waist and pulled me against his side, a clear power play to remind Fredrick that I wasn't just anyone. Wolves and their games…

"I have to say, when I heard about this, I hardly believed it. That little human here in hell? That was the sort of thing I couldn't miss."

I tried to stick my hands into my pockets before remembering that dresses didn't *have* pockets. "The world is a crazy place."

"So it seems. I never attend these things — I find hell a depressing place — but this was worth the travel. Not to forget that Troy in the games is a surprise as well. I would ask how that happened," Fredrick's gaze dropped to where Troy's are was wrapped around me, "But I don't think I need to."

It took me a moment to realize *why* I disliked him so much.

Troy.

It was the tension Troy had, the way he wanted me nowhere near anything pack.

"Have there been any more cases of werewolves going crazy?" I asked.

Fredrick's smile fell. "Yes, a few. I've stopped putting them down and converted an old storage area we had into holding cells. Now that I know it isn't some sort of infection, I am hoping we can fix it."

I frowned. "How do you even know what happened? It wasn't like we had time to leave a note."

Fredrick turned his gaze from me Troy, like a question, as if he wasn't sure Troy *wanted* him to answer.

The gesture annoyed me.

Thankfully, Troy shrugged, a safe response.

"The mage with you enabled communication between Troy and me. We've spoken a few times since you arrived there."

"No one ever thinks to tell me about this stuff, do they? Maybe I had people to call."

Troy lifted an eyebrow, his polite way of calling me out for the blatant lie.

Everyone I cared about or spoke to was here, in hell, other than Gran who I was pretty sure could have talked to me whenever she wanted.

"Shut up," I muttered before elbowing Troy.

He pressed a kiss to my head and released me. "Go on. I have a few things to discuss with Fredrick before the second round starts."

I pressed my lips into an unhappy line at the reminder of the competition, of the dangers, that we weren't just at some party.

Still, I did as he said, spotting Grant. He wasn't talking with someone I recognized, but given how human they looked, I had to guess mages.

Grant spotted me before I approached, but he didn't reach out, not like Hunter and Troy had.

Because of that, I didn't reach for him, either, letting him set the tone.

"Ava," he said, voice friendly but careful. "This is Jameson Cleric and his apprentice, Victoria Brown." Grant gestured toward me. "This is Ava Harlin."

Jameson, a man who appeared to be in his forties with a pair of round glasses, stared at me with no attempt to hide his displeasure. "I've heard your name a lot in recent weeks."

"Well, that's vague and mildly threatening," I said.

His eyebrow lifted, as if he hadn't expected my response. "I am the acting Magistrate and given there was a mage in the competition, it was expected for me to attend once we found out."

"But he isn't in the guild."

Jameson's gaze moved to Grant's in question.

"I am so tired of people trying to decide what I should know. Out with it."

"Grant's position in the guild is tenuous."

"And what does that mean?"

Jameson didn't wilt at all, despite my hard look. "It means if you wish to know more, you should ask him yourself. I am here because it would be improper for someone from the guild not to be present."

"And that someone had to be acting Magistrate, who I would imagine is the highest up in the guild?"

Jameson didn't answer the question, telling me that all mages were as annoying as Grant when it came to information sharing. "It was nice to meet you, Ms. Harlin, and I suspect I will be hearing more of you in the future. Grant, please think over what I've said."

"We both know that won't happen.," Grant answered.

Jameson only nodded, as if he'd expected no other answer, before leaving, the woman Victoria on his heels.

"What was that about?"

"History, and not the fun kind." Grant hadn't removed his gaze from the two, not until they were far enough away, they blended into the party. Only then did he turn back toward me, offering me that charming smile of his I knew so well.

The one I also knew hid whatever he really thought.

"What was he talking about?" I asked to derail whatever Grant was going to say, because no doubt it was all about changing the subject.

"Nothing important."

I crossed my arms like a defiant kid.

He rolled his eyes and let out a sigh as if I tested his patience. "It is an old story that now is not the time to tell."

"Let's go with simple here, since you told me you wouldn't lie to me anymore. Are you in the guild?"

"I didn't lie about that—it simply isn't an easy answer."

"You said you killed people and you left."

"Leaving the guild isn't official. Most mages who leave or are kicked out are fairly unimportant. The guild isn't worried about them. Let's say I left the guild but they see it differently."

"So you said 'I'm out' and they said no?"

Grant nodded. "That sums it up fairly well. They leave me be for the most part, but apparently this was deemed important enough to send the acting Magistrate himself. That's almost enough for me to be honored."

"But why is he here?"

Grant shook his head. "I don't know, but I can assure you it isn't anything good. Jameson doesn't show up unless he thinks there's a big payoff for him. My guess? He's hoping I get weakened enough in the competition that he has a shot."

"A shot at what?"

Grant's gaze wasn't on me, having moved in the direction Jameson had gone, his eyes narrowed for a split second before he turned back toward me, his face wiped clean for the suspicion. "It doesn't matter.

Others have tried before him, others will afterward. Now, have you eaten? Given that this time there are actual beings from the living realm, I believe there is a table of non-disgusting food just that way."

I offered Grant the same look he'd given Jameson, one that said I know damn well he was up to something even if I didn't know exactly what.

Then my stomach gurgled, and I realized putting nothing but tea into an empty stomach wasn't a great combination.

"Fine," I muttered, giving in.

Grant gestured toward the side wall, and I followed.

He was keeping secrets, but what was new? If I waited for Grant to be honest with me, I'd starve to death first.

Chapter Eighteen

The food was good, but the company left a lot to be desired. Grant remained for a short while, but before long, he left me to fend for myself.

At first, I couldn't seem to help but nurse a hurt from the fact that all four men didn't have time for me.

They had spent *so much* time following me—even when I'd told them to get lost—and yet suddenly they were all too busy?

Then I watched, carefully, and noticed how each spared glances my way. The reality was that they were getting ready for a second round in a game that had killed so many already. Then I noticed how they watched their opponents, how the two teams circled each other, and I realized this was part of their game. They were sizing each other up, getting ready to go into the final battle where only one of them would walk out.

Feeling abandoned would have been petty.

Or so I told my hurt feelings.

"I can't say I get the appeal."

I turned to find someone *far* too close to me, and the blue jumpsuit he wore let me know who he was.

One for the team facing off against my team.

He was tall—at least seven feet—and looked similar to the man who had tried to plant me. Except, where that man had been twisted and burned, this one appeared quite nearly human in form, other than the size and the dagger-like claws that tipped his fingers.

He turned his head, as if surveying who was around, and it gave me a look at some of his back.

More ridged claws ran down his spine like some dragon, and they shone as they caught like as if made of silver rather than bone.

I took a step backward, wanting *far* more personal space.

He chuckled as he looked back at me, and when he spoke, I realized his teeth were every bit as sharp as the rest of him, and a long, forked tongue darted inside his mouth.

It was a miracle he sounded so normal…

Or maybe that was part of the translation Grant had mentioned.

"I'm not going to hurt you. Well, not here, at least. Harming Lucifer's guest of honor would be a foolish mistake, and I'm far from foolish."

"So what are you doing here?"

"Do you know how many of these I've been in? More than Hunter, more than any other being."

"Why do you keep entering then?"

"Because the prize is worth it. Do you have *any* idea how valuable a favor from Lucifer is?"

"Not really, no."

He curled his lips into a smile that was chilling because it showed the points of his sharp teeth. "He can't release a soul from the afterworld for good, but he can allow one to move to a new level."

"Are you working your way up the ladder?"

"No. Too many rules in the other levels. I tried that, but I ended up getting sent back here. No, I use my favor the same way every time. I get a ticket back to earth."

"I thought you said he couldn't release people."

"He can't. The tickets don't last long. I can inhabit a newly dead body for a few weeks, perhaps a month at most, then I slip back here. Still, even a visit is worth it."

"I'm not really interested in your vacation plans, so are we done?"

"Not even close. See, Hunter and I, we've never faced off before. He's undefeated, as am I. I don't like to leave things to chance, however."

"That's good, because you don't have a chance."

"Ferocious for something so little," he said. "One swipe with my claws and you'd be done for. Worse, you aren't entirely mortal, are you? Do you even *have* a spirit? Would you go to an afterlife? Immortals give that up, but you?" He spoke as if the answers were all hypothetical and not talking about my real, actual life. He also moved on as if the answers were all together unimportant. "Tell your precious team to back out. They can forfeit, giving me the win I deserve."

"You wouldn't be asking for that unless you thought you couldn't win fairly. You *know* they'll beat you, don't you? You don't have any leverage."

"That's where you're wrong. They might win, but so might I. If I come out on top, and if you don't do as I say, if you don't have them forfeit, then I'll spend the weeks I have there peeling your flesh from your bones.

I can't touch you here, but we both know you won't be here forever. And, if I win, that means you won't have your protectors anymore."

My chest grew tight, especially because the seriousness in his gaze told me he damned well meant it. This was a creature capable of exactly what he was claiming.

I looked to the side, to spot Kase who stared right at us, that red rimming his eyes showing he didn't care for the creature to be so close to me.

I lifted my hand to tell him I didn't need him riding in to save the day.

After another sharp look, he turned back to his conversation.

The competition was our only chance at real answers, at figuring out where the spirits were going and who was behind it. Even if Lucifer didn't know anything, his favor could help us stop it. I could ask him to help us fight the shadow once we found it.

Plus, if my team forfeited, they'd be gone and unable to help me.

Or, more realistically, they'd be going through that dead zone on foot to get back to the palace, something that was probably more dangerous than the creature in front of me.

I shook my head and forced myself to meet the gaze of the creature from the blue team. "Not a chance."

His eyes widened as if he'd been certain he could threaten me into compliance. "You're making a very foolish choice."

"Probably," I admitted. "But that's for tomorrow Ava to deal with. Today Ava says to go get ready. My team is about to kick your ass."

He straightened to his full height, and for one split second I thought he'd lose control, that he might just forget that whole 'no killing honored guests' thing.

"I suggest you follow her exceedingly good advice."

I never thought I'd be happy hear Lucifer's voice, yet there we were.

The competitor nodded, then bowed before leaving, his hands curled into tight fists.

Once he was gone, I let out a deep breath I hadn't even realized I was holding.

Lucifer snorted. "So not quite so brave as you pretend?"

"I learned early that it's more important to *look* tough than it is to actually *be* tough."

"I've found that lesson sounds reasonable until forced to back it up."

I recalled trying that with a bully once, and how I'd put my hands over my nose to catch the blood after they'd put me down with one punch. "Do it well enough and you won't need to back it up." I turned to actually look at Lucifer, finding him in a similarly fantastic suit—this one a navy blue rather than the black pinstripe from before.

I hated to admit he was handsome, but he was. Not in the way where I wanted him, but in the way where I couldn't really deny it.

"Why did you not take his offer? You said you would do anything to keep your team safe."

"Because until I can stop what's happening with the spirits, they won't *be* safe. Until I can figure this out, until we can fix it, no one is safe."

He tilted his head, as if surprised that I'd answered without manipulation. "And you believe you *can* stop it? Because, from what I know of your attempts so far, you've had little luck. You have failed to even locate a suspect. Well, besides me, and I think you know you missed the mark there."

"Like you've done any better. I'm your only hope and you were wrong about me, too. Looks like we were both shitty detectives. "

"I never believed you were behind it. "

That caught me off guard. "What?"

"I knew you could not have orchestrated it."

"So why did you ruin my whole week and drag me here?"

"Because of what happened when you tried to find that first spirit."

I frowned, thinking back to what Hunter had said, that other things could *feel* that. Hunter, the warden, Lucifer.

It seemed I was luckier than I'd realized that nothing worse had happened…

"That's it? You don't even care about the whole world-ending thing?"

"I care about the spirits, but my influence at the moment is limited to here in hell, and seeing as the spirits aren't *here*, there isn't much I can do. You, however, are potentially *far* more valuable. What you did shouldn't have been possible, and things that aren't possible are my favorite." That came across as far more of a threat then a compliment. As it turned out, the devil thinking I was valuable just didn't please me.

It was a time when I missed flying under the radar in life…

Things were so much easier when I didn't have everyone looking my way.

"I hate to be the one to tell you, but if you think I'm going to be useful in any way, you've wasted your time.

I am, at best, a fucked-up medium." Good thing I wasn't wearing the bracelet, because I was pretty sure I'd get one hell of a shock for that statement.

The more time passed, the more I learned, the more I accepted I wasn't human, at least not in the strict sense. No matter how badly I wanted to be, no matter how much I wanted to be just like everyone else, I guess turning into some sort of ghost creature was a good way to shock me out of my belief.

Lucifer exhaled sharply, a sound that said I was being foolish. He gestured to the side of me without addressing my statement. "It is nearly time for the competition to begin. We should take our seats."

"Wonderful. It's been almost a whole day since I had to sit on a skull. I miss that incredibly gross feeling."

Lucifer sighed, then pulled a cloth from the inside pocket of his suit jacket and handed it to me, leaving the one in his outer pocket free from me stealing it. "Mortals are tiresome. I remember now why I don't allow them in the palace."

"Well, maybe remember it next time you decide to *summon* one, because this wasn't my idea of a great time, either."

He crossed his arms as I spread the cloth over the seat and lowered myself into it, grimacing at just how uncomfortable bone furniture was. "Your mouth will be the death of you," he said before taking his own seat.

He was probably right.

Watching both teams come out made me question not giving into the blue team's demands.

The blue team had behemoths of men on it along with one woman who was tall and had horns that went up from her temples then twisted back to meet behind her head. They looked like the sort of people who would kill someone for nothing more than being in the wrong place at the wrong time.

It was a *far* cry from my team.

Sure, I knew what my boys could do—I'd seen it. However, where the blue team wore their viciousness on their sleeves, my boys didn't look nearly as intimidating.

A fear crept into me.

What if I'd picked wrong? What if one of them *did* get killed? What if it was all my fault?

I met Grant's gaze, and all those worries must have shown on my face because he gave me a smirk and *winked*.

The arrogant bastard. Still, it helped. He knew what he was capable of, what the others were. Grant was not the self-sacrificing type, especially not without milking the hell out of it. There was no way he'd just allow himself to be killed off without even an ill-timed joke.

It let me draw in a breath, to remind myself that they'd survived one round and a few attempts over the night.

An announcer called both teams, this time calling out each member individually. When the teams had been introduced the last time, the crowd had gone crazy for the blue team. The crowd had been almost deafening with fanboy and fangirls.

This time, however, things had changed. When the woman gestured toward the black team, those standing around went wild.

She went through each of them, as she had the other team, and there was no doubt the crowd had taken to my boys.

Hunter threw his arms up and spun as if the cheering of fans were the best thing he'd ever experienced. Of course, before I could get too jealous, he turned toward me, winked, then blew a kiss.

Grant lifted one hand, all cockiness and confidence.

Kase nodded, hands folded at the small of his back, reminding me a bit too much of Lucifer's demeanor.

Troy, however, was always the odd man out. Discomfort showed in his stance. Where Hunter and Grant lived for the affection, and Kase seemed comfortable with it even if he didn't puff his chest, Troy looked as if he'd rather fight any of the other team if it meant he didn't have to endure being the center of attention.

Then again, he wasn't a fan of his other form, and a fight like this required it. No wonder he didn't relish the activity — he had to show an entire group of people a part of himself he loathed.

"I wonder what they want," Lucifer said when the teams filed out and the shimmering image appeared before us, this time of a slightly different but similar arena.

"What?"

"Your team. I know they came for you, but I wonder what they would request as their favor. The favor belongs to the team member who makes the killing blow on the final creature they face. My bet would be on Hunter, given he has done this before, but Kase killed the creature in the first round. What will they ask for?"

"How would I know?"

"Because I suspect nothing they do here is for themselves. Being here benefits them little."

"If we can't deal with the spirit mess, I think that involves everyone."

"Not really," he said.

"Pretty sure the whole living and afterlife bleeding into each other is a big scope problem."

"They're more adapted to such a world than mortals. In fact, they may prefer it."

I shook my head. "No more humans, no more new immortals. And you keep proving you know more than you let on."

"Everyone knows more than they let on. Anyone who shows their entire hand is a fool."

"So *help* me already, would you? You've wasted my time, risked my life, and for what? For something you think I can do?"

He twisted to look at me despite the teams walking into view in the arena, as if the competition had little value to him. "Believe it or not, I don't want the world to end, either. I rather like the living realm, and my power would be lessened were the barrier between the afterlife and the living world broken."

"So *tell* me what I need to know already. Stop playing games."

A screeching from the arena drew my attention back, and in the center was something I didn't recognize. A woman creature, sort of, but with elongated arms and legs and pointed nails. White hair flowed around her in an almost ethereal way, as if it defied the laws of gravity despite appearing corporeal.

"What is that?" I asked.

"A banshee."

I frowned, trying to recall if Gran had ever taught me anything about them.

Nothing.

Lucifer huffed, as if my lack of knowledge were an annoyance to him. "They scream when someone is about to die. Of course, they are often the cause of death. See, that scream? It is something that can be lethal to the living and the dead. Banshees exist in the living world, but their screams cross the barrier into ours."

When she screeched again, I covered my ears even though I'd bet the barrier filtered some out.

Sure enough, two from blue team collapsed to their knees, and Troy shook his head, stumbling backward.

Grant waved his hand, his lips moving, before walking up to Kase.

Kase nodded, though I couldn't hear what they said to each other, and opened his mouth. Grant ran his thumb across Kase's fang, then use his bleeding finger to leave a smudge of red on each of Kase's ears. He did the same to himself, to Hunter and Troy, and as soon as he did, as soon as he left that blood mark, the screaming didn't seem to affect them anymore.

"This is why I dislike mages in my games," Lucifer said, a clear pout to his voice. "They like to ruin my fun."

Lucifer's frustration was my gain, and I leaned forward to watch.

I understood the main issue. The teams needed to avoid killing the banshee before taking out the other team, or they would be locked into another round. However, the black team had the advantage here, due to Grant's trick, which meant the blue team would be smart to try and kill the banshee and hope for a more favorable opponent the next round.

For that reason, the two still on their feet on the blue team rushed forward, toward the screeching woman at the center of the area. They moved slowly, as if the sound waves from her physically pushed them backward.

While Hunter and Troy weren't harmed by the screaming, they didn't move much faster. It seemed Grant's spell could protect them from some of the damaging effect but not free them entirely.

Hunter and Troy went in opposite directions, with Troy headed for the two people on the ground and Hunter for the ones who went for the banshee.

"Agree to submit to me tonight," Lucifer said.

"Excuse me?" The words startled me enough I turned my gaze from the arena to his.

"You heard me. I need to test something, and for that, I need your complete compliance. No fighting me, no hiding, no lying."

"Why would I do that? It seems to me my team is doing fine, and if they're the only survivors, they're the winners, so they'll get all the special treatment tonight. What reason would I have to do what you want?"

He lifted one finger, and the banshee's scream intensified in time, as if he controlled it.

Hunter stumbled as he reached the two, shifting to his dragon form, the smoke spreading out and his scales catching the light. Still, even as he moved, it was clear the sound affected him. He pounced on the two, and I jerked my gaze away so I didn't have to see what happened to them.

Troy fell to his knees, but his body changed, his back bowing, his bones doing that popping thing when he started to lose control.

Red leaked out of Grant's ears, his face pulled into tight lines that screamed of pain.

"Do you really think I can't make this far worse for them?"

Just as I was ready to think it was a coincidence, he lifted that finger higher, raising the pitch of the scream, and this drove even Kase to the ground, his fangs bared.

Even still, Troy had the upper hand with the two members of the blue team. He twisted, his real form much larger and stronger than either. Plus, with the increase of the banshee screams, they were all but useless.

With one swipe, Troy ended both of the team members on the ground so only the black team remained, though not in great condition.

"See, you have nothing to bargain with," I said. "My team already won."

"Not yet they didn't. To end the round, they have to kill the banshee." He lifted his hand, and the screaming intensifying until a warm trickle down my neck said my ears bled as well.

And in the arena, it was worse. All four men were on the ground, twisting, and none could reach where the banshee stood at the center, her mouth open, that horrible sound making the area around her blurry.

"They won't be able to survive this long," Lucifer said. "Even with Grant's trick, she can overcome it and end them all."

"Then you won't have a winner *or* my help."

"But without your compliance, you're useless to me anyway, and what do I care about a winner? I only set this up to give me leverage to use you as I please. Understand that I don't care about the competition, about your precious immortals or about you. I play to win, mortal, and I always do."

My stomach rolled at how easily he'd maneuvered me, and how he'd set it all up against me. Try as I might, I didn't see another option. The banshee would kill them if I didn't agree.

"Okay," I whispered. "I agree."

Lucifer dropped his hand, the banshee's scream quieting.

It was Kase who rose first, who showed that astonishing speed as he rushed the woman, grasped her chin and snapped her neck.

Her body fell still to the ground, and the crowed exploded into applause.

"I will see you tonight," Lucifer said before rising from his seat and walking away, as if I were no longer important.

Then again, I wasn't.

He'd outsmarted me, and I had no idea what he wanted from me….

Chapter Nineteen

I was amazed that the guards heeded my request when I asked to see the black team. I had to assume Lucifer had already approved it. He probably knew that if he didn't allow it, he'd have to deal with my complaining.

Down one floor and across the courtyard, the guard stopped in front of a door with had another guard.

"You have one hour," he said. "Then Lucifer wishes to see you."

I nodded, then slid into the room, closing the door behind me.

Inside was a huge room set up with seating and tables full of food. Doors sat the sides, likely the quarters rooms off the main area.

A woman walked from one of the rooms, her eyes drunk with lust and her hair messy. On her heels was Kase, a spot of blood on his lip, his hand on her lower back.

I froze, the sight painful in a way I hadn't expected.

Kase lifted his gaze to mine, an uncomfortable moment of silence as if he wasn't sure what to say.

Instead of saying anything to me, he escorted the woman to the door, then knocked.

"But I don't want to go," she said in a slur, turning and pressing her lips to Kase's.

He set her aside, firm hands on her arms, then peered at the guards. "Please return her. I am quite satisfied."

Satisfied.

How satisfied would he feel if I kneed him right in the groin? Then again, if he'd already finished, I suppose he didn't really need to use that equipment anyway.

When the door shut again, leaving us there, he didn't speak right away. *Leave it to Kase to play the long game.*

"I told Lucifer to pick ugly donors. I should have also specified men for you."

He let out a slow sigh. "I didn't sleep with her."

"Of course you did. She looked like the poster child for just rolled out of bed."

"She wanted to, yes, but as you saw, I sent her away after feeding."

When he tried to reach for me, I pulled back and stormed past him. "You made it pretty damn clear that resisting wasn't possible when you fed on Troy. Or was that just a game to see what you could get me to do?"

"Werewolves are different. The blood is more potent." Even as he spoke, there was a quiver to his voice that reminded me of when he'd fed from Troy.

I gave myself that moment to recall, to remember how his lips had looked at Troy's throat, how I'd wrapped my lips around Troy's cock, how lost to it all we'd been.

Then I spotted the blood on his lip and my passioned chilled.

"You can't be angry that I had to feed, Ava. If I don't feed, I die. While I would happily feed from only you, that isn't possible, so we are in this situation."

I narrowed my eyes, wanting to argue it more because I really didn't like the thought of that other woman pressed up against him, of the way she'd kissed him, of how his lips would have looked at her throat.

I *hated* it, and it being unfair to be angry didn't really matter.

Still, I took a deep breath and tried to let it go. Reality sucked some of the time, and this seemed just another example.

Besides, the memory of the blood that had leaked from his ears as well told me that he had probably needed to feed.

"What happened?" he asked. When I furrowed my eyebrows, he continued. "The banshee quieted for no reason. I doubt Lucifer leaves much to chance, so I assume that was due to you? What did you promise?"

I grabbed a bottle of water from the shelf and took a drink before sitting to explain. I told him about my deal to submit to Lucifer.

He didn't speak, and yet the tension inside him made me want to scoot farther down on the couch.

He waited for me to give every detail, to tell him everything that had happened before he answered. Finally, he set his arm on the back of the couch and frowned. "You should not have agreed."

"You could have died."

"Trust me, I know. I have never encountered a banshee before. It feels as though your brain is dissolving. I could not move my body, couldn't think or see. Even still, you should not have agreed. Who knows what Lucifer wants from you?"

His words were strange in that they were honest. He would have rather I left them to die just to avoid becoming entangled with Lucifer?

What an idiot.

I shifted to my knees and shoved his shoulder. "If you really think I was going to just sit there and let you *die*, then you really are a fucking moron."

He tilted his head, that blank expression he wore when he thought I were being entirely irrational. "You have no idea what Lucifer will ask of you, and you're now obligated to comply. Do you not recognize how dangerous that is?"

"I *recognize* that if you all died, I'd have been—"

Alone.

The word made me freeze as I realized how true it was and how stupid it would have been to answer.

Not speaking it aloud didn't change the truth, though. If they'd died, I'd have been alone. Not just to figure out the spirits, the shadow, how to escape hell. No, I'd have been on my own after finally finding something that made me feel as if I belonged.

The thought was worse than death, worse than anything Lucifer could do to me.

Kase stared at me, his eyes still as he seemed to read my face.

I shoved him again, as if that would explain the things I couldn't say.

He caught my wrist and tugged me forward, into his lap. "You are a foolish woman, Ava, and you take too many risks."

"And you're an idiot who doesn't understand women at all."

"Perhaps." He pulled me closer, but I leaned back and gestured to a spot of red still on him. There was no way I'd kiss him, not with another woman's blood painting his lips.

He wiped it clear. "I wish I didn't have to feed from others," he admitted.

Instead of answering—I couldn't say anything that would make either of us feel better about it—I leaned in and brushed my lips to his.

His breath was warm when he exhaled, that tiny release he always did, as if he couldn't quite believe I was there.

Still, he kissed me back, and I kept my hands from grabbing at him, no matter how difficult I found that level of restraint.

He broke the kiss too fast, though. "There isn't time."

"I can be quick."

He chuckled lowly, a rare sound I cherished, before shaking his head. Even still, he didn't move me off his lap.

I peered around. "Where is everyone?"

"Hunter is trying to find information about the creature for tomorrow. We knew about the banshee in round two because that what's that Persephone let slip, which was why Grant could prepare for it and have the spell ready. With any luck, he gets information again."

"And Grant?"

"Sleeping. Without knowing what we're facing tomorrow, he needed to try to recuperate as much of his magic as possible."

I smothered my disappointment. The last thing I wanted was to risk them not being at their best because I was being overly needy and didn't let him recover. Still, it was hard, because what I really wanted was to reassure myself that he was fine. I recalled the blood that had leaked from his ears, the way he'd been thrown to the ground.

Grant was tough—I couldn't deny that—but he wasn't quite like the others. He could be killed far more easily.

"And Troy?"

"Meeting with Fredrick. I was able to get rid of Colter, but apparently the pack alpha is harder to throw."

"Why would he want to see Troy?"

Kase shrugged. "In my experience, people in positions of power do not like it when others can challenge them."

I thought back to Troy's story, to what the last alpha had done. "Is he in danger?"

"Not while here, I'm sure. A non-competitor killing a competitor would look poorly on Lucifer, so I doubt Fredrick would try anything so blatant. I suspect he is feeling Troy out, seeing if the new fame is going to his head. It is a foolish worry, because I have never seen a more grounded wolf in all my years."

"Is that why Colter came?"

"Hardly. Colter and I have an understanding. He is aware that if I wanted to, I could take the coven. I don't care for that sort of power or responsibility, so Colter runs it and I do as I please. It works well."

My gaze shifted to a closed door again, as if drawn there.

"You can feel him, can't you?"

"What?"

Kase nodded toward the door. "That's Grant's room. You keep looking there, as if you know it's his."

Did I? *I have to, right?*

I blew out a breath and shook my head. "I should get going. Lucifer is expecting me.

"I heard the guard. You have another forty minutes before you're expected there. Why don't you go check on Grant?"

"I thought he was resting."

"He is, but I would bet he'll sleep more soundly after seeing you, and you will be more focused in dealing with Lucifer after seeing him."

I didn't even bother to argue. It *was* what I wanted, and I wouldn't bother him for long...

The room was dark when I closed the door behind me, but after a moment, my eyes adjusted. A huge bed sat in the center of the room, large posts stretching up and over the frame. The blankets were bunched at the foot, as if Grant had kicked them off, and he rested on his back in the center.

He didn't wake when I closed the distance, something that made me nervous. Worse, when I reached the side of the bed, I noted that he looked much worse than I'd expected...

His eyes were sunken in, and even in the dim room I could tell his skin was ashen. Red had soaked into the pillowcase, and dried blood created a trail from his ear and down his neck.

It was odd to see him so still, so quiet, and so fragile. I recalled how I had met him, how he'd stood on my porch looking like some untouchable rebel.

His tattoos had surprised me that day, since I hadn't spent much time with men who were covered in tattoos. As time had gone on, though, I'd stopped even noticing them.

When he'd stripped down to nothing, when I'd had him at the same time as Hunter, I hadn't been hung up on each twisting pieces of colorful ink. There had been too many distractions.

It meant this was the first time I got a *good* look at him, at the expansive artwork marked into his skin.

I crawled into the bed, rewarded with a muttered curse from Grant. His voice was rough and filled with pain, but when he cracked his eyes, when those green eyes met mine, he offered a half-smile.

I stretched out beside him, careful not to jostle him.

"Are you here to take advantage of me? Because unless you have some little blue pills, I don't think I'm going to rise to the occasion."

"Is everything a joke to you?"

"Usually, yeah. It makes life more fun." He groaned as he rolled toward me, on his side. "Are you okay?"

"Yeah, I am."

"Wish I could say the same for us."

"If you knew what was coming, how did it hurt you this much?"

"Because when Persephone told Hunter about the banshee, I expected a regular ol' one. Most don't get much over thirty years, if that. All that screaming drives them mad. What I did would offer full protection from any run-of-the-mill banshee, but leave it to me to underestimate Lucifer. The one he found was one hell of a surprise. I don't think I'll get rid of this headache for at least a week."

I went to reach for him but froze before I made contact. I didn't want to risk hurting him.

He let out a rough chuckle, then caught my wrist and tugged my hand until it rested against his chest. "I'm not that fragile."

"You don't look good." My hand on his chest, feeling the thump of his heart against my palm, helped. "I thought…"

Grant pressed my hand tighter to his chest as if to prove a point. "I'm fine, really."

I sighed, focusing on the steady beat of his heart. "I hate how much waiting there is. I always figured things like this would be all go, go, go. Instead, I'm putting on dresses, going to stupid parties, and I just keep getting my ass handed to me by Lucifer. You end up getting hurt, and for what? We've been in hell for days and I don't think we're any closer to figuring this out than we were before."

Grant stroked his thumb over my wrist. "Oh, I see, we're having a pity party?" He sighed, then released me. A wave of his hand and a whispered spell occurred a moment before something fell onto the bed between us. I pushed backward to see what it was.

Between us sat a bag of chocolates, and I frowned. "Did you just magic us some chocolate? I thought you needed rest to recuperate your magic."

He smirked, the grin fuller as if annoying me perked him up. "Chocolate is needed for pity parties. I'd give you wine, too, but you are a mean and handsy drunk. Though, if I heard right through the door, if you're doing to see Lucifer, maybe mean and handsy is the way to play it."

I picked up the small bag of candy and chuckled at how simple it was. Leave it to Grant to be the one to try and make hell normal.

"Now, lie down and hush," he said. "I'm supposed to be resting."

I did as he said, twisting so my back was toward him, then let him scoot as close as he wanted to. As it turned out, that was right up against me, because he groaned as he slung his arm around me.

"We are getting closer," he said. "It may not seem like it, it might not feel like it, but we're getting closer. That's how this sort of things works. The worse it gets, the closer you are to the center."

"Sure. You're half-dead, we're still stuck in hell, no idea who that shadow is and now I'm stuck having to submit to Lucifer."

"You're forgetting something. "

"Oh yeah? What am I forgetting?"

He tapped my hand that had the bag in it. "You've got chocolate."

I looked down at my hand and the candy in it, then laughed softly and settled in. "Well, I guess we can't lose, then."

"I'll put my money on you and chocolate any day."

I rested against him, choosing to take the short amount of time until I had to deal with Lucifer to relax.

We lay there for thirty minutes until I knew my time was running short. I offered Grant a quick kiss, and was disappointed to find the main room empty, Kase having taken off.

When I returned to my room, before heading to see Lucifer, something sat folded and wrapped in tissue on my bed. I picked up a note at the top, unfolding it to find perfectly written letters and Kase's name at the bottom.

I recall the first time seeing you in this. You faced down Colter in it, and I think you need to remember that. Maybe you didn't need something new – you needed something old. Gran was willing to retrieve this for me, and I am sure the price will be high. Make it worth it.

Kase

I frowned as I tore open the tissue, then found the item inside.

A smile crossed my lips…

It was times like this when I had to admit, no matter how scary and closed off he was, he had his charm…

Chapter Twenty

Lucifer's room was empty when I entered, but the guard left me in it anyway.

I supposed that made sense. What was I going to do to Lucifer? Even unattended in his room?

After a few minutes, Lucifer appeared, walking into the room. He was as put-together as ever, a glass with dark amber liquid in it, a white collared shirt on with a vest that matched his slacks. The cuffs of his shirt were undone, and he'd rolled them up to his forearms as if the day had been too much.

When his gaze landed on me, he stilled for one long moment. "You are an enigma, Ms. Harlin." He didn't say it with any affection, as if it charmed him at all.

Still, I pulled the edges of my robe as if it were the finest of suits.

Lucifer came closer, eyebrow lifted as he peered down. "Do you have penises on your clothing?"

"Yep."

"And you think this offers you some sort of protection?"

"In my experience, penises tend to make all problems worse."

"So why wear them?"

"Because they're as absurd as the rest of my life."

He looked me up and down again, before shaking his head, as if he'd realized that no answer I could give would make any sense.

"You know you cheated."

"If anyone doesn't cheat, they don't care enough about the game."

"And you don't care at all that you didn't win fair and square?"

"What story have you heard about me that makes you think I care about being fair?"

I opened my mouth, but nothing came to mind. I hated when someone made a good point.

"So what now?" I tucked my hands into the pockets of my robe. "I'd like to get through whatever it is you've got planned as quickly as possible."

"Are you not worried about what it is I want from you?"

"I just figure whatever it is, worrying about it won't help. I made my bed, now I have to lie in it. I just hope to fuck you aren't in it also." The joke came out thin, the first time I admitted to just how worried I was about that particular concern.

I *really* didn't want to have to have sex with him. He hadn't implied he wanted that at all—in fact, he'd treated me like a child he had to put up with more than anything else—but I still didn't trust him. All the horror movies I'd seen where women stupidly sleep with the devil and ended up birthing some demon spawn came back to me. I wasn't ready to raise the antichrist…

Lucifer caught my chin in a grip that was nothing like when Kase did it to me. It was rough and none-too-kind. He forced my eyes to his red ones. "Let me be clear. I have no interest in you physically. I will not now, nor in the future, compel you to have sex with me." Even the way he said it made it clear the idea was not in the least appealing, especially when he tacked on "*ever*" to the end of his statement.

Which should have pleased me—and it did, somewhat. Still, being so soundly rejected made me wonder exactly what his type was.

Not mouthy humans in penis robes, clearly.

Stop worrying about the devil finding you attractive, damn it.

"So what do you want? If you planned this all, it has to be important."

"Indeed, it is. It has been a long while since I've had to do this much work to get my hands on a mortal. Then again, we both know there is more to you than meets the eye."

"You use a lot of words to say nothing."

"And you have a death wish with the way you speak to those who could kill you."

"News flash. Everyone could kill me, so if I was only mouthy to people who were weaker than me, I'd never talk again. Besides, if you wanted to kill me, you could have done it already. Whatever you need from me, I'd guess you need me alive for it. I doubt you'll murder me over a little sass. What sort of king of hell keeps that position if he can't stand up against some snark?"

Lucifer rolled his eyes and the gesture felt like a win. How many could claim to manage to annoy the devil enough to make him act like a teenage girl?

He set his drink down, then picked up a box from a side table against the wall.

He placed it in front of me, and I backed up. "The last time I opened a box from you, I got sucked into hell."

"And since you are already here, what are you worried about?" He leaned down and flipped open the lid, but instead of that horribly smoke that had escaped the last time, only a dark interior sat. He reached in and pulled out a piece of paper and a pen. After jotting something down, he handed it to me.

There were words, but like the sign on that bar, I couldn't read them at first. It took a minute for them to shift and form something coherent. "'Wear more appropriate clothing next time.'"

"So you can read it."

"Yes, and did you really invite me here to insult my outfit?"

"No. It just seemed a worthwhile message."

I handed the piece of paper back. "Grant said that language is thought to thought which is why I can understand."

Lucifer shook his head. "Verbal language is like that, not written. This has happened before?"

"A sign in one of the little towns. I saw the weird scribbles, then they sort of shifted before my eyes and I could read it. What language is that?"

"An old demon tongue, one of the basic written languages used in hell. You shouldn't be able to read it." He frowned, then nearly whispered, "I wonder..." He wrote something else, then handed the page back.

Again, the letters were foreign, meaning nothing to me at first. They were written differently from the other language, with more flowing strokes that reminded me of cursive. Finally, they also shifted and when I could read them, I sighed. "'You are an adult and should dress like one.' Who knew the devil had such bad jokes?"

Except, when I looked at him, he didn't look amused. There was a light there, in his dark eyes, one that said he was far too interested in the fact that I could do that.

"What language is this?"

"An exceedingly old one, one before there were men, before demons, the uniting language of the first. There are few who can read it."

"So why can I?"

"What happened in that field?"

The question caught me off guard. "What?"

"You lost your corporeal form. What happened, exactly?"

I wanted to ask how he even knew about that, but his answer wouldn't be useful. He'd just tell me that he knew everything that happened in his realm. I'd be annoyed and no better off, so I kept the question to myself. "If you know that, you know as much as I do."

"What happened in the shack? How did you do that? What did it feel like? What were you thinking?" He rattled off the questions as if he had a list already prepared.

"A crazy man tried to cut me up, I have no idea how I did it, it felt uncomfortable and I was thinking that I really didn't want to die." Each answer I gave was full of 'you idiot' attitude. What did he *think* a person who was going to be killed by a machete-wielding maniac would think?

"So it was a reflex? A useful one, at that." He met my gaze. "So do it now."

"Do what?"

"Turn incorporeal again."

"I can't. Don't you think I've tried since then?"

"I could try to kill you. It worked the last time."

I held my hands up. "Whoa, now, let's leave that to plan B."

"You agreed to submit to me," Lucifer pointed out.

"And I will, but you're asking me to do something I don't know how to do. I think you picked the wrong person for whatever it is you're looking for."

"I am an excellent judge of character. I have followed you since the night you tried to contact that spirit, when you reached somewhere you shouldn't have, have seen glimpses of what you've done, of what you're capable of. I have no doubt you can do exactly what I want."

"Well, unless you have a how-to guide for it, I'm open to suggestions."

Lucifer sat back. "I would normally suggest relaxing. Often fear and other *emotions* can keep a person from accessing powers they have." He said emotions as if it were an entirely inconvenient fact he was above.

"Are you telling me it's performance anxiety?"

Ah, there was that wonderful annoyance in his expression again. "Ambrosia can help when a person is unable to control their feelings."

"There is no way I'm having any of that."

"I believe you offered compliance."

"I didn't realize that meant ingesting that disgusting substance."

"You argued less when you thought I might demand you sleep with me."

"Sex is sex. I can get through that no matter how gross I find the partner. Consuming weird corpse plants is something else."

"I don't think I appreciate the way you refer to sex with me."

"Typical man. Even the king of hell can't let it go if someone doesn't want to sleep with him."

He reached into the box one last time and pulled a small metal orb. "Our deal requires your submission to my requests. Since you are unwilling to do as I ask, the next step is to use ambrosia to relax you and try again."

My stomach churned because I couldn't stop thinking about those plants, about the way that hand, buried under the dirt, had moved. The thought of consuming that in any way made me sick. "I'm going to be honest and say I don't think I could even swallow that if I wanted to."

"Lucky for you, swallowing isn't necessary."

I went to make a joke back, but he took that moment to hold the orb in front of me and twist his thumb across the edge. It clicked and a green powder sprayed into the air in front of me.

I jerked backward, but he brought the orb with me. My nose burned even after I tried to snort, to clear anything from my nostrils.

It didn't work, and that same clouded-thoughts feeling I'd had after drinking last time came back.

It might have been a different delivery method, but it sure as fuck was the same sensation.

I twisted my head, and this time Lucifer allowed it.

He tossed the orb into the box. "That will work through your system quickly. Powdered compressed ambrosia is far more potent than the sort you drank in that bar."

"Of course you're the sort of a person who drugs someone against their will."

"I have been exceedingly patient with you. You offered me one night of submission, one night where you will do as I ask. Instead of that, you have complained and fought me. I am well within my rights to forfeit your deal. Do you understand what that means?"

Honestly, right then I didn't. I was pretty sure I was at the point where I was amazed by the size of my own hand, so contractual consequences weren't something I was grasping.

Thankfully, he didn't require an answer. "You were given your team's life. I can take that back should you push my patience much further."

That woke me up, even past the still-creeping haze from the ambrosia. I had no doubt Lucifer could and would do exactly as he claimed.

"I'm cooperating," I said, dizziness swamping me. It was good I didn't have to walk because I was pretty sure I'd end up flat on my face. "But even with your gross plant powder, I've got nothing for you."

"We will give it time to work." He rose, grabbed a water from the bar area, then set it before me. "While we wait, I am curious…why are you trying so hard to solve this issue with the spirits?"

"I live in the world, don't I? It sort of is my issue."

"I have seen humans from the start, and if there is one thing I have learned, it is that they are more than willing to sit back and let someone else take the risk. So, Ms. Harlin, what is it that makes you feel this is worth you risking yourself for?"

My words felt liquid, as if they sloshed around in my head then poured from my lips. It seemed the ambrosia was good for more than just trying to get some power of mine to work. It also made me answer questions I had no business answering. "You ever wonder where you fit into the world?"

"No. From the start, I have always known exactly where I belong."

"Well, aren't you lucky? Most of us don't get that." I shifted and leaned backward, the room spinning. I'd sure had a larger dose than the last time.

"It isn't all it's cracked up to be."

When I fell over toward Lucifer, he set a hand on my shoulder and pushed me back the other way.

"The reality is that knowing where you belong does not mean a person is content there." He took another drink as if watching a show. "How are you feeling?"

"Pretty damn good." And…I was.

It was better than the alcohol, as if it reached my bloodstream faster, as if it smoothed over edges the alcohol left sharp. "So, you going to let me in on your little plan?"

"Why do you think I have one?"

"Because I know your type. You always have a plan." He reminded me of Kase—an unflattering comparison. Someone who was always a few steps ahead and playing close to the chest so no one could guess his moves.

All I knew for sure was that he was out-maneuvering me by a long shot.

"What do you remember about your parents?"

"Nothing." I frowned, then shook my head. "I saw a something, in a dream, but I don't think it was real. I saw a woman rocking a baby, and she called it my name. She told it the spirits couldn't hurt it."

"So your mother knew what you were? What you could do?"

"Maybe. Or maybe she just abandoned me like everyone else, and I just want to believe she cared at one point. Abandonment issues can play one hell of a trick on the psyche."

"And your father?"

I shrugged. If Lucifer wanted information, he was barking up the wrong hell-tree. I knew less about my parents than I did about myself.

"I heard Lilith is your daughter," I said.

He nodded before going to the bar to pour himself another drink. "Yes. I have many children, but she was the first."

"And how do you measure up as a daddy-o?"

He paused, as if he'd never considered the question before. "Lilith was different. My other children were created, how should I say — the more traditional way. Lilith was not born but made, much like Adam."

I thought back to what little I had heard about such stories. "She was Adam's first wife?"

Lucifer nodded before taking his seat again. "Yes. As a means of balance, Adam was made by" — he hesitated, as if unsure how to phrase the next part — "you would think of him as God. Reality is always more complicated. A compromise was decided that between Adam, forged by him, and Lilith, forged by me, we would have a mix of influence. However, our children were much as we are, stubborn and difficult. Adam wished to dominate, and Lilith wished for freedom. They were incompatible."

"So then the whole 'Eve from Adam's rib' thing happened?"

Lucifer nodded. "Lilith was set aside for her failure, and God created Eve from Adam, a more biddable female for him. Of course, you women showed him, didn't you? I don't think anyone expected quite so much in the way of bite from you."

The joke didn't land as I thought about the woman I'd seen, about Lilith, about how lonely that life had to have been. *To be created for a single purpose and to fail in it?*

"So she was just cast out?"

Lucifer took another drink, a slow one as if he didn't care for the subject. "She has always yearned for freedom, has always loathed control. She was made sterile, so she could never carry on her line since she rejected what was laid out for her, but she has always been exceedingly smart. It was Lilith who created the first vampire."

"I thought she was sterile?"

"She is. She could never bear children or create life on her own, so instead took dead bodies and breathed a semblance of life into them. She created the first vampire, and it was God's anger over it that forced them into the darkness. She didn't create all immortals, but they all have a certain amount of credit to her, because it was her work with vampires that sparked many of them into existence by that defiance. They are the children she was denied."

"So why don't I know that? Why haven't I heard that before?"

"Because she also believed that freedom was the most important gift any could give another. She didn't believe in raising or taking any part in their lives because she saw that as a sort of control. I think she finds solace in their presence whether or not she has a connection with them personally."

I blew out a slow breath, the story harder and harder to follow as the ambrosia lessened my focus. "And your other kids?"

"Many have positions of power here in the afterlife. Some have chosen to live on earth. Some are mortal, some immortal. Many take after whatever their mother was and thus live the life she had. Countless I don't even know about."

"Father of the year, huh?"

"Live as long as I have, bury as many offspring as I have and you will realize that they matter little." He caught my chin, turning my head as he stared into my eyes. "You're ready."

"You care to tell me for what?"

Lucifer went to the door and spoke to someone outside. Afterward, another person followed him back in.

The man was dressed in a simple pair of jeans and a shirt, making him completely out of place. "This is her?"

Lucifer nodded.

"How deep should I go?"

"As far as you have to. I need to know if I'm right."

And boy did *that* sound like something I was not going to enjoy with these two...

Chapter Twenty-One

The man who sat on the table in front of me had a thick red beard and bright blue eyes. He took my chin and stared into my eyes in a way that made me lean in, as if drawn to sink deeper into his gaze.

It felt like sliding into a warm bath, as if something pulled me down and surrounded me.

I could feel him inside my head, his metaphorical fingers slipping along the edges of my brain, not painful but not comfortable either.

"What are you?" he asked as if to himself.

Still, I answered. "I don't know."

His eyes narrowed — not out of anger but as if concentrating — and I cried out at a sudden pain in my head, as if that gentle stroke had become a jab.

As soon as it happened, it eased though didn't disappear entirely. Flashes came to me, moments of my life. Different foster homes, the Christmas I spent at a friend's house, one of my only real Christmases, the times I spent in Gran's shop. They were tiny moments of my life, the good and the bad, and he sifted through each of them as if looking for something specific.

"How much ambrosia did you give her?" he asked without breaking eye contact.

"More than enough. I'm not sure she'd survive anymore."

"The synapses in her brain are unlike anything I've ever seen," the man said, frowning before digging deeper into my mind, causing another lancing pain. Even still, I couldn't pull away.

"Am I right?"

"Maybe. You're asking me to identify something that hasn't ever existed."

"Force it out of her. She went incorporeal. If she takes that form here, I'll know I'm right."

The man pressed his lips together and yet another sharp pain consumed me, as if he'd poured molten lava through my head. After a moment he shook his head and released me. "I can't."

"Because it isn't there or because *you* are unable to?"

The man rose, rubbing at his temples. "I don't know. I *feel* what you're talking about, but I don't know if there's enough of it to matter."

Lucifer crossed his arms, looking less pleased. "I hope you don't expect a full payment for this."

The man turned his eyes toward me, a resistance there. "As long as I never have to go into her head again, I'll take no payment at all."

Lucifer waved him off, the man rushing away.

It hit me as hilarious. The whole situation, how even the devil couldn't seem to make heads or tails of me. Wasn't that my place in life? Or in the afterlife, it seemed.

"What's so funny?" he asked, tone sharp.

"Everyone wants to understand what I am, and no one can figure it out. The thing is that I've spent my whole life trying to be one thing—normal. Now here I am, at the other side, in hell, and it is that same question. It never goes away, never stops. What am I?" I laughed again, knowing my voice had a hysterical edge to it. "After everything I've seen and lived through, and I finally figured out it doesn't fucking matter. I mean, if you and your brain melon baller there can't figure it out, maybe that's it. Maybe that's the end."

Lucifer came forward and leaned in closer, as if he could peer through my eyes, into my head that this friend had dug through, and see something he'd missed. "It matters, Ms. Harlin, because if I'm wrong, we're all fucked."

Even if I'd wanted to say something back, even if I'd *had* something to say back, the ambrosia overpowered me at that point. The spinning room lost definition, and it was Lucifer's dark eyes that haunted me as I passed out.

It seemed I was a girl who couldn't hold her ambrosia.

* * * *

I groaned as the throbbing in my head made me wonder if I was actually going to die. When I cracked my eyes open, I was sure of it. The light stabbed at me like needles, and I decided dying was preferable.

"Why do you have a pair of boxers?"

I flinched at Gran's voice, twisting to see her standing above me.

Above? I looked around to find myself on the ground beneath the large tree in the courtyard.

And sure enough, I clutched a pair of boxers I didn't recognize in my hand. "Whose are these?"

"I figured one of your men."

"None of them wear silk boxers."

I pushed myself up to sitting, my stomach rolling.

Gran held her hand out and took them. "These are Lucifer's."

"What?" If I'd felt sick before it was nothing compared to now. "Why do I have Lucifer's underwear?"

"That I can't tell you."

"How do you even know they're his?"

She held them up and showed the interior band where *Lucifer* was embroidered.

"He has his own name on his underwear? Why?"

"Maybe because people like you steal them."

I rubbed my eyes with the heels of my hands and filed that away for worry another time. "I thought ambrosia worked until I took one of those pills. I am feeling very much not drunk enough right now."

"I put two of those pills in your mouth a few hours ago then let you sleep off the rest."

"Why does my head hurt so much? I didn't have a hangover last time."

"You were drunk enough to try and climb the magic tree with Lucifer's stolen boxers. I'm going to guess you had a lot more than you did last time."

I frowned, then recalled before that had happened. "That man stuck his fingers in my brain!"

Gran patted her side. "Maybe I have another pill…"

I got to my feet and waved her off. "I'm not still high. Lucifer had some guy with a big red beard dig around in my mind trying to figure out what I was."

"Good thing you were drugged then. That sounds like a lot rougher than you like your sex."

I gave her a glare. "How long until the next competition?"

"They called for it a few minutes ago."

I glanced around the empty courtyard. "So where is everyone?"

"Lucifer is holding the final round local-style. He set up a spot just this side of the dead zone."

The loud, low sound that chilled me rang through the palace, telling me it had started.

Lucifer knew where I was because he seemed to know everything. He'd done this on purpose, which meant I had to get to the competition *now*.

I rush toward the doorway, Gran on my heels despite the fact that she looked far too old to be running that fast.

Please don't let me be too late.

I made it to the top of a staircase that led down to the outer courtyard. The arena sat on the outer edge, between the palace and the dead zone.

All four men still stood, letting me pull in a rough breath. The short run had winded me, telling me my exercise routine was sorely lacking.

At the center, in front of the crowd, sat Lucifer in the same throne—or perhaps a replica. It seemed he rather liked the whole skull motif. At least he was consistent.

He turned toward me, a smirk on his lips that said he'd planned it all.

But *what* had he planned?

He looked far too pleased given that the night before, as far as I recalled, he hadn't learned anything useful. Or maybe he'd gotten exactly what he'd wanted, and I just didn't understand. Whatever it was, I could bet if he was happy, I wouldn't be.

Another sound echoed through the open space, and in the center of the area where the men stood, the air shimmered with green like some sort of force field. Darkness moved beyond it, but I couldn't tell what it was.

A large, sprawling staircase sat between the arena and me. Past that, the crowd of onlookers stood, their backs to me. Even though I didn't have any idea how I could reach the men — or even if I did, what I could do to help — I took off down the stairs.

The shimmering brightened, then disappeared as it had before, revealing what creature Lucifer had chosen for their final fight.

Silence fell, the crowd seeming to take a simultaneous breath and step backward. Anything that forced that from a group of immortals was not a good thing.

In the center, between the men and the crowd, was a shadowed being that made my blood freeze. It was something I'd seen before, something I'd lived my whole life hearing about.

The thing Lucifer had picked for them to fight, the thing they somehow had to kill despite it being impossible, was a *reaper*.

Chapter Twenty-Two

The reaper didn't move at first, floating there, clothed in black fabric. I understood the whole grim reaper myth, now. Clearly people who repeated the myth had caught a glimpse a reaper and twisted the facts.

I pushed myself faster, somehow managing to not miss a step or go tumbling down the stones despite the lack of a guardrail.

Reapers were almost indestructible. They weren't really alive or dead, not tied to the living or the dead realms, so they couldn't be harmed by either beings.

That meant Lucifer had placed before the men something they had *no* chance of actually defeating. He'd set them up to die, because once the round started, there was no forfeit.

Lucifer did nothing without cause, though. I'd learned that if nothing else, so what was he trying for?

I shoved past the tightly packed bodies of people who saw this entire thing as a spectacle, just entertainment for them.

It was so much more to me.

Any other time, I'd have been hesitant about barreling into countless hell creatures and immortals, but right then I had bigger issues at hand.

Past the gathered people sat the chairs for the VIPs, Lucifer at the center, the one to his side, my chair, empty.

When I tried to pass him, he caught my wrist to pull me to a stop. It reminded me that he was *not* human, as his strength seemed to make a mockery of even Kase. It was like a statue holding me back.

"You're going to get them killed," I snapped.

"I am doing nothing."

"You *know* they can't hurt a reaper."

"They've seemed fairly capable up until this point. Perhaps they'll surprise us all."

I couldn't pull my gaze from the arena, from where the men had spread out to flank the reaper.

It moved, side to side, as if examining the situation. Then again, reapers had no enemies, no reason for fear.

It floated toward the crowd, not at any sort of speed as if worried. However, when it hit the boundary where a line of rocks sat, it bounced backward.

"You trapped it in there with them?"

He nodded. "It isn't an easy task, but it is possible."

"I thought they were untouchable…"

"By normal means, yes. There are a few ways to restrict their movements, at least for a while." He released my wrist. "Of course, doing so has the unfortunate side effect of agitating the reaper."

I turned back toward the arena to find, sure enough, the reaper shifting in quicker motions, side to side, before heading toward the ravine. It bounced off a wall there, too.

My head pounded, a sharp ache as if I'd heard some horrible screeching even though it didn't seem real, even though no one else flinched.

"That's what it sounds like," Lucifer said. "Most people can't hear it, have no idea what a reaper actually sounds like, but you can, can't you?"

I didn't answer—I doubted he really wanted me to. Besides, I couldn't explain it. I could hear it but I couldn't. It was an odd sensation, where the pain told me I sensed the sound even if I couldn't identify it.

Each time the reaper bounced off a wall, my headache increased as if it screamed louder.

It moved toward Grant, who lifted his hands in front of him. The quick motion that normally would have thrown back anything that neared him had no effect. At the last moment, just before it struck him, Kase rushed forward, yanking him clear.

The reaper hit Kase instead, and while it was not entirely corporeal, it still interacted with him. He pulled back, as if seared by the contact.

"If the reaper had touched Grant, it would have been able to sever his soul from his body. Lucky for you all, Kase doesn't have a soul in the same way. Not that the reaper won't be able to kill him eventually."

"What do you want?" I forced myself to look away from the arena, to look directly at Lucifer. "You always want something. You put them in a no-win situation for a reason, so *what* do you want from me?"

He curled his lips into a satisfied grin. "I don't know what you're talking about."

"Don't play game with me. Just tell me."

"You said you would do anything for them. Well, now is the time. I don't lie, and I am telling you that unless you do something, that reaper will kill all four of the men you claim to care so much about."

"What am I supposed to do against *that*?"

He sat back and crossed one ankle over his other knee, as if the entire thing didn't matter to him.

My head ached from that sound and from the mental gymnastics I had to perform to try and work out what I needed to do.

In the arena, Kase moved much slower than he had before — a sign that the reaper had hurt him — and the others simply dove out of the way when the reaper charged. Even as I watched, it was clear that it wasn't so much attacking *them* as it was trying to escape and didn't much care if they were in its way.

My feet moved before I could think about it, before I could figure out my plan. I just knew I had to do something. I couldn't sit there and watch them get slaughtered in front of me.

When I reached the line of rocks, I paused. Heat came from it, like a warning. I turned to spot Lucifer, and the look on his face was pure expectation.

He'd *pushed* me here, to do this. Even though a fear struck me, a sense that crossing that line wasn't a good idea, I knew damn well Lucifer wasn't going to kill me.

He wanted me to do this, and while I didn't know what or exactly why, it didn't stop that I needed to. I remembered Grant's words, when he'd told me that asking if something was possible was pointless if it was my only choice.

I drew my hands into fists and forced myself across the line of rocks.

Heat seared me, but I pushed through it. It felt like trying to walk through a waterfall of lava.

At the other side I collapsed forward, into the dirt. Even though the barrier had only been perhaps a foot wide of space, it had felt like crossing miles.

"You have *nothing*?" Kase asked, voice less controlled than it usually was. "What good are you?"

"Well, I'm sorry, but fighting a *reaper* wasn't ever one of the things we considered," Grant shouted back.

I shoved myself to my feet to find the men moving, all faster than I could, and the reaper following the line of the barrier, looking for an escape.

"You have got to be kidding me," Troy snapped from farther away, and that tone said he'd seen me. It was his strictly for me annoyed voice.

Smoke surrounded me for a moment before it took form as Hunter—naked, but I was used to that—stood just in front of me. "You need to take a few steps backward, shadow-girl." He set his hands on my shoulders to shove me backward, through the barrier.

When my back hit that line, however, a searing pain than before overcame me. It forced a scream from my lips, and even with his quick shove, the wall held like a one-way path that wouldn't allow me out.

Hunter yanked me away from the barrier, a curse on his lips. "She's trapped in here," he called out.

"We *will* talk about this as soon as we are out of it," Kase all but snarled in my direction, his finger pointed at me like that was scarier than what we currently faced.

Grant came over, breathing hard, then grabbed my hand. He flipped it over, and I wasn't even startled when a sharp pain spread through my palm. I'd gotten used to Grant slicing my hand at his whim.

He did the same to himself, whispered quick words before grasping hands with me. The blood mixed, and I ignored the risk of bloodborne illnesses because, again, that was a worry for another day.

If we got one.

He released my hand, then pressed his bloodied palm against my forehead along with a sharp word in a language I didn't recognize. "You are an idiot," he said with no sense of affection.

"Is she protected?" Troy asked from across the arena.

"Best I can do. No idea if it'll work against *that*, though. They don't teach reaper defense in the guild." Grant turned away, but I caught his wrist.

"Lucifer wants me here."

"What?"

I tugged at his hand, trying to get him to pay attention to me. "I don't know why, but he planned this. He pushed me to be here now, to come into the arena. He wants me here."

"Lucifer is a sadist who enjoys watching people tear each other apart for fun. I think you're giving him way too much credit."

I released Grant's hand, frustration eating at me. I tried to figure out what I was supposed to be doing. What was the plan?

The scream of the reaper increased again, a driving pain through my temples. I clutched my head before lifting my gaze to find the reaper still and staring at me.

It did it the way the last one had, when I'd first gotten into hell. It still ignored the others, but it saw me.

Grant set a hand out as though to push me back, to keep me behind him. The chivalrous movement was sweet but stupid. The reality was that the reaper could go *through* him if it wanted.

It seemed to bore its gaze into me even though I couldn't spot any eyes because of how the hood hid its face. If it had a face… The sound increased again, as if it were trying to speak to me.

It came forward, and Grant tossed his hand up. A rush left his palm like a spark of black lightning. It arced across the space and struck the reaper, throwing it back against the barrier.

Everyone froze.

"I thought you couldn't hurt it?" I asked.

"I wasn't sure that would work," he panted, looking exhausted. "I haven't exactly faced off against a lot of reapers to test, and that took a pretty big chunk of my power."

I opened my mouth to answer but that pain was back, driving me to my knees, forcing me to cover my ears to try and block it out. It didn't work, though, the sound still bleeding through.

Across the space, the reaper was up again and almost vibrating. What was it waiting for?

Kase, Troy and Hunter came closer, placing themselves between the reaper and me. Seeing them — or at least their backs — created an odd feeling.

How many times had people given a damn about me? My whole childhood had been a matter of not being important, of people walking away because I was too much work, too difficult, too unimportant.

I'd spent my whole life trying to fit in, trying to find somewhere I belonged, and here were these four men, men who had their own lives, men who I hadn't proven myself all that useful to, and they had placed themselves between the danger and me knowing damn well it would probably kill them.

They wanted me — they *valued* me — and even if I didn't understand it, it brought back I'd told Lucifer. I'd do anything to keep them safe, and for the first time, it seemed I'd found people who would do the same in return.

So when the reaper did its version of 'come at me, bro', I acted on an impulse so deep inside me, I couldn't place it, had never fully embraced it. It was like a whisper I'd ignored all my life, a part of me I'd refused to ever acknowledge but that had always been there.

The spark along my back that I'd felt before, when I'd turned into some sort of ghost, spread over me. It was stronger this time, though, and instead of fighting it, I threw myself into it.

That same sensation ran over my skin, through my body, down my limbs until my hands faded away, going incorporeal.

Whereas the last time I'd rejected this, this time I gave myself over to it entirely. I threw away all the worries, all the fears, all the desires I had to be normal.

Fuck normal.

I would be whatever I had to to keep safe the men who had risked everything for me.

I moved faster than I could track, able to pass around the men, my feet never touching the ground.

The reaper stilled, staring at me, and I could see it in a way I hadn't before, as if I could make out details that had been hidden. The fabric was clearer, and it hung forward over a shadowed face.

It spoke, and while the words were still impossible for me to make out, they no longer hurt. It came forward a few steps, but I lifted my hands.

It was then I realized my hands were shadowed and covered in darkness, like a robe. From my palms, a force went out, knocking the reaper backward.

It hissed, then barreled toward me.

Something stirred inside me, like an ancient whisper from somewhere I couldn't identify. It spurred me on, and I reached for the same power, for what I'd used a moment before to drive it back, but unleashed all I could.

The reaper screamed, this time the sound audible to me.

Instead of being driven backward again, it seemed locked in place for a moment before it shattered, devolving into mist then into nothing.

Had I killed it?

I twisted to find all four men staring at me, eyes wide.

"Ava?" Hunter asked.

I answered, but the words didn't leave my mouth. It was that pressure in my temples instead, just like it had been when the reaper had screamed.

"I don't think she knows," Kase said.

I wanted to ask what I didn't know but again, the words wouldn't come.

Grant lifted his hand and waved it into a circle, and a shimmering space of air appeared with a mirror in it.

And there, staring back at me, wasn't the face I recognized. It wasn't the dark hair and the green eyes I knew so well.

Instead, a dark figure hovered there, and the undeniable truth hit me.

After all the years of trying to understand what I was, of wondering where my skills came from, the answer was there, and it was one I wasn't ready for.

I was a reaper….

Chapter Twenty-Three

My knees hit the ground hard, the sharp rocks and sand digging in. Yet, oddly, I *liked* that, embraced the spark of pain. It reminded me that I was still alive, that I was there, that I was me again.

When I'd been in that other form, I hadn't been able to touch the real world—I hadn't been a part of it.

Sure, I didn't love the pain in my knees or the way my cut hand got dirt in the wound, but at least it was something.

I lifted my head and peered past the men—I didn't really want to see how they looked at me anymore—to find Lucifer leaning forward, for the first time fully invested in what had happened.

And the way he smiled said he'd gotten *exactly* what he wanted.

He rose and walked to the edge of the barrier, then raised his voice as though addressing the crowd despite his gaze not leaving me.

"We have a winner. In a rather surprising turning of events, the winner of our competition and the recipient of any favor I am capable of giving is Ava Harlin, our not-so-mortal guest of honor."

Murmurs from behind him started up—then again, a mortal had just won their precious competition—but a lifted hand by Lucifer silenced them.

"You planned this," I accused.

Lucifer nodded at the barrier, and it fell. He stepped over the line of rocks, then reached out his hand.

I took it, ignoring that I probably got blood and dirt on him. He pulled me to my feet, staring down at me with far more interest than made me comfortable.

"So I'm going to guess you got what you wanted?" I asked.

"I did, Ms. Harlin."

"And why did you want it? What did you get out of all of this?"

He released my hand, his lips curling into a cruel and calculated smile. "We will see."

And that did not make me feel any better.

* * * *

My hand ached, and, for the first time, I wished I'd had a chance to see Kase. Nothing like a little vampire blood to chase away the injury.

Funny, since it wasn't all that long ago that I had recoiled at the thought of him healing me. It seemed I'd realized there were a lot worse things in the world than a few drops of blood, especially if they managed to do away with the wound.

I wasn't sure if that was a positive change or not.

I hadn't looked at or spoken to any of the men. Lucifer had sent me off with a guard right after he'd declared me the winner, and I'd gone without lifting my gaze.

Fear gripped me. I recalled how I'd looked in the mirror Grant had created, how my reflection had shown nothing of who I had always seen.

How could anyone accept that? I couldn't, and for that reason, I'd not met the gazes of any of the men.

The idea of them seeing me differently created this pit in my stomach, a fear that something I'd found might be gone.

What would I do if I found disgust in Troy's eyes when he looked at me? If Grant watched me with suspicion, or Hunter flinched from me?

Even Kase, who didn't seem startled by anything, might not touch me with the same gentle stroke of his fingers after seeing that. I'd risked everything for them, and they might have decided I wasn't worth it anymore.

Reapers weren't immortals. They weren't like *anything* else. It would have been easier to accept I was some sort of freaky hybrid of an immortal, but a *reaper*?

The things Gran had said before came back to me, when she'd said I was more than I realized, that I wasn't supposed to be. She'd been right.

Too bad I hadn't listened.

A knock on the door came a moment before a guard came in. "It's time." His tone came out careful, respectful, his gaze hesitant.

It was an entirely different reaction than I'd had before, when I had been stared at like a new chew toy. The mortal in hell, the one who sat to the side of Lucifer for some reason. The guards had been amused at best, but now?

Now he gave me the same suspicion given to the far larger and scarier folks.

I nodded, walking past the guard at the door. He moved backward to leave more space between us, as if he didn't want to risk coming into contact with me.

A muttered insult rested on my tongue, but I kept it in.

It wasn't this guard's fault that I was in a testy mood, and taking it out on him would be unfair. He had one job—to take me to the stupid official audience where I would ask Lucifer for my favor before the end of the entire party and competition ordeal.

And what I was going to ask, I still had no idea. I'd expected for Hunter to figure that out, since he understood what a person should ask. However, since I'd been the one to land the killing blow on the reaper, I was awarded the actual favor.

I was still dressed as I'd been during the fight, during the night before. In short—I was a mess. Penis robe and all.

At least I didn't turn back into my normal old self naked, as Hunter did. Then again, Hunter became that smoke creature, but it was still a *real* creature. When I transformed, I hadn't been just another form of my same energy. Instead, I had been something entirely different.

It was odd to not have Persephone at my side. While I didn't love her cheery nature or distractibility, I'd grown used to it. When I reached the courtyard, I spotted the woman in question there, in her seat, trying very hard not to look at me. She'd still attended—she'd just not wanted to walk with me for the first time.

That same unease that had haunted me since realizing what I was crept into me again. Persephone, who had managed to see good in the devil—who I was pretty sure had no good in him—had written me off.

She had chosen to avoid me, to not look at me, as if I were suddenly different.

I am, aren't I?

I walked forward, spotting on the other side of Lucifer extra seats filled with none other than the black team.

Even still, I tore my gaze away before seeing any of them clearly. I knew where they sat, saw Kase, Grant, Hunter and Troy all looking well enough.

I wasn't brave enough to face them, not yet.

"Approach," Lucifer said, crooking his fingers.

I tucked my hands into the pockets of my robe, missing those moments before when the spells tattooed on my arms had kept me hidden.

Others stood around, faces I'd seen over the last few days, including Fredrick, Colter and the acting Magistrate.

All of them eyed me as if trying to understand me, as if trying to see what they'd missed before, trying to see the monster beneath, the one I'd hidden.

"You have won a favor from me. It must be something I am capable of giving. It must be something with a definable consequence. That means you cannot ask me to give you a good life. You could ask for two million dollars. You can ask me to kill someone, but you cannot ask me to make you immortal, unless you were asking me to find a person to turn you into a specific type of immortal. Should what you ask be impossible for me, I will tell you, and you will not forfeit your right to the favor."

"That's a lot more caveats than I thought would be involved in a favor from the devil," I said.

"I am a careful negotiator. And, no, you cannot ask me to make *you* king of hell or the devil. I've had people ask, and as that is a birthright, it isn't something I can give away."

I snorted. "Trust me, I don't *want* your job."

"Good to know. Now, Ms. Harlin, the question falls to you. What do you want?"

I didn't know. Nothing came to mind. Nothing seemed important enough. I could ask him what I was, but even if I had a good idea now, I doubted he knew much more than I did. I could ask about the shadow, about the thing I'd come looking for, the reason behind all of this, but he hadn't seemed to know. I could ask him to take care of the shadow, but according to his rules, it wasn't a definable consequence if he didn't know who the shadow was.

"Can I wait and ask for my favor later?"

He nodded. "You have one year to claim your favor. Just prior to the time running out, I will call you here again for a last chance, and you will be given a method of transport here in case you come up with a favor in the meantime."

It wasn't ideal, but at least I'd have time to think.

I opened my mouth to tell him my choice, that I wanted to wait, when a scream echoed out from behind me.

He lifted his gaze, a quick motion that showed the first real moment of surprise from him.

I twisted to find chaos engulfing the people behind me. The crowd shifted like something alive, and the movement was so varied that I couldn't identify *what* was happening at first.

It was violent, fast and coated with splashes of red.

After a moment, my eyes narrowed in on one grouping, on a tall female demon who raked her claws against the throat of another. She moved from one to the next, her motions fluid and lethal.

Her eyes, it took me a moment to realize, were black. They were the same as Olin, as Paul, as Troy when he'd been taken over. The only explanation was that the shadow was *here* and infecting immortals.

That was the piece I needed to fit the rest together. At least twelve other immortals in the group were in the same frenzy, casting chaos through the crowd, forcing others to defend themselves.

Still, in such a small area, there wasn't much of a defense any one person could put up.

I backed away until something grabbed my arm. I twisted, fist drawn as if a punch from me would do *anything*, but Troy grabbed my hand.

The time to worry about what he thought about my revelation could come later as the screams increased.

"Let's go," he said, yanking me backward.

"Their eyes."

Grant came up and nodded. "I saw. We need to go, *now*. Lucifer has already bolted and when the devil leaves a party, it's time to *go*."

And, for once, I couldn't agree more. We rushed backward, past the thrones, past the tree, away from the bloody chaos of the immortals.

"Can't you create a portal now?" I asked Grant.

"Lucifer hasn't removed your tracer yet."

"Of course he hasn't," I griped, feeling like it was yet another time Lucifer had screwed me over.

He was on my list of least favorite people.

"Gran," I said, trying to pull to a stop.

Troy would have none of it, my useless objection nothing to his strength. "Gran can take care of herself," he reminded me.

Which was true, I guessed.

We took the staircase up to put distance between ourselves and the violence, but as we turned a corner, a vampire I didn't recognize but had seen with Kase and Colter appeared. Those eyes of his made me shudder, especially when they locked on *me*.

Kase moved past me, nothing but a blur, before he hit the vampire.

Troy didn't give me time to watch or worry. He pulled me the other way, but our paths of exit closed quickly. A demon with wings landed on the edge of the walkway and Hunter took on that one. A creature stood farther down that Grant incinerated on the spot. A man who looked like the one who had tried to plant me forced Troy from my side.

Everywhere we went, more of those immortals with the black eyes stood in our way until only Grant and I rushed from one spot to another. He seemed breathless, and I recalled what he'd said about how magic worked.

What happened if he ran out? He could do away with most of the things that opposed us with a flick of his wrist, but his words became slower, clumsier, and when we turned a corner, he stumbled.

Two lumbering, twisted beings blocked our path.

Grant cursed, then opened the closest door and shoved me in.

I tried to go back, but he was quicker, closing me in. He uttered a quick spell and a shimmering light engulfed the wood. I knew before I even tried that he'd barred it, but I pulled anyway.

The idiot had put himself on the wrong side of that spell!

I knew, of course, that he'd done it on purpose. Grant, despite his failings, would have kept himself on the outside to give it every last bit of fight he had.

I screamed his name against the spell, the door, the frustration of being locked in with *nothing* I could do about it.

I tried to reach for my other form, for the power I'd found, but it didn't work. Was there a limit when I could use that? Was it my fear?

All I knew was I couldn't seem to grasp for that burning sensation that had consumed me before.

I slammed my fist against the door when I had nothing else to do, nothing else to try.

"Well, well," came a voice from behind me, one I'd heard but didn't immediately recognize.

I twisted to find Lilith there, a smirk on her lips that was *exactly* like Lucifer's.

I could have thought it was a coincidence that I'd ended up in her room, or that she was hiding like me, but there was no way to believe something so innocent.

I took one look into her eyes, into the sadistic pleasure on her face, and got the same feeling as I had when I'd faced her — or the pieces of herself she'd left in others.

Lilith was the shadow, the thing that had been stealing spirits, that had driven the immortals mad, that had nearly killed me in my dreams, and here I was, stuck alone in a room with her.

Chapter Twenty-Four

"So it was you?" I asked, not bothering to play dumb.

"You can't be as surprised as I am about you." She walked with a confidence and gait that was downright impressive. If I didn't hate her so much, I might have liked her. "I couldn't see you before, just glimpses of this dark mist, just a *feeling* as you shoved the slivers of myself I left in others back, when you removed me entirely from that werewolf."

"Are you wanting an apology for that?" I crossed my arms, knowing damn well that there wasn't anything I could do if she wanted to kill me.

"I didn't understand what you did or how, and when I heard Lucifer had a guest, when I heard rumors of him looking into the missing spirits, I'd though it might be connected. Of course, one look at you, and I put that thought aside. How could *you*, some useless mortal, be the thing plaguing me?"

I wasn't so useless when I was fucking up your plans, was I?

"So you set up all of that out there just to get me alone?"

She shrugged. "I have my skills, but I'm not as strong as those bodyguards you had. Besides, this way things stay quiet. They'll find your body, blame it on one of those poor possessed immortals, and no one will be the wiser. A good tactician knows her strengths."

I took a step backward when she took one forward, a game of me trying to keep enough space between us for something else to happen. Anything. "You *know* what you're doing could shatter the entire balance between the worlds, that you could destroy everything, don't you?"

"Of course I do."

"So why do it? Because last I checked, you *lived* in the world, too."

She tilted her head, as if surprised by what seemed an obvious question to me. "I've lived a very long time, half-breed, and I've learned that just because something *is* doesn't mean it should be. This world was built on subjugation. From the start, when I refused to do as I was told, I was cast out and someone more biddable put in my place. From there it spread like an infection, and now the entire world is built in the image of kneeling, domesticated mortality."

"So you want to destroy everything because you were a jilted lover? Really?"

Her eyes flashed, a moment of anger before it smoothed away. "Hardly. I just want to free everyone."

"You take people *over*. You make them do things they never would otherwise. How is that freedom?"

"Because I don't make them do anything. I don't whisper in their ears or force them into anything. I take away that control, those rules they'd taught themselves to believe in. You say they'd never do those things because it makes *you* feel better, not because it's true. What I make them is what they *really* are without a lifetime of rules placed on them. I reduce them to their true nature."

I thought back to Troy, to the way he'd snarled and roared, to how he believed her lies, that that was all he really was, down deep, and I rejected it. I *knew* Troy. What she'd done wasn't freeing him—it imprisoned him. "You can use all the excuses you want, but you're nothing but a kid who wants to flip over the boardgame because they're losing."

She let out a harsh laugh. "Do you know what ousted you? It wasn't until I saw you in the arena, when I saw what you became. A reaper hybrid has *never* been before, but it took seeing that to make me realize you were the mist I saw, that you were the only one capable of doing what you did, of reaching inside a person and yanking out that sliver of me. Nothing else could sever that bond, especially without destroying the original spirit. If only you hadn't tried that, I would have left, thinking you nothing important."

"So what now?"

Lilith curled her lips into a chilling grin, one that made my blood freeze. There weren't many options for what *that* meant.

She lifted her hand, and a flame danced in her palm. "Hellfire," she said. "You had a taste of mine before, didn't you?"

Without meaning to, I touched the scarred skin she'd left me the last time she'd tried to kill me. Sadly, it was looking like this time would be far more successful.

"It won't hurt for long," she assured me, an almost sad tone to her voice. "It's an unfortunate thing to have to destroy you, really. Killing something that has never been is a travesty, but you've left me no choice. I've spent too long planning for you to ruin everything, and you are the only one who could ruin it." The flame grew taller in her palm, stretching up toward the ceiling, the temperature of the room increasing.

She lifted it to her lips and blew, the flame shifting like a blowtorch.

I covered my face with my arms — a useless reflex — but nothing burned.

I turned to find Gran between us, but she didn't look like the old woman I knew. Instead, it was the glimpse I'd gotten before, her pointed ears, sharp cheekbones and bright green eyes. She held a hand up that diverted the flame around us both even as the air turned stifling and hot.

Lilith stopped and took a step backward. "Why am I not surprised to find *you* in my way?"

Gran dropped her hand. "You know better than this. I *warned* you about this!" Her voice was that of a much younger woman, so different I'd never have recognized it as Gran. Still, it fit with her true face.

"You told me nothing, like you always tell people nothing."

"I told you what you sought would destroy you and everything you wanted."

"But even you don't know what your foolish, vague prophecies mean. You're a fate, not a god. You can only see the picture, not the pieces."

Gran shook her head. "Your pride has always been your biggest problem. You're too afraid of looking weak to ever find real answers."

"And you're always standing in my way," Lilith shot back. "This time I won't go easy on you. I did before because Lucifer would have been furious if I'd hurt you, but I don't care what he thinks anymore. My work is too important. Step aside."

Gran didn't move. "No."

"You'll risk yourself for some freak of nature that never should have existed?"

Gran spread her arms out, the clearest *I am not moving* motion I'd ever seen. "You're right, Lilith. I can see the puzzle but not the pieces. I saw the chaos you'd bring so long ago, saw the fear in you, but I had no idea *this* would be how you'd do it. I also saw the part Ava had to play, even if I didn't know exactly how."

"Well, then you're more blind than I ever thought, because you dying isn't going to change a thing." Lilith lifted both hands and struck, a mixture of fire and smoke flinging toward us. Gran moved, rising her hands to shield us as she had before, but there was *so much* more this time. The magic reminded me of what the other Older One had used to drive Lilith out of the tent what seemed like a lifetime ago.

She pulled her hands apart, then shot a blast of power at Lilith, knocking her back.

A shout from outside echoed in, a roar I recognized, but the door wouldn't budge.

Lilith pushed herself away from the wall. "You're stronger than the last time we did this. Not that it matters." She went back and forth with Gran, both taking strikes, both tiring, but neither getting an upper hand. I stayed by the door even as they shifted, dodging and blocking each other's blows.

Though, it seemed clear Gran was tiring quicker.

A hit from Gran sent Lilith tumbling into a table, the furniture shattering beneath her.

Lilith growled, a sound that had no business coming from a body that look like a young beautiful woman, before she shoved herself upright. "Enough!" Her gaze moved from Gran to me, her lips curling. "I don't need to beat you," she said. "I just need to take out the thing in my way."

She lifted her hand, and I knew it was over. She was done playing, done talking, done *waiting*.

A blast of that hellfire left her and sailed right for me.

A split second before the fire hit me, something stood in the way.

No, *someone*.

A cry left Gran's lips as the hellfire struck her instead of me. She didn't block it or divert it as she had before, but consumed it. In fact, when it hit her, it seemed as if the entire flame were sucked inside her, taken right from Lilith's palm.

The door didn't open but exploded inward, shards raining through the room, leaving tiny cuts on my bare arms.

Lucifer walked through the debris, his eyes a swirling mixture of red and black. He'd never appeared so monstrous before. He lifted a hand and Lilith was pinned to the wall by an invisible force. "You," he said in a voice I'd never heard.

His smooth, deep voice was replaced by something that echoed, something old and evil and terrifying. It was the voice I'd expected to hear call from the abyss, but it left his lips all the same. "You dare to create this sort of chaos in *my* home?"

Lilith grabbed at her throat as if she could pry off whatever held her in place.

He let out a growl before she dropped to the ground in an unceremonious heap.

"I expected one of my wayward offspring to be behind this, to betray me, but you? The first? My favorite?"

She lifted her gaze to his, the same defiance there I'd seen in his. They were related — there was no doubt about that. "You made me knowing I'd never fit with Adam, that I'd never be what he wanted. You *created* me to fail. It's your own fault."

Lucifer lifted his hand as if to grab her again, but Lilith reached into a pouch on her thigh and withdrew a small orb. It looked like the one that had transported me before.

She slammed it against the ground, shattering it, and she was gone, disappeared as if she'd ever been there at all.

It left just Lucifer, me and Gran's unmoving body.

Chapter Twenty-Five

I'd never realized pain this deep could exist, that a person could be entirely hollowed out. I'd suffered before in my life, but they had always been *my* suffering. They'd been times when life hadn't gone the way I wanted, when I hadn't gotten what I needed, but in the end, they had been my pain.

Staring at Gran's still body, stretched out on a stone slab in the courtyard beneath the large branches of the tree, was a whole different sort of pain. I could endure anything, it seemed, but loss.

No matter how much I'd shaken her, when I'd screamed and cried, she hadn't moved. Her skin had grown cold, her lips still and lacking the smile I'd known most of my life.

It didn't feel possible.

"Ava?" Troy's voice was careful, as if unsure of his welcome.

I didn't answer.

I didn't have it in me to answer.

It all seemed like too much work, like effort toward something useless. I'd pressed forward, I'd done what I was supposed to and in the end I'd failed. Lilith was gone, I had no idea how to proceed and now the one person who had known me the longest was dead.

Even without my answer, Troy came up beside me, a still and steady presence I hadn't realized I needed.

"How can she just be *gone*?"

She'd seemed so full of life, so impossible to end. Gran had been the moon, something that I expected to always be there.

The fact that she wasn't shook me to my core.

Troy took my hand in his and squeezed, not offering any stupid platitudes, any 'I'm so sorry,' bullshit that didn't mean a thing.

He left me alone after a minute, and even though the others filed in, even as Kase, Hunter and Grant stopped by as if to remind me that I wasn't alone, even if I wanted to be, nothing took away the sting, nothing fixed the foundation that was broken. It felt as though forever I'd trip over the cracks made by losing her, as if I'd never getting my footing again.

I knew what I was, but the one person I wanted to talk to about it, I couldn't. The one person who made sense of everything was gone.

Lucifer came up to me, and when he spoke with his normal voice, without the horror I'd heard in that room, it felt disingenuous. "I may not have always gotten along with Gran, but I respected her. I can't say that about many people."

"Don't you talk about her," I snapped, not caring that I was speaking to Lucifer, that he could do anything he wanted to me. "This is all your fault. You think I haven't figured it out? *You* wanted me here, you knew what I was and you put that reaper there to draw that out of me. You did it all just so whoever was behind it would target me, right? You used me as bait, and she paid the price for your stupid plan."

Lucifer didn't deny any of it. How could he? I was right, and he didn't regret any of it. The asshole was an 'all's well that ends well' sort of egomaniac.

"She died protecting you. She would have been happy for that to be her ending."

I turned away from her to face him, to find him dressed in all black other than a red rose pinned to his jacket like some funeral wear. "She shouldn't have died at all! Don't you get that? She wasn't supposed to die." I planted my hands on his chest and shoved, wanting to hurt him, to hurt *something* if it would just make me feel a little better.

Maybe if I did that, some of the pain inside me would dissolve.

He didn't move, as solid as ever. "Yes, I used you, because I had to. I needed to know who was behind this before it was too late."

"Don't you talk to me about the greater good."

"Why do you think Gran was here? She came to hell because she *knew* what needed to be done. She did nothing without knowing the consequences, but still she came. She made the choice to save you because you are the only person who can stop Lilith. Gran was a fate, able to see how choices fit together, and she decided that your life was worth more than hers."

"Well, she was wrong," I whispered, crossing my arms and turning my back on Lucifer.

"I've never known Gran to be wrong before. Do you know what she told me the first time we met? She was a child then, an outcast from her people because of her gifts. She came up to me — I could travel to Earth back then — and she knew what I was. Her eyes turned white and she said, 'You will give up what you need for what you think you want.' I should have heeded that warning, but I didn't, and she was right. Thousands of years later, I lost the thing that mattered more to me than anything else just as she said I would."

"If you're expecting sympathy for your little sob story, you're going to be waiting forever."

"No. My point is that Gran knew nearly everything. She sacrificed herself to put you where you needed to be, and you lack the luxury of falling apart, Ms. Harlin. You do not get to mourn or pity yourself or lament your place."

"Fuck you," I spat. "Fuck you and your daughter and this whole fucking place!"

"So you will allow Gran's sacrifice to be in vain? You'll let Gran throw away her life for nothing because of your own short-sided stubbornness?"

I shook my head, trying to see Gran past the tears in my eyes, trying to spot the woman I'd relied on so much inside that corpse. Her spirit, like all immortals, was gone, snatched away, and it left me with *nothing*.

"Death is always in vain," I whispered before leaving. Lucifer could go to hell — or stay there, in this case — because I was out.

I'd followed this damn mystery. I'd done what I was supposed to, and what did I have to show for it? Lilith was *clearly* stronger than I was. She'd killed Gran — the only family I had — and if Gran couldn't stand up to her, what chance did I have?

I reached my room again, exhausted and wanting nothing more than to sleep for…well, ever. Or at least until the world ended and I didn't have to care about anything anymore.

I lay on the bed, curling in on myself as if I deflated. How had I not realized how much Gran had meant to me? She was the only person in my life who had always been there. As it turned out, even when I was just a baby, she'd *been* there. She was the only good constant thing, and now she was gone.

Something tugged at my senses, an all-too-familiar sensation that made me want to cry. I was so sick of everything wanting a piece of me, of everything wanting something from me.

"Go away," I whispered to the room, to the thing that watched me. When it didn't, I opened my eyes. The darkness, the same one I'd seen in my dreams, the one that had chased Lilith away when she'd been a shadow in my dreams stood in the room as if waiting on me.

And, for the first time, I realized exactly what it was.

A reaper.

It stared back at me, still as if trying to get me to understand something.

That felt like my whole life. The universe trying to tell me shit without coming right out and saying it. I was forever trying to keep up, trying to decode it.

Even so, the reaper stared.

I didn't sit up, even as I snapped, "What do you want from me?"

Just as last time, it didn't respond.

I pushed myself upright, wishing I had that other power again, that I could blast this reaper as I had the last. When I couldn't seem to do that, I went with trying to use my sharp words to disintegrate it. "If you want something from me, how about you actually *do* something? Say something. Stop being so goddamned cryptic!"

Even as I screamed, it didn't move. It tilted its head, the only sign it heard me at all.

I leaned forward, bent over and carded my fingers into my hair, frustration eating away at me. "All I want is to get to see Gran again. I did what everyone wanted me to and I still lost, and now I don't even have someone to help me figure out what to do. I can only take so much…"

The reaper came closer, doing that same thing it had before, as if leaning down to look into my eyes for a moment before it disappeared.

Great. Alone again.

As quickly as it happened, the reaper was back and beside him?

Gran…

Or, not exactly. I could see through her — a spirit? I'd never seen any type of immortal spirit.

Not that it mattered. I went forward and tried to touch her, tried to wrap my arms around her, but I passed right through her.

It made me despair again. So close, but always out of reach from what I wanted.

"Well, I didn't figure I'd see this place again."

I could have cried at the sound of her voice. *Oh wait, I was…* "I'm so sorry —"

She cut me off with a wave of her hand. "Oh, you hush. I don't have much time, but if I expected you to be sorry, I wouldn't have done it."

"Why did you? I'm not ready to be on my own."

"Of course you are. You were where I was headed my whole, very very very long life. You think I didn't know? That I didn't see this? Of course I did."

I wrung my hands together, wanting to stay right here, in this moment, the place where Gran was still here and everything wasn't falling apart. "I can't do this, Gran. I can't lose you—I can't beat Lilith."

Gran moved over and sat on the bed—or at least it looked like that, since she wasn't really there. She patted the spot next to her until I sat as well. "You can beat her. I've seen it—the first thing I ever saw, back when I was a kid. You're the only one who can." She shimmered, fading.

"Don't go," I pleaded.

"That isn't up to me. In fact, I can't believe I'm here at all." She glanced over to the reaper who stood there, waiting. "Your buddy here tore me from another place, from wherever I was. Even I didn't know that was possible."

"How?"

"I think he knew you needed it."

I thought back to when it—he?—had helped me before, back when he'd helped me understand how to save Troy, when he'd shown me my mother. "Who is he?"

She shrugged. "Even I don't know everything, and it's time for you to stop asking me. You don't *need* me to tell you what you need to know, what you need to do. You already know it."

I hated how much like goodbye that sounded. "Please, don't do this."

"It's done. I've tried to teach you this and you've never accepted it. Sometimes things just are. This is one of those things. You can't lie down and stop just because you don't like it. You've been pushed out of the plane, and you can't stop it, now. You can't stop moving, but you can decide where you're going to go, now." She faded again, and the reaper came forward.

He reached out, and when he made contact with Gran, she disappeared, leaving the room silent and feeling empty.

Still, the reaper remained. It waited, watching me, as if to see what I would do now.

I wanted to curl back up and fade away like she did. I wanted to give up, to make this all someone else's problem, but the reaper stayed. It watched me. It reminded me of exactly what Gran had said, her parting words.

You can decide where you're going to go now.

"I can't just stop, can I?" I asked the reaper as if he would answer. "No matter how tempting it is to give up, I have to keep going."

He remained almost deathly still other than the floating of cloth around him, as if I knew damn well what the answer was without him.

A knock on the door came, and it opened without me having to answer. Funny that I had thought I was alone, because Troy, Kase, Grant and Hunter walked in. It was written in their expressions that they'd given me a little time to myself, but they were done letting me suffer alone.

The reaper remained, and while they caught sight of it, it must have been my lack of fear that made them not react.

"So, what's the plan?" Hunter asked.

And there was only one answer. After seeing Gran, after being given that last moment with her, after pulling my head out of my ass, I had only one direction I could go.

Lilith had better watch out, because I was coming for her, and I was going to bring hell down on her when I found her.

She'd fucked with the wrong reaper.

Want to see more from this author? Here's a taster for you to enjoy!

Grave Concerns: Saving the World & Other Bad Ideas
Jayce Carter

Excerpt

"I could tear your soul right out of your stupid, entitled body!"

The man I yelled at stared at me as if I were crazy, but that didn't even slow my tirade. He might think I was a nutjob—and maybe I was—but that didn't mean I wasn't fully capable of doing exactly what I'd threatened.

"You're insane," the man said.

"You're the one who's attacking that poor woman who works here."

"She made my drink wrong."

"So?" I set my hands on my hips, giving him my best *melt him into the ground right where he stands* look. "You think you're entitled to everything you want? You think the world revolves around you?"

There, beside us, stood the barista we argued over, her dark eyes wide. In fact, she looked far more concerned about our interaction than she'd been about him acting like a spoiled brat. When I had been standing by the bar, waiting for mine, he'd brought his back to tell them they'd made it wrong.

"It really is okay," the barista told me. "It's not a big deal. I can just remake it."

"No," I responded. "It's *not* okay. People can't just expect others to be perfect, to have it all together all the time. He needs to be understanding."

"I don't expect perfect," the man said. "I asked for iced and she made a hot drink. That's it."

"So? She's trying, damn it. She's the one working, so you should just say thank you and move on. What makes you so special that you think you'll get whatever you want?"

His mouth hung open, like he'd never dealt with someone telling him off before. "I wasn't even rude," he argued. "All I did was ask her to remake it."

"She's doing her best," I repeated for what had to be the tenth time, that same thing that stuck in my head. "She's just human, and maybe she's having a bad day. Maybe she recently lost someone she cares about. Maybe she went to hell and is now in some sort of existential crisis because she doesn't know how to bring the person responsible to justice. Did you ever think about *that* or did you just decide to criticize her?"

The chime above the door rang, and when I turned, I realized *maybe* I'd gone just a little overboard.

Troy walked in, and I doubted he was there as my friendly neighborhood werewolf, just making the rounds.

Which meant someone had called the police on me.

For what? A little disagreement?

Or maybe because I told him I'd rip his soul out of his body…

"Finally," the man said as if Troy were his saving grace.

"You called the police?" I muttered *pussy* under my breath, low enough that Troy wouldn't catch it.

The sharp look in his silver eyes said he had. *Stupid werewolf hearing.*

"You are going to get arrested," the man said in the mocking, self-assured voice of a kid who had tattled to mom on his sibling.

"I doubt that." I leaned in and kept my voice low. "Because I'm fucking the detective."

Then? Just when I was pretty sure my childish behavior couldn't sink any lower, I stuck my tongue out at him.

At least he looked shocked.

My high horse didn't last long, however, not when Troy wrapped his large hand around my upper arm. In a different, sexier moment, I might have even liked his macho bullshit. "I'm very sorry," he said to the man as he pulled me toward the door. "I'll handle her."

Handle me?

I would have told Troy exactly what I thought about that, but he lowered his voice to all but snarl into my ear, "You should probably keep quiet."

The rumbled reprimand shocked me into silence. Troy *never* used that tone of voice with me. He was typically soft spoken and the most likely of the men in my life to let me get away with...well...everything.

So his sharp tone kept me quiet until he opened the passenger-side door of his car and tossed me in. By the time he'd gotten into the driver side, my brain had started working again and I realized that I didn't let *anyone* talk to me like that, not even my sort of boyfriend who turned into some sort of wolf creature and had plenty of weird emotional hang-ups.

"Don't you manhandle me," I snapped.

"What was that?"

"What was what? I was protecting the staff against a male Karen. That's called being a good person. Not my fault you don't recognize it."

"You were arguing with a stranger so aggressively that the staff called us about *you*."

I crossed my arms and sat back. "He was getting mad at her over one little mistake and she was trying her best."

He let out a long sigh, as if my words had been more telling than I'd meant them to be. The damn man was far too observant. "I know it's frustrating to not have any leads."

Frustrating didn't even *start* to explain it. After Lilith had killed Gran, after I'd sworn she would pay for it, everything had stalled out. Swearing revenge like that was supposed to be some sort of catapult to action. It was supposed to lead almost immediately to a big showdown where things got resolved. People didn't swear to make someone pay then spend six weeks doing absolutely nothing about it.

It was said revenge was a dish best served cold, but it turned out I lacked the patience for that.

It didn't matter how much I wanted to rain hell down on her—I had no idea where she even was, and neither did anyone else.

"I thought we'd have *something* by now," I admitted, letting my head fall back against the seat.

Troy set his hand on my thigh, the weight of it reassuring even when I didn't want it to be. Something about him having my back never failed to make me feel a bit more optimistic. "Ava, you survived hell. You faced off against Lucifer. You destroyed a reaper. You'll get through this, too. It just may not be as fast as you'd like."

"Hell was easy. We knew which way we had to go. This, though? I've got no idea where to even start."

He squeezed my leg. "You look exhausted. Are you not sleeping well?"

"I've got enough horrible things going on in my life when I'm awake. Why should I sleep? Just so I can dream about the mist there?" Just saying it made me shudder.

I'd had those nightmares all my life, but since going to hell, they'd gotten worse. I woke up choking, coughing, gagging and clawing at my throat with the memory of that damn mist. Even after I was able to breathe, I couldn't shake the horrible drowning feeling.

"You can always sleep at my house," he offered, his voice having lost its sharp edge, having quieted as if coaxing me to agree. This was the sweet man I was used to.

"You might be able to scare away most things, but I'm afraid you aren't the best dream catcher." Despite what I said, he had a point. Even if he couldn't keep the damn dreams away, no doubt it would be better to wake up next to him than alone.

But I wasn't that girl, the one who threw away everything for a man—or four of them—so I didn't agree. I'd survived these dreams my whole life, so I could deal with them alone now.

"What if Grant gets some ambrosia? You slept and didn't dream when you took it before," Troy pointed out.

"I'm not ever touching that stuff again. I saw it grown in body parts—I almost was the body some was grown in—and that made it lose its magic. No thanks."

I kept to myself the fact I hadn't actually seen Grant. He and Hunter had both all but disappeared upon our return.

It stung.

After everything, they had just dropped off the face of the earth — or hell, whatever — without a word.

Was it because of what I was? Maybe the reality of sleeping with a reaper was a turn off they couldn't ignore anymore. Fucking the cute, eccentric girl who talked to ghosts was one thing — getting naked with a reaper must have been a hard limit.

Cowards.

"What's wrong?" Troy asked, probably having caught my expression.

"Nothing," I lied.

He sighed, the sound telling me he knew I was lying. "Ava…"

I turned to face him. "It's just more of not knowing where to go, of not having a plan, of being totally and completely stuck. You know, same old, same old."

He pressed his lips together, as if he knew there was more I wouldn't say, but he shook his head. "Why don't I drive you home?"

"What, no handcuffs?"

That glow in his eyes started, the one that said he really wanted to do just that.

Not that I'd gone without…

In the six weeks since we'd returned from hell, I'd ended up in bed with Troy countless times. Always at his place, and usually because I went there, because I craved his scent, his taste, the feeling of his strong hands on me.

It made me wonder if there wasn't something to this whole mate thing, some bond that drew me to him, that made me need him like I hadn't before.

Or maybe I was just addicted to his stupid knot.

That was *very* possible.

He inhaled, slowly, the glow of his eyes brightening. *Right*. He could smell me, always knew when I was thinking such things. There weren't a lot of secrets in a relationship with a werewolf.

He leaned forward, as if drawn by the smell of my desire, driven by the need to satisfy me.

I put my hand up and over his face, stopping him before he could kiss me. "No time."

His groan was muffled by my palm. "I can be quick."

"No, you can't."

Normally, that would have been a wonderful compliment, because the reality was that I never left Troy's bed unsatisfied. In fact, I usually fell asleep there because I couldn't stay awake another moment, not after he'd had his way with me, some wild part of his wolf needing to turn me boneless like laying a claim.

He nipped my palm before sitting back. "Will you at least promise to stop harassing strangers? I don't want to get called out on you again."

"I wasn't harassing anyone." At his lifted eyebrow, I blew out a long breath. "Okay, so I may have threatened to rip his soul out of his body."

Disapproval flooded his expression.

Which, I guess was fair.

Maybe that wasn't the smartest thing I'd done recently. Or, maybe it was. It hadn't been a very good six weeks.

"I know you're frustrated, Ava. I know you want to find Lilith, that you want to handle this, but going off the rails isn't going to make it happen any faster. If you end up in jail or rushing into trouble, it isn't going to help. You need to relax."

"How am I supposed to do that? Yoga? Meditation? *Tea*?"

"I have tomorrow night off. What if we go out?"

I paused at the offer, it taking me off track. "Like…a date?"

He nodded. "We're involved, aren't we? Let me take my mate out, have dinner, act like any normal couple."

"I don't think you get to use the word normal, not when we went to hell, had a threesome with a vampire and your penis gets stuck inside me when we have sex."

He let out a rough laugh. "You're impossible, you know that?"

"I've heard that before, yeah. So, you're not going to arrest me?"

"Not today." He caught my arm, as if calling me on the fact that I hadn't actually agreed to the date. "Dinner tomorrow?"

Maybe trying to date like some happy couple wasn't the best idea in the middle of everything else, or maybe that was exactly why I needed it right then.

"Okay," I said, inexplicably nervous. Then again, when was the last time I'd had a *real* date planned?

Maybe never? Certainly never with someone I actually loved.

I went to get out of the car, but he didn't let me go. Troy shifted his hand to the front of my shirt, then tugged me in until he could take my lips in a possessive kiss, in one that screamed *mine* in a way that melted me.

Whether it was him or his wolf leaving a mark on me, I didn't know, and honestly, I didn't really care.

Being claimed by both of them was fine by me, and one of the few things going exactly right in my life.

Home of Erotic Romance

Sign up for our newsletter and find out about all our romance book releases, eBook sales and promotions, sneak peeks and FREE romance books!

About the Author

Jayce Carter lives in Southern California with her husband and two spawns. She originally wanted to take over the world but realized that would require wearing pants. This led her to choosing writing, a completely pants-free occupation. She has a fear of heights yet rock climbs for fun and enjoys making up excuses for not going out and socializing.

Jayce loves to hear from readers. You can find her contact information, website details and author profile page at https://www.totallybound.com